CERES STORM

CERES STORM

DAVID HERTER

TOR®

A TOM DOHERTY ASSOCIATES BOOK

NEW YORK

CERES STORM

Copyright © 2000 by David Herter

This book is printed on acid-free paper.

Edited by David G. Hartwell

A Tor Book
Published by Tom Doherty Associates, LLC
175 Fifth Avenue
New York, NY 10010

www.tor.com

Tor® is a registered trademark of Tom Doherty Associates, LLC.

Library of Congress Cataloging-in-Publication Data

Herter, David.
    Ceres storm / David Herter.—1st ed.
        p.   cm.
    "A Tom Doherty Associates book."
    ISBN 0-312-87493-6 (alk. paper)
    1. Life on other planets—Fiction.   2. Interplanetary voyages—Fiction.   I. Title.

PS3558.E7938 C47 2000
813'.54—dc21   00-031684

First Edition: November 2000

Printed in the United States of America

0 9 8 7 6 5 4 3 2 1

To

Briony and Harry
aka Mom and Dad

and

Leoš Janáček

ACKNOWLEDGMENTS

With love to my dad, Harry; my sister Capt. Melissa Smith, USAF, her husband, Marlin, my nephews Thomas, Alexander, and Levi; my brother Justin and his wife, Lisa; my famous sister, Jarrah. Bill Tuttle helped me brainstorm, and came up with a few of the core ideas. Lael Schultz was a constant friend; her husband Zach was my first reader. Gene Wolfe taught me the most. David Hartwell was the ideal editor. Lucius set me up. The music of Leoš Janáček and Harrison Birtwistle provided direction, as did the works of Vance and Bester, and Henry Green. I'd also like to thank Susan and Sean Draeger, Susan Adams, Chris Schelling, Ted Chiang, Becky Morris, Terry "tergod" Goodman, Scott Herman, Tori Miller, Vito and the gang at Koen Pacific, Jim Minz, Scott Hilsen, David Lockwood, Sandy MacLaren, Arinn Dembo, Pat Swenson, David Silas, David Remy, Don Keller, Shira Daemon, Edith Scott, Ellen Datlow, Grant Fjermedal, the Cast and Crew of Clarion 1990, Scott Williams, Bob Althizer, Carol Jones, Tim Lewis, Jim White, and, of course, Trisha Yearwood.

1

STORM

He was called the *Leader*, young Daric—the *demiurge* by some. Hard to grasp, I know, but he was *sole and singular*. The crown of a stellar empire! And if you were unlucky enough to be summoned to the palace, you were made to scatter your shades beforehand—no shades in the Leader's presence, ever—and once there you would bow, inwardly and outwardly, and you would sing the Leader's anthem, and sing it well, like this . . ."

Grandpapa canted back and swung up his arms, as he did whenever he sang old songs or wept over the lost worlds of his youth. "From pole to pole and planets wide," he began, in a robust tone.

Sitting on the stone floor below, Daric watched Grandpapa grope the air, as though to clutch the stars on the distant ceiling.

" 'Cross warp and weft of stellar tide . . ."

Daric squinted up. His shade called the ceiling a *domical*

vault. The painted spiral of stars was faded, flaking. The ancient galaxy was drizzling on Grandpapa, settling into his threads. One day, Grandpapa might seize up and become just another artifact in the turret, and he, Daric, would no longer have to climb the stairs at nine and noon and eighteen.

Grandpapa deserves your respect.

He thought, The last time Jonas was up here he told me the painting—

The fresco, Daric.

—was crumbling, that it might fall if it isn't sealed, but KayTee's grant says we can't touch it.

Not the Krater-Tromon Clan, but a local group, the Ares Historical Foundation.

Daric shrugged, then hid the motion by stretching his arms. I should show respect to Grandpapa, he thought, peering up at the golden man-shaped bulk atop the silver stand, whose lips, closing now as the song ended, were carved of jade.

"Years and years and years ago, young Daric. So long, only the molecules remain. We breathe it now, you realize?"

Daric nodded.

"Years and years and years," said Grandpapa, his voice low and spiky, like the distant grind of gears in the basement. "His enemies turned him into a tree. Something your pillow won't teach you, not one of the *official* lessons. They used a slow virus, to taunt him. And oh, how he raged! He contemplated a freeze and a long sleep, perhaps a retreat to Parson's Planet for rejuvenation. But in the end he did *nothing*, for his great age had finally given him wisdom, as it must." Grandpapa's silver lids narrowed over his ruby eyes. "He looked back across the millennia, discerned cruelties and petty truths. And then . . . then he was no longer the Leader, but an *oak*."

Daric pulled his tunic tighter about his narrow shoulders. "A tree? Why would he want to be a tree, Grandpapa?"

"Why not? He'd lived a long time. Not a hundred years, but a *thousand*."

Grandpapa leaned toward Daric, eyes widening. "He'd dominated the solar system and soon the nearby stars. His enemies were right; it was time to retire to a stationary attitude. And if one had to be a tree, then an oak would do. He acquiesced, and in one last ruse—a departing gesture of sorts—he had himself planted in a wild forest."

"Where?"

Grandpapa quickly raised and lowered his arms. A shrug. Where?

Daric studied the fresco overhead, the yellow, blue, white sparks forming a spiral that filled the ceiling.

He wondered, Is it true, Shade? About the tree?

Grandpapa straightened. "It's half-past noon. Did Jonas mention a chore for you? A special chore?"

"Yes, Grandpapa. At breakfast."

"He told you to behave, and follow your shade's instructions?"

"Yes, Grandpapa."

"Then you will do well, my boy." Grandpapa raised and dropped his left arm; the session was over.

Daric arose, then climbed down the winding stairs, pulling his sheen up from his collar and over his head. In the Atrium he consulted the instruments and recorded the noontime numbers—calm weather, null activity—fulfilling the rules of the grant.

Twelve thirty-five. We are late today, Daric.

He followed the curving wall to the window, leaned his forehead against the glass, and looked down. The turret's shadows, cast by the sun and Dayblown Phobos, stretched across either side of the lake to the orchard. Above them a flash of gold was Aver, Jonas's hawk, wheeling near the boundary. Beyond, the Tharsis plain stretched to the vague, seething horizon.

He thought, How old is this turret, exactly?

It's been here for four hundred seven years.

More than four hundred years beside the lake on the Tharsis plain, he thought. Four hundred. Almost forty times my life. Right, Shade?

Yes, Daric. Very good.

More than eighty times yours.

I'm older than that, Daric. I was once Jonas's shade, remember.

Aloud: "Where did Jonas say he was going?"

To tend the orange trees.

Daric continued down the stairs, past his room to the front door, across the grass to the circular lake.

We don't have any oak, do we?

No. But we have a relative, the maples, beside the rhododendron.

He looked at the trees, then turned. The turret was silhouetted by the sun, with Phobos, the oblong moon of yellow-white brilliance, to its right. He studied the turret's flat top and tried, not for the first time, to imagine Grandpapa's room up there, beneath the spikes of the sensor equipment, never to be discussed with visitors.

Daric, your brother mentioned a special chore.

He walked backward across the grass, listening to the water rippling on stone, and stopped precisely at the lake's edge.

He smiled. "It's time for me to ride my wheel."

Jonas would like you to go to the workshop.

Daric raised his arms and turned in place, so that the turret, the burning moon, the lake, flashed by, faster, faster, with the orchard streaming behind.

His shade was unruffled.

Grandpapa and Jonas would like you to go to the workshop, Daric.

He dropped to his knees beside the lake and felt the ground

pitch and yaw. He remembered the ship that had landed last summer beyond the perimeter markers, the pilots who had descended, bewinged; the stories they had told that day, while Jonas fetched help in the city, of the weightless world, of the sun and stars beneath your feet.

You can play later.

"To the workshop," he said, and stood. But first he would walk around the lake, which he knew without asking was one hundred eighty-two steps.

Halfway there a sweet breeze came from the orchard—

... hyacinth, white rose, pine ...

—and stirred the water, bright with sinuous threads of Phobos, while beneath swam Daric's fish over the bed of plum algae.

To the workshop.

He rounded the corner, running his palm along the scarred stone, and stopped at the door in the back. He opened it and hopped down the stairs, one, two, three, four, five, six, into the basement. Lightlines illuminated the bulky machineries topped with silver globes, and a trail of bare floor through the head-high cartons of apples and carrots and squash.

Listen now, Daric. Grandpapa and Jonas have asked us to perform a task. A special task.

But his eyes had found the tools scattered on the workbench beside the stairs. With these Jonas was able to fashion or repair anything they needed. Daric had often stood here beside him, and watched the old man's determined eyes, nose twinkling in the overhead light, rough hands delicately wielding these tools.

Tools that now lay free for Daric.

Listen. Grandpapa and Jonas wish us to travel into Oppidum.

The city?

The dirigere is due to pass within the quarter, so you must call it quickly.

"Is Jonas taking us?"

Jonas is tending the orange trees.

"But I've never . . . How could I pay?"

We'll need coins and a century rose. This has been arranged. But first, get the linkpad. You'll find it in the drawer, upper right.

Wary, he touched the corner of the workbench, grasped the brass handle, and pulled open the drawer. The linkpad, a square wafer the size of his hand, was inside. He lifted it. He had never been allowed to hold this before.

Press flower, stone, water, number, heat.

Daric's hand hesitated.

Flower, stone, water, number, heat.

He touched the symbols, aware of his shade's voice—which was calm and deep, like Jonas's voice—speaking behind his head.

Sun, flower, stone, stone.

When he touched the last, the wafer glowed for an instant.

There. Now for your currency. Look in the chest.

He turned to the wooden chest, on the floor beside the workbench.

Inside.

Daric fought the urge to turn round on himself, to face his shade.

"It belongs to Jonas."

Touch the brim, it will open for you.

He did so, and the lid raised, revealing an interior of green cloth, on which were laid two century roses and a bright scattering of coins.

Take one rose, and the coins.

His mouth became dry.

They were put there for you, Daric.

Surely this was a test of some sort, and Jonas would appear behind him. He would smile kindly, as much with his wrinkled eyes as with his mouth, and shake his head saying, "No, boy, that's not the way to do things."

We will need a century rose, and coins for the trip.

Daric knelt. He lifted the rose by its glass stem and looked down at the petals, to find his own face and the roof of lightlines reflected, as if in small pools of blood.

How long will we be gone?

Until evening, Daric. Now, the coins.

He scooped up the coins, counting seven. He slid the rose into the deep left pocket of his tunic, and the coins into his right, then sealed both pockets.

Now lift the edge of the cloth.

Chewing his lower lip, Daric lifted the cloth, revealing a gold necklace and a medallion shaped as the old Martian rosette.

It's protection. Take it.

"I can't..."

Ask it.

"You are Daric. You are authorized."

He nearly dropped the cloth. The rosette had begun to glow.

"You are Daric," it said again, a kind voice, like his pillow's. "You are authorized."

"I can't take Jonas's things."

The medallion, glowing near his fingers, reasoned, "You have been authorized, Daric."

Trust us, Daric.

He chewed his lower lip. Let me find Jonas, he thought.

Jonas is tending the orange trees. Remember, he told you to follow my instructions, and said that he trusted you to do your chore well, by yourself.

I remember.

He hesitated, then took the medallion.

Outside, Daric. We're late, and the dirigere will soon be here.

He stood and climbed the stairs, heart beating in his throat. His shade had never been so urgent before, had never asked of anything beyond the routine. Now ...

Around the corner to the lake, Daric paused, focusing on the sky above the orchard. A shape hovered in the distance, south over the Tharsis plain.

"I recommend you hide me, Daric."

String it around your neck.

He looped the chain over his head and tucked the medallion beneath his shirt.

A dirigere. He had often seen them passing in the distant sky beyond the boundaries. Now it was coming here, for him.

He stood still, while the shape became clearer. A strange blue fish, he thought, with a down-curving snout, a puffy body, and a flat, stubby tail.

It's approaching faster than it seems, Daric. Hurry.

As he walked to the lakeshore, an alarm chimed beside the front door. The dirigere had crossed the outer perimeter.

Daric squinted up.

The craft, its hull shimmering in the Phobos light, sailed serenely down toward the orchard. Windows glinted on the underside, and from upswept wings in the back rippled scarlet banners decorated with the white KayTee cross.

Watching it, he was reminded of how his fish, after eating, would lazily drop to the bottom of the lake.

You'll need to get farther from the turret, Daric.

He could hear it now, a soft huffing.

Look to your left.

An oval of light fell on the shadowed grass, while music stained the air: a sharp, three-toned fanfare. Then a voice called out from above, "Greetings from the *Alectryon*. Stand on the light and await pickup, sieur."

Daric complied.

Do nothing. Remember what your pillow has shown you. The ship will pull you inside.

He looked up, trying not to blink as the dirigere dropped, over the pine trees now, dropping still, the hull darkening. Warm air rushed across his face, and he smelled something sweet and acrid, like burning flowers. Then the Phobos light was lost, and with an inevitability new and frightening to Daric, the ship made as though to gently crush him.

He felt a downward tug on his skin as he left the grass and the orchard, passing through the dirigere's hull to find himself lifted into a wide, bright room.

"Welcome aboard the *Alectryon*, young sieur."

A steward clad in a black, gold-piped uniform stood beside him, a woman. She nodded curtly, extending her hand, palm up.

Set two coins upon her palm.

He did so, and after an amused perusal she slipped the coins into an invisible pocket. "This way, young sieur." She led him along a narrow corridor, then up spiral stairs into a salon. The decor was bronze and bright wood, with wide oval windows.

His vision grayed for an instant.

Your sheen's adjusting to nano-particles, Daric.

"We'll dock at Oppidum within the quarter."

Daric was disappointed by the dozen or so passengers lounging on the lumpy chairs; clearly they were local members of the KayTee—*raised*, perhaps, but not the long-limbed offworlders his pillow had shown him. As he walked toward the stern they ignored him, tending their drinks or reading squares, several arguing to the empty air, though Daric knew they were *linked*.

Two chairs were set beside the aft port window, the nearer one taken by a woman with a dark cloak and long black hair that trailed down, like vines, to the carpet.

She was gazing out at the clouds.

"Pardon me, madame," he said, stepping over her hair. The ends raised and flicked, but the woman did not look at Daric as he climbed on the chair.

Below, the house dwindled into a heat haze, reduced to the size of a toy; and the orchard, which had always seemed world enough to him, was now a green and gold ring on the vast Tharsis plain.

Squinting, he tried to find Jonas, or Aver, but could see only shimmering leaves and lake water.

The dirigere began to turn.

He sank down on the cushion. He remembered the promise that they would return by nightfall—but what of his duties? Had Jonas really been told he was leaving?

Yes, Daric. Jonas knows.

But why—

You should respect your Grandpapa's wishes, Daric.

He leaned close to the glass and peered straight down, trying to find home.

"Child?"

A weight on his shoulder: a braid of black hair bound with golden thread. He turned, and the hair tickled his neck through the sheen. The braid was but one of a dozen sprouting from the top of the woman's head, some to entwine behind her, others to dangle.

"Shall I help you open a better portal, child?" Her face was narrow, with prominent cheekbones. Her eyes were oblong and green, yet had none of the twinkle of Jonas's eyes.

"Yes, please," he said.

A pendant made of dark, glassy wood was fixed to her forehead. Like another eye, Daric thought.

The woman leaned forward, reaching for the floor with long, spidery fingers. Daric was fascinated by her cloak, the black material patterned with faint purple flowers, and how it contrasted against her nut-brown skin.

She tapped the floor with three fingers. An oval section faded, revealing the distant ground.

"Kneel over there. Can you see it?"

"Yes, thank you."

The orchard was a colorful ring, brightest at the orange trees.

The turret was indistinct from its shadows, the long one falling across the lake, and the shorter one darkening the grass.

He tried to imagine Grandpapa up there under the fresco, but could not. All had been suddenly made to vanish, as Jonas would make his smaller tools or a spoon vanish behind Daric's head.

You have my company, Daric.

He said nothing, aware that the woman—whose luxurious cloak jostled and spread of its own accord against the window—was watching him.

"Is that your home, child?"

He looked up, staring at the pendant.

"Yes," Daric said.

Mori symbol.

"It's an old place, a *cenotaph*. Do you know the word?"

"No."

Mori?

He looked below, where shreds of cloud sailed above the plain.

"What's a child up to, going into the city alone?"

"I'm helping out my brother." Staring with fascination at the clouds, he added, "He's busy with the orange trees."

"Ah, so there it is. My name is Thola Nee Montyorn."

Remember your manners.

He straightened to his knees and offered his hand, which she grasped gently.

"Daric, madame."

She let go. "A cenotaph means a monument, Daric. A monument to something old and gone."

"It's my house."

She smiled, as gently as she had shaken his hand. Her teeth were the brightest he had ever seen.

Daric said, "It's been there for four hundred and seven years."

"You should feel lucky to live in such history. According to the steward, it once belonged to the Mind of Mars."

"Who?"

"You've never heard of him?"

"No, madame," he said truthfully. "We care for the house and the grounds. On behalf of the Ares Historical Foundation."

Enough, Daric.

"You're a bright boy."

Say thank you.

His eyes strayed to the portal and the red rock below. He might have been close enough to touch it.

"Thank you."

You've seen Aver fly this high, Daric.

"The Mind of Mars lived in your house. Back when it was part of his palace in Chryse—elsewhere, child, before Dayblown Phobos was born."

Daric nodded.

"That's an old phrase. From a poem. *Dayblown Phobos.* Have you heard it before?"

Tell her no.

"No."

"Does your shade know?"

You don't have a shade.

He looked up to find her tending the cloak, which had begun to sinuously sail across the carpet to the farther chairs.

He said softly, "I don't have a shade."

"No? I don't suppose many do these days."

Thank her, Daric, and take a chair closer to the front, so you can see Oppidum when we arrive.

"Pillows must suffice," she said, "so far from Plexus Foley."

"It was nice to meet you, madame." He stood up and looked across the salon.

"You're leaving?"

"I want to find a chair . . . to see Oppidum."

"But you can see it from here, child. We're at the perfect angle for the approach."

He looked past her, out the window, and forgot his shade's request. He climbed onto his chair. They were passing through thick clouds, surrounded by whiteness, and might not have been moving at all. Curious, he stared into it, tried to see beyond it. Soon the clouds began to shimmer with sunlight and break apart, a mist alive with rainbow colors that quickly dispersed, revealing the city on the horizon.

Daric pressed his forehead to the glass.

As with all such cities on his world, Oppidum was encircled by a fundamental, rising from the Tharsis plain to a height (he estimated) a thousand times his turret. From this distance it appeared to be fashioned from the same russet stone of the plain—Oppidum wore it like a smooth skirt, and from its compass rose hundreds of towers, gleaming like sapphire, gold, and ivory, topped with spires that swayed and reeled.

It's beckoning, Daric, to the unraised inhabitants of Old Mars.

Rather, the motion reminded him (and here he bit his lower lip and tried to ignore the presence of his shade, who, sometimes, could be sensed in thought, about to speak), it reminded him of a sandfink he had found dying in the orchard, one whose hundred legs still twitched, still pawed the dirt.

He asked, "How many people?"

The woman touched his shoulder. "Under six million, child. The fundamental sees to it."

He cupped his chin.

Horns sounded faintly through the salon.

"Oppidum, next five stops," the steward called out.

The dirigere turned. Oppidum was hidden below, while passengers stirred and gathered their things. They're coming home, Daric realized. It's part of their day, like visiting Grandpapa is part of mine.

Moments later, as they crossed the fundamental, the city seemed to open under his eyes, pulling back its towers—the spires curling, uncurling—to allow Daric to see down to what the shimmering moonlight barely touched, crisscrossing ramps lit with tiny yellow globes, in which a faint surge of color and shadow was really people, leading his eye down layer by layer to a darkness lit by more points of light, and a further darkness below, yawning like a pit, where faint luminous clouds could be discerned. He remembered the rhododendron bushes last spring, where he had tried to see through the tangle of branch and flower, down to the soil where blazebugs were building a hive.

Closer, he noted craft drifting like pollen to and fro, and smaller, darker objects that zipped, impossibly fast, like flies.

The gens, Daric.

"First stop, Concourse Tharsis," the steward called out.

Looking up he found another dirigere dropping, slowly turning, among the towers. And farther away, a beam of green light drawing down a huge ship—what his pillow had called a *schooner.*

"First stop, Concourse Tharsis."

Daric straightened and stretched his neck. Remembering his manners, he turned to the woman and said, "Thank you."

She smiled, gathering her heavy cloak about her.

What was her name?

Madame Nee Montyorn.

"Madame Nee Montyorn," he added, with as much a bow as he could manage.

Again she smiled, showing her wide lustrous teeth. "What's your stop, child?"

The first.

"The first."

She scrutinized him, ignoring the hair rising from the carpet to twine about her bare forearm. "Surely you wish the third, and the Concourse Elysium."

"The first," he said. He turned to the window in time to see the other dirigere stop below a swaying russet spire.

"We're friends now, aren't we, Daric? You've charmed me, and I feel bound to help you."

Thank her, but we must go.

"Thank you, madame. You've already helped me."

"Have you wandered it alone before?"

"No, madame. But I have directions."

She looked past him, out the window. A gen had darted up, to float alongside. It resembled a chip of the blackest rock, nosing in beside them, zipping anxiously back and forth, up and down. The sunlight did not touch it.

"Have no fear, Daric. They never trouble innocents."

The thing remained by as their dirigere began to slowly turn and drop, down to a writhing spire that uncurled three tongues of freckled stone. They fixed, one by one, to the hull.

"First stop, Concourse Tharsis."

Daric bowed low to the woman and hurried toward the stairs, and was soon dropping to the depths of Oppidum.

He stood above a rushing crowd—a river made of people.

You must be careful, Daric. Follow the concourse to your left.

But Daric did not move; his eyes were drawn into the crowd, true *Citizens of the Worlds* striding the concourse in colorful, rippling, flashing robes, their long faces held high, luminous clouds trailing at their shoulders, sometimes darting from one to another.

Their communion.

He could see *his* people amid the Citizens, the local Martians, shambling in comparison, and being perfectly avoided. And here: six void mariners in black robes, stalking at the edge of the crowd, their wary, waxen faces moving right, left, right.

We must go on.

He stepped from the aperture and paused, looking up past

yellow globes to the structures rising against a fragmented sky, curling and uncurling at the top. Beside one, the dirigere had become a breeze-blown bud, separating from a tower to drift away.

Yes, Daric, Oppidum is a garden.

He thought, We're below the surface.

Yes.

Aloud: "What am I to do?"

The concourse stretched away on either side, curving out of sight. A dozen spans to his right stood a girl his own age, his own size.

We are to go to the Heliotrope, an establishment in the Cosmopolis, and there make a purchase with our century rose.

She had red hair straight to her shoulders, wore a plum-colored dress to her ankles, and stood with hands folded in front of her, clearly at ease, against a black edifice with a purple gloss. Daric, who had never had friends his own age, envied her this ease.

She looked in his direction and smiled, or so Daric thought. He followed the edge of the crowd, alongside a tall Citizen with a white moth—

A weeform . . .

—flitting at his shoulder.

The girl's eyes and lashes were red. "You look lost," she said.

"I might be, actually."

"My name is Pen, which is short for Penthesilia."

"Daric."

He offered his hand. She did not take it.

We must find our way to the Concourse Elysium.

"Welcome to Oppidum, Daric," she said, smiling. "The prize of the Krater-Tromon Clan. In my opinion, more charming than all of Triton."

Behind her, in the distance, a gen darted up beside a billowing green-glass façade. The nearby crowd slowed, some stopped. A shop tender was gesturing angrily at an insect—a weeform—which flew ragged spirals around his head. Then it froze, wrapped in white light, as the tender stumbled back, and bowed. More of the passing crowd slowed to watch, others hurried along, as the gen darkened further and cast a shadow at the weeform, which vanished.

The tender nodded vigorously, bowed again, and backed into his shop.

Pen was watching it, too. "You don't have to worry about the gendarme, Daric. They're quite fair, even a bit lax this far out. That bug—it probably broke the rules—its rules, from the Scales."

Rising to a height above the crowds, the gen continued down the concourse.

"Where are you from, Daric?"

He looked back, into her strange eyes, and said, "I live in a house . . . that once belonged to the Mind of Mars."

"It must be an old house."

"It is."

Her feet were bare, and seemed to float above the ground.

If you wish, Daric, she can lead you to the Heliotrope.

"So, you've come to Oppidum in search of something. I'll be your guide. Tell me where."

"The Heliotrope."

She frowned.

Below the Concourse Elysium, in the Cosmopolis.

"It's below the Concourse Elysium, in the Cosmopolis." Feeling clever, Daric added, "I've been sent to fetch a parcel for my brother, Jonas."

"The Cosmo isn't KayTee property, but I'll lead you there. Here's the catch: You'll have to let me suggest other places to visit. Would you like?"

He unsealed his right pocket and groped the coins: five remained.

You don't need to pay her.

"My services are free, Daric. A courtesy of Krater-Tromon."
She gestured to the concourse. "Shall we? I know a shortcut. Ares
Lane to Blue Square and then . . . Well, come on."

He followed her into the crowd, glancing up at the dark
buildings and fragmented sky.

"This way, Daric."

They turned down a narrow street with glowing green bricks
underfoot. On either side were figures in tattered robes gesturing
at the passersby. Twelve in all. Closer, Daric could see their
mouths working frantically, spittle flying, though he could not
hear them talking. The third, an old man with a faded rosette
tattoo above his eyes, stood beside an aquarium. As Daric stopped
in front of the stall the old man's voice ached out: ". . . the glorious mimir . . . seer in time . . ."

Pen said, "They're in costume. This is the hallowed eve, the
only day they can do it."

To Daric, the old man sang, "Behold the great mimir, seer of
all that was, all that is, all that shall be." A melody hinging on
four notes. "Reveal the truths, illumine the wonder, the terrible
wonder, of existence . . ." Four notes that were really two notes,
the KayTee fanfare; it made the words sound jagged. "From the
fabled rivers of the planet Last, where time is water . . ."

Daric had heard of Last. In the hours while Jonas fetched
help for the ship that had landed beyond the orchard, the pilots
had sat with him in the kitchen, their white wings folded behind
them, and had told him of the Limbus Realm, the stretch of fabled
planets beyond the rim of the galaxy.

Last, where time falls like water.

He studied the aquarium. Floating inside was a creature
nearly as large as the tank, its scaled skin the color of mustard,
with bristled fins and slitted eyes that stared (it seemed) at nothing
in particular.

"Is it really from Last?" he asked, doubtful.

Pen said, "He's a local, Daric. They like the old holidays."
Let us continue.

"The mimir swims a wheel made of water, made of time. Ask it a question, young sieur, young sieur," sang the old man. "Learn the mysteries, the mysteries, of your future."

Daric turned to the girl and was surprised to find her plum-colored dress flickering, parts of her hair disappearing. She looked down, then smiled. "Grottoes do this. I'll be better on the other side. Watch."

The mimir forgotten, he followed Penthesilia, watching how her feet seemed to float an inch above the ground, how her scarlet hair brightened and faded, like fire.

She's a ghost, Daric. An eidolon.

When they neared the tunnel's end she turned to him, smiling. "It was never that bad on Triton. I've heard from friends," she said, slowing, walking alongside him now, "it never happens on the core worlds. Absolutely never. It always works perfectly. Like this. See?" She held out her arms. Her dress was once more complete.

Daric stopped. He studied her eyes. "Does it hurt, when that happens?"

Penthesilia reached out to take his hand, but her own had no substance: He pawed the air for it. "I'm an ad, Daric. My job's to lead you to your destination. Which we can't do by standing here."

He stretched his shoulders. "I needed a rest."

"Out and about, Daric. In and around. So says the healthy mind." They began to walk once more.

Another moth flitted overhead.

"They escape, sometimes," Daric said, gesturing. "Last year we got a flurry. At my house." He had been in the Atrium, had seen the dials flash. A cloud of metal insects across the Tharsis plain. "So we monitor the perimeter. And Aver watches, too. That's my brother's hawk."

They stepped into a plaza of bright blue tiles.

"We all have our kismet," she said, but his attention was on the tiles, which jutted up to form benches and tables, in the distance swelling like waves, frozen against the surrounding structures. "I've been fairly judged by the Scales and now serve the Krater-Tromon Clan, to help rebuild the home system, for the greater glory of the Heliocratic stars. I recited that, could you tell?"

Daric looked over, and nodded.

"I learned it from Peer Tromon himself. He visited Oppidum last year. Not in person, of course. A doppel." Looking down at her feet, Pen added, "You never see the real one on Triton, at least I never did."

He spoke her name slowly: "*Pen-tuh-suh-lay-uh.* Is that right?"

"Very good, Daric, though Pen will do, really."

A familiar smell—baking bread. A series of stalls racked with breads and pastries, with steam rising in perfect spirals overhead.

We don't have time, Daric.

He counted the coins in his pocket.

"Daric, these are vendors. Cuisine from the *ancient ancient*, of a sort. For the tourists."

As he walked toward the stall—

This is not your sort of food, Daric.

—the smoke darted toward him, enveloping his head.

His sheen tightened, tingling from scalp to chin, and he reached for Penthesilia—whose hair was now gray—and fell onto the gray stones.

"Daric?"

His vision blurred.

"Are you all right, Daric?"

Lifting his head brought dizziness.

You've had a slight reaction.

"My machineries are not injured, Daric."

Penthesilia said, "What just spoke? Daric? Is that a necklace?"
Micro-elements, Daric. They have withdrawn.

Those passing saw a boy, face upturned, unkempt black hair
falling away from his ashen forehead, eyes squeezed shut, mouth
crimped. A boy who looked not only ill but unraised, whose
features—the narrow nose and pallid lips, the telltale hair—
looked *simple*, whose clothes—the rust-colored tunic two sizes
too large, the leggings and shabby boots—marked him an orphan
of the natives, without doubt.

The sheen relaxed. Daric breathed deeply and looked down at the
tile beneath his knee, whose pitted gray surface was flooded with
blue.

Penthesilia was leaning over him.

"I'm all right."

*You've had a slight reaction to micro-elements, but nothing
serious, Daric.*

He stood, arms held out should he fall again.

"Daric, are you sure?"

"Yes. Just a slight reaction."

The vendors, tended to by their spirals and eddies of smoke,
scrutinized him.

"This way," Penthesilia said.

He followed her slowly, groping his left pocket for the century rose, checking the stem and petals.

"How do you feel, Daric? Good to walk?"

"Yes, thank you."

When they were halfway across the plaza, he looked up from
her flashing white feet and said, "Do you have trees here?"

She slowed her pace and held her hands behind her, palm up
against her skirt. "Trees? Well, we have a garden at the KayTee
core, with fauna from home. There's dulcis trees, and some faille,

and birithmius shrubs. I can read you a list if you'd like. What about you? Any trees?"

Around him the tiles began to sparkle as Dayblown Phobos topped the spires overhead.

"We have maples," he said as the light spread across the plaza, sparkling pale red on the blue tiles. "But no oak."

Tyrian purple.

"Tyrian."

"And what?"

Daric said, "The color around us . . . now . . . is called Tyrian purple, I believe."

"You're very astute, Daric."

The glow deepened, and the buildings became shadow. Daric looked down at her white feet on the purple stone.

"Thank you."

"Is that why your brother let you come into the city alone?"

"Actually, he had to tend the orange trees."

"And did they once belong to the Mind of Mars, too?"

"I don't suppose," he said, impulsively adding, "What do you know about him—the Mind of Mars?"

Penthesilia glanced over and slowly—somehow strangely—blinked. "The Mind of Mars. He saved your planet from the Whirlwinds, didn't he? Long ago. The entire system, I think, except for the Earth. And he left the moon burning as a reminder. A warning. That's all my trove has, Daric. But if you want to know about the garden, I could recite every variety of flower. Or at least I could try. Shall I?"

"Please."

She did, finishing as they reached the other end of the plaza.

Ask her how far.

"How far is it to the Heliotrope?"

"Sorry. I go on, don't I? Nothing is really farther away than anything else, Daric, once you know your way around. Are you feeling ill?"

"No," he said. "Thank you."

"This way." She pointed to an alley between the buildings on their left. "The Concourse Elysium will lie on the other side."

They left the purple tile for dim walls, shadow. He followed Penthesilia around a curve to find the walls narrowing, around another to find darkness lit by yellow lines. Penthesilia's hair faded, then brightened, a fire he followed as they worked their way toward a third curve and the end of the alley.

"Here we are," she said, beside him on the landing that led, by hundreds of steps, down to a field of red stone. "The Concourse Elysium."

More narrow that the Tharsis, the Elysium was nearly empty, curving away from him on either side; those figures in sight were the unraised locals, or the stalking shadows of void mariners. A series of luminous columns occupied the center, each containing a creature.

Statues, Daric.

He squinted, then thought, *They're moving, Shade.*

"See the Grawls, there?" She pointed at the third column, a creature with four long, double-jointed legs, hunching shoulders, a long neck, its squat, fang-filled head slowly sweeping back and forth. "The Cosmo's past it."

Wary, Daric followed her down the steps and across the concourse, looking up at the creatures, who repeated the same sluggish movements; one raising a taloned hand in greeting, another squatting to leer at the empty stone below. "Where are they from, Pen?"

"From here, I suppose," she told him. "But they represent the creatures made by the Whirlwinds. There's an inscription . . ." She pointed to a plaque on the third column.

It says Grawl, Phoenix, Arizona. That's on Earth.

"It's for the tourists, Daric, from the Heliocracy. That's what they're coming to see. We're supposed to say, Imagine these things being alive *right now*! On Earth, the Whirlwind Planet!

And it could happen here, too, you know! They like to be scared. Peer Tromon told us."

He gazed up at the Grawl, wondering if his pilots had seen anything as strange.

Onward.

Daric continued around the pedestal, then waited for her to take the lead. She walked toward a ramp dropping into shadow. A figure hurried up, a mariner with billowing black robes, whose head was wreathed in blue smoke trailing a scent of roses.

Daric's vision grayed for an instant.

"We're now in the Cosmopolis, Daric. It belongs to the mariners."

Following her down, he was reminded of the levels below the workshop at home, where Jonas often disappeared for the entire day, and where he—Daric—was refused access.

Her feet flickered as the ramp leveled off.

The Heliotrope is directly ahead.

They were approaching a black wall.

He stopped.

"That's it, Daric. They don't mark the door. The customers feel the shrine, of course."

Tell me now. What am I to do?

Thank Penthesilia, and ask her to leave.

Tell me what I've come to buy.

An advantage.

His shade placed peculiar emphasis on the word.

"Second thoughts?" Penthesilia had stopped beside him, hands clasped in front of her.

He chewed his lower lip. "I want you to come in with me."

She can't, Daric.

"I'd like to, Daric, but it's not part of the KayTee. My resolution would be poor, and the tender might refuse me access."

We need to go in alone.

Penthesilia slowly blinked, and a moment later said, "You

wouldn't be able to find your way back, would you?"

"No."

"All right." She nodded. "All right, Daric, I'll stay and help, if I can."

"Thank you."

Penthesilia stepped forward and disappeared. Daric followed, through the wall, into the Heliotrope. The floor was sunken, the ceiling domed, and everything gilt and glowing, a lustrous carpet inset with tangerine tile that stung his eyes, brilliant tables and tall chairs all about; while ahead, along the arc of the wall, a long, low bar consumed in blue flames.

To his left, looking out of place, was an object sprawled on a black pedestal, what might have been the gnarled roots of a tree, mottled blue-green and gold.

"The shrine," said Pen.

He nodded.

"Where shall we sit, Daric?"

Among the empty tables, two patrons brooded like shadows; nearby, a blue-skinned mariner in black robes glared down at his open hands; across the room another—a woman with white hair curled around her throat—leaned back in her chair, asleep, it seemed.

Only the tender behind the bar noticed their arrival, his round face glancing up over the flames.

To Daric's left the wall was decorated with four long bones, each as tall as he, the ends crossed to form a square.

He chose the table beneath them, and sat heavily. Beside him Penthesilia cautiously lowered herself onto the chair, her dress settling an inch above the golden cushion. She smiled and contrived to rest her arms on the armrests, but finally folded her hands in her lap.

"A chidder, eh?"

Daric looked up.

The tender shambled toward them, his hands working at a

lump of silver, squishing it in the middle, then pressing it flat between his palms.

"What would a chidder be doing in my establishment, one? Ill, are you, two?"

A moth flitted near the tender, over his bulging brow and piggish eyes.

Daric said, "No, sir. I'm not ill."

"Two, going to collapse? You look simple, chidder."

Tell him you've come to buy a drink.

"I've come to buy a drink."

"Three, drink with what?"

The rose.

Daric unsealed his left pocket, reached inside, and carefully withdrew the rose. As he raised it the moth darted down, its wings suddenly glowing, casting a light onto the petals.

"Ah," said the tender. "Ah, one, I still wonder, what is a chidder doing in my establishment. But three, a drink with that, I agree. Allow." He reached out: Each finger bore a scarlet stain at the knuckle.

Yes, let him take it.

The tender lifted the century rose and appraised it in the moth's fitful glow.

"She's fine enough. Four, what vintage?"

Solus Alpha Intra-Data, current minus ten.

"Solus Alpha Intra-Data," Daric carefully repeated. "Current minus ten, I believe."

"A premium? You buy for someone else, five?"

"No, sir, for myself."

The tender looked from Daric to the century rose, then back. "Two, you're a chidder, and look ill. If the gens come here you're not known to me. You're a chidder from the farms. You've no business with drink. But I'll fetch it. I'm fond of roses, that is known. Your lectrice has to leave. Go. Shoo-shoo." The tender waved his hands at Penthesilia, who watched him without expression.

"Daric," Pen said. "Should I report him to the Scales on Triton for refusal to transact? I've instantaneous contact with my trove, you know."

The tender's eyes had strayed to the rose; he pursed his lips, then said, "The Krater-Tromon get nothing but praise from me, of course. I shall return."

The moth darted up to the roof.

"What are they, Pen? The Scales on Triton?"

"It's a place, Daric. Larger than Oppidum. Somewhere you never want to go. Trust me."

Daric nodded. "The Scales on Triton," he said softly. He looked at the bones, noting their pitted but polished surface. "I wonder where these are from." He stretched his shoulders, straightened his legs beneath the table. "I collect bones. I have two hundred and thirty-eight, mostly fish and small animals."

"Really? Where do you find them?"

"I have a lake. So I have fish bones. And sometimes I find animal bones in the orchard. But I don't recognize these."

Penthesilia slowly blinked. "Neither do I."

Letting a moment of silence pass, he ventured, "Have you been to the Scales on Triton, Pen?"

Her eyes left him, looking over his shoulder. Daric turned in time to see the gen float clear of the wall. In the brilliant light, it cast no shadows and seemed a chip of dark, starless space, moving now at head's height toward the blue-skinned mariner, who looked up briefly before finding his drink again.

"Yes, Daric," Penthesilia said. "I have."

Silently, the gen continued over the patrons and paused beneath the apex of the dome—while the tender made himself busy behind the bar—then reached the wall, passed through, and was gone.

Daric looked for the moth: It fluttered wildly near the top of the dome.

"Six, seen what a gen would do?" The tender approached, holding a bulb of blue liquid. "No, not seen, six? Eat my establishment *entire*, is what. You'd all wake up beetles, is what. Here, your order, four, Solus Alpha, Intra-Data, current minus ten. And here, mindful of six, your change." He dropped some narrow translucent strips on the table—seven of them, patterned with black lines—and set the bulb beside them.

"Thank you, sir," Daric said, putting the strips in his pocket. Is this the correct change?

Drink.

Daric raised his eyebrows.

"You got a quarter to soak it up. Use a dome. Then you leave—rolled out or no."

The tender touched the table and disappeared—or, rather, their table was now covered by a small, radiant dome.

Now?

"I thought you were buying it for your brother," said Penthesilia, her hair flickering.

First you must pull the sheen from your face, Daric.

Daric stared down at the bulb of blue liquid.

Drink it now?

I'm here to help you absorb it, Daric.

Couldn't I bring it home?

Information must be consumed in the Cosmopolis. Pull the sheen from your face.

Daric reached beneath his chin and found the rib, then lifted the sheen up and over his head, feeling a faint tingle.

"Is that a nano-sheen?" Penthesilia shut her eyes, then opened them.

Drink it quickly.

"Daric, I don't think that's a good idea. What about your reaction to the food?" She leaned closer.

Drink, and we will return to Jonas and Grandpapa.
Daric lifted the bulb, looking into the blue liquid.
"Daric, I can only make suggestions, I realize, but . . ."
Now, Daric. For Grandpapa and Jonas.
He sipped. A faint taste of lime.
All of it.
He sipped again, swallowed, then drank the rest in four gulps.
Good. Now pull your sheen back down.
He did, then swallowed a final time and leaned back.
"Daric?"
The dome brightened further, and seemed to consume Penthesilia. He was now alone; more than alone, for his shade, too, was suddenly gone. Daric sensed it, as if an ever-present hand had been lifted from his shoulder.
Shade?
The aftertaste was tart; he swallowed back acid.
Fear began as a stomachache that spread, reaching up his throat, burning with each beat of his heart.
Shade, please say something.
Aloud: "Shade?"
"Daric, are you all right?"
Wait. Wait. His shade *hadn't* left. Daric could sense it, elsewhere, not far: *turned away*; and now, as Jonas, while he was otherwise engaged, would sometimes give Daric a tool to play with, his shade gave him . . .
Daric's eyes burned. He blinked rapidly, unable to see the dome but sensing it rise.
His shade gave him . . .
A volley of horns, echoing wildly.
A memory of mine, Daric. While I work.
"Shade?"
His shade nudged him again, sounds and images flowing, frothing. Daric reached out, and a familiar voice was heard.
"He was *the Leader*, young Daric."

Daric fell back onto a stone floor.

Floating overhead, under a red stone ceiling, was Grandpapa.

Again, the horns sounded.

"Hard to grasp, I know, but he was *sole and singular*."

Grandpapa, a golden man, entire, sitting on a silver chair, gazing down with brilliant ruby eyes. "During his thousand-year rule he galvanized mankind, pushing it beyond the boundaries of its world, then its solar system . . ."

The wall around them was lost beneath canvases—paintings such as those Jonas had often done, but instead of the orchard, or Phobos starscapes, these were planets, hundreds of them, green, gold, crimson, *tyrian purple*, some banded and swirled, others rendered in abstract dabs and blotches, in finger scrapes. Planet to planet, they echoed the horn tones, and found echoes, too, on Grandpapa's hands as he nervously tapped his knees—stained green, gold, crimson, planet colors.

The air was hot, stifling. A high narrow window dropped sunlight across Grandpapa's shoulder.

"He was feared, despised, and dreadfully adored. *My Glory*, they called him. And on that fateful day . . . Are you listening?" Grandpapa's jade lips froze, half-open.

Daric nodded, aware of a roar, vague in the air, thrumming in the rock beneath his hand; the ancient Martian sea.

"On that fateful day, when the virus threaded leaves into his hair, pushed up roots from his miserable toes, the Leader mustered all his formidable energies to *fight* it. He was the *demiurge*, after all. The god before God. He directed his thaumaturgists to seek antidotes, and when they found none he put them to the Pain Dragon. He opened his hoard of genetic essence—*unthinkable before then*— in order to grow another body. He considered a pilgrimage to the fabled Parson's Planet. Oh, yes, young Daric, he *raged*. But then, finally, one warm night such as this, far from our beloved Mars, he acquiesced, ordering those few who loved him to carry out a final wish. To bury him in a wild forest of oak, of *Quercus lobata*, bury all his essence, including the vials, which, in the end, as the seasons passed, were wrapped in roots."

Grandpapa's chair turned in place, then floated up to the window. His eyes burned in the sunstruck glass.

"Young Daric, there is dire business at hand. The Storm approaches. They've awakened it—dormant since the Leader's *transmogrification* eight thousand years ago. Now, Earth's been lost. Trillions dead or sublimated! The autochthons rise. And our planet is next—this dear world we helped rebuild, once ruined by Him—soon to be lost again. Devoured, young Daric. Unless you help, and become my fingers and toes."

Daric's voice: "Will we be devoured, Grandpapa?"

Grandpapa was quiet for a moment, glaring down at the paintings. "We destroyed Fear long ago, but Panic remains. We shall use Panic. You must go to the basement . . ."

Shade?

"You must use the Machineries. The followers—it was a gift of theirs, you see, upon my awakening."

This isn't me, Daric told himself.

"Listen, you must fire up the Machineries."

He shut his eyes and turned away, into sunlight.

. . . oh Myiepa oh Rhea oh Alendra Six oh Tethys oh Cyprine Two . . .

Daric opened his eyes to a bright sky. Not Mars, but where? Perhaps Earth, with the whirlwind creatures nearby.

. . . oh Barnum Five oh Cybele oh Pluto . . .

He was staring up at the table's dome. His shoulders ached. He was out of breath. He had spat up some drink, which now tingled down his chin to his neck.

. . . oh New Io oh Isidis oh . . .

Not his shade's voice, but many voices. The words reminded Daric—

. . . oh Coeus Alpha oh Parisbeta oh Regio oh . . .

—of the pilots telling him all the planets they had visited before falling beyond Daric's orchard.

. . . Onomule oh Paul IV oh Betelguese oh . . .

He shut his eyes, then opened them again, relieved to find the other Mars, the other Daric, lit by horn volleys, had left him.

. . . Dorland's World oh St Ives oh Amenthes oh Rupes . . .

He studied the back of his hand, which was stained blue.

"Daric, should I get the tender?"

Penthesilia sat beside him, her hair alive like flame.

What time is it?

He wiped his mouth again.

Is it night?

Allowing his arms to fall to either side of the chair, Daric thought of dusk at home: how the surface of his lake would darken as the sun left the sky, allowing him to clearly see the scurrying fish—

. . . Xerxes V oh New Hester oh Pyrmides oh . . .

—while he sprinkled their food on the water; how the kitchen would begin to smell of boiled cabbage and carrots, Jonas's favorite; and later, during dinner, how the sound of Grandpapa singing the Martian anthem—all five verses—would echo dryly down the stairwell.

. . . Amalthea oh Groje . . .

"Daric?"

Penthesilia was a *soul*, he now understood. A Krater-Tromon soul, serving *indenture*, seeking *realization*.

"Can you stand up?"

He was trying to rise from the chair when a face breached the radiant dome above him, a familiar face, with three oblong eyes, a kind smile. It hung, silent, like a half mask, while the eyes took in his sprawled body. Then the lips parted, revealing brilliant teeth. "Child."

The woman from the dirigere.

. . . oh Styx oh Pleidra oh . . .

She stepped in, her slender neck, dark cloak, and then her hair sliding into view, ropes of black hair uncoiling, more spiking through the brilliant dome, like the legs of a spider, as she assumed Penthesilia's chair.

"Daric," the woman said.

Penthesilia's face flickered, lost in the woman's hair, until she stood and moved into the next chair.

With long fingers the woman stroked his forehead. "Can you talk?"

Again, Daric tried. She watched his eyes, then lifted the hem of her cloak and wiped his mouth, his chin, his neck.

He stared at the pendant, the third eye in the woman's forehead, and listened to her voice rising from the chorus: "You drank all this?"

She held up the empty bulb.

He tried to nod.

"A void mariner's dose. Were you being foolhardy? Or was it your shade?" She shook her head.

"I'm going to alert the tender," Penthesilia said.

Without looking away from Daric, the woman said sharply, "You have no business here. I will care for him." She stood and stepped through the dome.

Daric stared at it, wondering if she—this woman he had never seen before this afternoon—had been a vision, summoned by the voices. But then she reappeared, streaming through the dome to set a bulb of clear liquid on the table. "This will help. Drink."

She lifted it to his lips. Daric was terrifically thirsty, and quickly gulped down half the syrupy liquid.

"Enough." She pulled the bulb away. "Now relax."

Gathering her cloak through the dome, as if conjuring it out of nothing, she sat down beside him, then touched the side of the table; the dome dimmed to morning blue.

He listened to the voices, tried to sense his shade. "Do you remember me, child?"

He studied her pendant, the dark, segmented form, realizing it was *chitin*, the body of the *Spiri* insect.

She watched his eyes. "The voices tell you something, I can see. Tell me."

A *symbiotic* creature, used by the Mori . . .

"It's important we talk now, child, while your shade is scattered."

"But he can't . . ." Penthesilia began.

"Tell this ad to leave, child."

"He can't talk."

"Child?"

"He had a reaction to food in the square. I'm going to stay with him, I've decided."

"Thing," the woman said, not looking away from Daric. "You interfere with the living. By the laws I choose a forfeiture. You are *done*." She raised her right hand, drawing her cloak over Penthesilia, through Penthesilia, who cried out and was suddenly gone. The woman now held a rose by its crystal stem, a century rose with petals shining like blood. "To your guardians, child, you are currency, too."

Pen!

Daric tried to stand up, tried to call out, but the woman— Madame Thola Nee Montyorn—leaned forward, her cloak stirring of its own accord, curling up like a dark wave from behind her head, rippling over both of them to create a second dome, a cave of darkness. Luminous teeth appeared, inches from his eyes. "You must listen to me, child." Warm breath touched his forehead. "Your future is a game to him."

He looked away, while the cloak cupped his neck and shoulders, and seemed to stifle the voices, so that he could hear his pounding heart.

In the corner of his eye, the teeth flashed. "Started long ago, long before Dayblown Phobos was born, before the Ceres Storm and the Whirlwinds, *from which time fled to us with hands across its eyes.*"

Daric tried to pull free, but only brought her face, her warm breath, closer.

"Calm, calm. Do you know those words? A poem written by another Daric, a century ago on Anchor Three. He calls himself Jonas now. Listen to what the voices tell you."

. . . Camphos oh Larain oh Pelrop IV oh Ares . . .

"Ask the voices, why would a child be sent alone into the city? To suffer drink and perhaps die, and in dying, with the blame only on him?"

He tried to rise, but she held him tight. "Calm, child. Think. We wish you to come with us. Away from dead Mars and the remnants of Sol. Consider, Daric, you've begun to change. Your mind has grown *larger.* For a time the stars will seem more vivid than your home, he expected this. Soon you'll realize this is not the place for you."

Daric struggled, but she held him, and her hair gently coiled around his neck, his arm and ankle. "I have a tincture, child. To help you rest. But—hold still—but we have to wait for the drink to subside. Please, calm, child."

He tried to fall from the chair, to push his arm under the cloak, through the dome.

The coils tightened.

Shade!

He choked, and the darkness throbbed with blood, thick in his ears.

"Thola Nee Montyorn?" A voice, calm, like his pillow's.

The woman relaxed her hold: Daric gasped for breath.

"Release the boy, Thola Nee Montyorn."

Her teeth flashed inches from his eyes. "What is this, child? What do you wear?"

"Release the boy. I am his protection."

Daric discerned a faint red glow, strengthening while the voice spoke.

"Clever, *thing*. You avoided our eyes."

"This I intended, madame."

"Quite clever."

"Release the boy. I have a phase beam locked on your cerebral centers, another on your *banule* confrere."

In the medallion's fitful glow, her nostrils flared.

She stroked Daric's chin. "Not a simple device, are you? But . . . of course." She drew a breath through her shining teeth. "I address *the Mind*. Always with your child, spirit and soul. But you kept silent while he was in pain. Why did you hesitate to help?"

"I give the required warning, madame."

"Child, ask yourself, why did it hesitate? Because its plans are not yours, child. Because it is using you. I have defenses, thing."

"A crude Heliocratic web," said the medallion. "I find it strange that the Mori are now pandering to raised technologies. True, I have slept for ages, much has changed. Nonetheless, eighty percent of your defenses are now undermined. My phase beam will fuse your cerebral tissues, Thola Nee Montyorn. You will wander the streets of Oppidum, an idiot."

Daric looked up: A red gleam lingered in her third eye.

She smiled. "Ah, so there it is. You . . . you misunderstand us. You redeemed yourself, partly, during the Whirlwinds. You called yourself the Mind of Mars and saved this planet. But we cannot allow the Leader to spin himself forever into the future."

"Provocative, but incorrect at a fundamental level—I am not the Mind of Mars. I am of the original Darius. Let the boy go."

Her lips touched his ear, and she whispered, urgently, "Child, it cares not for you. Nor does your shade. Remember, you were sent out *alone*."

"Madame, I will count to three . . ."

"See, child! He will not use his energies! He does not want the gendarme! This is *His* device, but it is not *linked*. Your home has always been quiet—must be quiet. I spoke the truth!"

"One, Thola Nee Montyorn."

The red glow waxing, waning.

She said calmly, "Daric, take off the device."

"Two, Thola Nee Montyorn."

"Daric. Choose."

The braids slipped from his neck. The woman pulled away, whipping free her cloak, swimming in blue.

"*Thing*, ask the child. Ask him. What shall it be, Daric?"

"Three."

Thola Nee Montyorn was a writhing shadow, and Daric said to it, simply, "Go."

She whirled round, her cloak and tangled hair misting into the dome.

Daric touched his throat, grimacing against the pain. He blinked.

The medallion said, "You did well, Daric."   .

He swallowed once, twice, then reached for the bulb and drank the rest of the liquid.

"Madame Nee Montyorn is retreating. Ten meters. Twelve. Fifteen."

Silence settled. He was alone.

No shade, no voices.

He reached under his tunic and lifted the rosette medallion.

"Fifty meters. I will continue monitoring."

He pulled the medallion over his head and dropped it on the table, beside the empty bulbs. He coughed.

"Daric?"

He wiped his mouth. Then he croaked, "What happened to Pen?"

"The Mori was in her right, Daric. The eidolon interfered, and was forfeit. But Grandpapa will be proud of you, Daric. Jonas will be proud."

"She was just trying to help me."

He shut his eyes. He tried to appreciate the silence, but was distracted by a sudden flash on his eyelids.

"Daric? A weeform has breached the dome."

He looked. The tender's moth flitted over the tabletop.

"It reads benign, Daric, but you should tell it to go. Madame Nee Montyorn continues to retreat, one hundred meters. I suggest you string me around your neck."

Daric was pleased by the change in the medallion's voice.

"Daric?"

It was afraid.

He straightened in his chair and wiped his mouth.

The moth darted away, then came closer, wings fluttering.

"Daric, I suggest you put me back on."

He reached up quickly, catching the moth. He clutched it, felt it tickling his palm.

"We cannot take chances, Daric."

His fingers were luminous.

Daric smiled, unknown to him a tight smile, lips compressed, draining them of color. He unsealed his left tunic pocket, then thrust his hand inside, flung the moth free, and withdrew, quickly sealing it up.

"Jonas will be angry if you leave me behind, Daric."

Cautiously, he stood.

"Daric, Grandpapa will . . ."

The boy emerging from the dome did not walk but *hobbled*, drawing the attention of the blue-skinned mariner, who turned his long, saturnine face to Daric, his eyes seeming for a moment a reflection of Daric's own—somehow both lucid and befogged—until Daric looked away and continued past the tender, who muttered, "Chidder, be rid of you!"

Daric stepped through the wall of the Heliotrope.

Wearily climbing the stairs, he looked up to find a man limping down, a white-haired man in a gray tunic, clearly unraised, somehow furtive, steadying himself with a hand flat against the wall; a stranger to Daric, until his nose twinkled, and his white hair caught the light as a limpid crown.

Jonas stopped above him, watching Daric climb. "Grandpapa told me where you'd gone. So I thought to find you."

Daric reached the stair on which Jonas stood and looked past him, toward the concourse.

Jonas drew an orange from his tunic and offered it.

A small, pocked sun.

Studying it, Daric thought of Sol, and the Heliocracy stars that burned between Mars and Plexus Foley. He could name them, he realized. He began to, silently.

Rhea, Alendra Six, Tethys, Cyprine . . .

"Take it. They're the best yet. I got three baskets."

He took it, regarding it blankly, then continued up the stairs. Jonas followed, both of them with difficulty, to the Concourse Elysium.

"Are you okay, boy?"

Daric was looking at the Grawl when a gen darted up beside him. It hovered, silent, close enough to touch.

"This way." Jonas took his hand, but Daric did not move. He stared into the gen. From here it was less a shape than a void, blotting out the city. This must be what space is like, he thought. It would suck him in; he would fall forever through that darkness.

Daric said, "I've done something wrong."

Jonas squeezed his hand. "Lies and such." He pulled Daric along.

"I stole something."

The gen followed for a few paces, keeping in Daric's periphery, then darted soundlessly away.

Jonas's grip relaxed, and he was quiet until they reached the dirigere tower. "Grandpapa has his reasons, Daric," he said finally. "All according to his plan."

Daric stared up past the city at the sky. He could sense the stars as glowing lines. And on the lines, numbers.

During the trip home he sensed them in the air, lines and numbers from Mars, from Earth and Mercury Scythe, from Onomule, Cyprisia, and Plexus Foley, and many more. The numbers glowed and were too quick to read; somehow the voices made the numbers, or were *inside* the numbers.

The dirigere landed beyond the orchard.

As Daric led the way through the pine, Aver appeared in a great rush of gold-tipped wings, alighting onto Jonas's arm. Jonas greeted it, then spoke the guarding sound, and the hawk nodded and leapt out, wings wide into the air, gone to shadow.

Home was quiet.

In the kitchen Jonas said, "Are you hungry, boy?"

Famished, Daric shook his head. He set the orange on the table. Jonas walked to the stairs, pausing as he did most nights so that Daric could hurry up before him. But when Daric did nothing but stare at the baskets of oranges against the white wall, Jonas began to climb.

Daric?

The voice behind his head.

Daric?

Farther up the stairwell, Grandpapa whirred and chirped. His waking noises.

Daric? You should eat an orange, as Jonas wishes. It will help restore you.

Daric climbed behind Jonas, remembering the dream turret, the painted planets, with Grandpapa floating up beside a narrow window.

"Ah, my boy."

Jonas had reached the top and stepped aside. Daric trudged up to find Grandpapa looming on the silver stand, glowlamps on either side. "Ah, my boy, my boy, my boy, my boy," Grandpapa said in a lulling tone, somehow musical, like the mellow grind of gears in the basement. "You have all returned."

Daric squinted up, past Grandpapa, at the peeling star chart. He thought he recognized what they stood for, each yellow, blue, white point.

Say hello to Grandpapa, Daric.

"You were obviously successful, Daric. I can tell by your eyes. But how—Jonas, how *successful* was he?" Grandpapa half raised his right arm, beckoning to Jonas.

"We don't know yet, Grandpapa."

"Hmmm. No doubt you feel your place in the stars, now. It will give you strength. And in time, a guidance of sorts. You stand at the beginning of a new life. Tell me, Daric, can you appreciate what you've gained?"

Daric looked from the painted stars to Grandpapa. "A moth," he said.

A moth?

"What do you mean?"

What's this?

Daric unsealed his pocket, his tight mouth tensing into a grin as the moth, bright as fire, hissed past his fingers—

What . . .

—and spiraled up, past Grandpapa—who awkwardly clutched at it—up and up, to strike the domical vault and sizzle there among the painted stars.

Grandpapa murmured, while Jonas, hands on his hips, peered up.

Daric, the weeform was not yours to take.

Grandpapa said, "An offering, eh? Why, the Leader often had his people bring offerings . . ."

"It's mine," Daric said flatly. "I'll want it back when it comes down."

Grandpapa lowered his arms. "You *must* tell us, how do you feel? What about your shade? What does he say?"

We're fine. Some slight matrixing problems, but all is well.

"I haven't heard from my shade, Grandpapa."

Daric.

Jonas scratched the edge of his nose, while Grandpapa canted toward Daric, whirring gravidly. "Hmmm, well. This is not unusual." Grandpapa straightened. "Don't worry, you just took more than you could digest. Tomorrow, Daric. Tomorrow your shade will return. We will discuss your new life, eh? What you need now is rest."

"Yes," Daric said.

"But first, you were asking a question earlier. About the Leader. Was it true? you asked. Was he really turned into a tree?"

"I don't care anymore, Grandpapa."

Daric.

I don't care.

Grandpapa trilled. "Brooding won't help, my boy. And I was hoping to finish the story."

Daric. Tell them my systems are fine.

"They buried everything that was the Leader, branch and bark and brain, and for a long time he stood in solitude, a noble oak, and turned his leaves to catch the sunlight, and groped the ground with his roots . . ." Grandpapa canted back, watching the moth.

Daric.

Hello, Shade.

"Alone, abandoned, he had reconciled his life to this, not knowing that his followers"—Grandpapa paused again, distracted, perhaps, by the vigorous paths the moth charted against the fresco—"that his followers would one day . . . seek him out . . . oh, but how would they find him . . . you ask . . ."

Daric, please.

And here Old Jonas, who was eyeing the moth, said, "I remember how that tale ends, Grandpapa. Yes, surely. I heard it long ago, on a night such as this. How could the Leader have guessed—or so it goes—that the weeping leaves would give him away?"

2

WHIRLWIND PLANET

*M*oving day, Daric.

A whisper, while he slept.

Today we leave Mars. You and I and Jonas and Grandpapa.

A whisper over Daric's dream of a forest, tall trunks diminishing on all sides, arranged in perfect rows, flourishing high overhead in a strange purple canopy, like countless domical vaults across the sky.

The suns and planets beneath your feet.

A whisper while he wandered the forest, accompanied by other figures in the distance, dark-robed like the void mariners.

Today we leave, Daric, and I'll be your guide.

While he searched the ivy for a rose.

Your trustworthy shade.

A certain rose, with petals shining like blood.

Penthesilia.

•   •   •

He awoke to trembling light and an incessant sound: *tick-tick-tick*. The jar on the bedside table.

His moth batted the glass, its light pooling up the curving stone wall behind, winking on the circle of empty hooks where his fish bones had hung. Otherwise the room was dark and quiet. His pillow was dead, had been dead these last few days.

Daric flung back his sheets and sat up.

Moving day, he thought. Jonas's already up, at work.

He swallowed, rubbed his eyes.

The moth's light touched a green bottle on the bedside table. His throat tightened at the sight—medicine said to soothe the effects of the information he had consumed five days earlier, a sour syrup that burned his throat and sapped the strength from his body, dimming the starlines. These last three nights he had not touched it, except to pour the correct dosage down the sink before bed, and Jonas had been too busy to notice.

He stood up, holding on to the table for support.

No dizziness.

"What time is it?"

Had he not nulled his pillow, it would have brightened to a nocturnal blue glow and announced, "Good morning, Daric. The hour is . . ."

Is the pillow just a pillow, Daric wondered, or is it Grandpapa, too?

He found his tan shirt and trousers beside the table, and struggled them on; then his tunic.

Is the pillow Darius, like Grandpapa and Jonas and you, Shade, and the medallion . . . and me?

He was still not used to rising in silence, to dressing without conversation from his shade. These last three mornings he had awakened early and gone outside—alone, much to Jonas's concern—to stand on the lawn beneath the stars and idly name them, face upturned to their radiations. With the voices silenced (the medicine had done this much) he was able to apprehend the countless lines, vibrant with numbers; from the core worlds of Plexus Foley and Iridani, from Osud and Hexel Terra, from distant Dombus.

Daric found his boots and slipped them on.

At sunrise Jonas would summon a ship. At noon they would raise Grandpapa from his century seat and float him down the stairwell. By dusk his home would be empty, all the stuff of Daric's twelve years packed into the ship that would lift, by nightfall, into the stars.

Because of me, he thought. All because of me. Right, Shade?

He looked for Grandpapa's finger, which Jonas had given him the night before.

I left it outside. In the grass. Didn't I, Shade?

With both hands he raised the jar.

"Good morning." He squinted at the moth—the weeform, he remembered—studying the blur of its wings, the white light of its body. "It's moving day."

The moth had no face, no eyes; it left a faint fog where it bumped the glass. Through the holes punched in the lid, he could hear the hum of its wings.

Daric stepped quietly from the room, pausing on the stairs. Light came down from above, and a soft sound, low and musical, like the grind of gears in the basement: Grandpapa's reverie. He could picture Grandpapa on the silver stand, canted back, head lolling, ruby eyes peering up at the vault and the fresco of the ancient galaxy.

Grandpapa had done little else for two days now.

Quietly, he continued down to the atrium, his light winking on the instruments—the oval dials of the Actuality gauges. Will Jonas tell the Ares Historical Foundation we're leaving? he wondered. That the readings won't be done anymore?

In the kitchen he made himself some porridge, mixed in sliced apples, and hurriedly ate; then, clutching the jar to his stomach, he stepped outside, into darkness.

The air smelled of soil, more pungent than during the day.

What time is it?

He listened for Aver, who had been out every night since Daric's return from Oppidum, guarding the perimeter.

The stars were mirrored in the circular lake. As he walked toward the shore, he searched for Grandpapa's finger, holding the jar away from him, the light trembling on the wet grass as he slowly turned in place.

Do you remember where I left it, Shade?

Behind the turret, the sky shimmered with the first faint light from Dayblown Phobos. There was no line for Phobos—its appearance always surprised him. Soon the burning moon would rise and roll across the dark sky, heralding the sun.

He found it by the shore: the fourth finger from Grandpapa's left hand, crooked in the middle, made of jade. Kneeling there, he set down the jar and began his chore. When Phobos topped the pine trees on the edge of the orchard, sending a writhing lattice of shadows across the grass, Daric had eight cubes of water beside him. Each held one of his fish.

He thought, How many more? Three?

Leaning forward, he raked the surface of the lake with the finger's glowing green nail, back and forth, as Jonas had taught him, dragging luminous threads of Phobos across the water.

By the fifth stroke he touched a silver wave, which was another fish.

"Hello," he said softly, lifting the finger with both hands, along with the fish, which depended from the tip in its cube of water. "Sleep," he said. "I'll wake you up when we reach our new home." The fish stirred the sluggish water with its tail, and gulped, staring at nothing in particular, it seemed. Daric studied the dull eyes as they hardened, thinking of the aquarium in Oppidum, the mustard-colored fish inside, said to be a *mimir* from the fabled planet Last.

And he remembered his friend Penthesilia, her long red hair and long purple dress, how she had been kind to him . . .

We leave today, Daric.

The voice spoke gently, behind his head.

For the stars.

Daric thought, She was my friend, Shade.

He set the cube down behind the others, then leaned back on his heels, thinking, How many more fish to go?

One more, Daric.

Machinery groaned in the house. The shore trembled beneath his knees; it was Jonas, already up and working.

He leaned forward and raked the water, once, twice, and thought of Penthesilia, who was now a rose. A century rose, tucked into the cape of Madame Thola Nee Montyorn.

Waves lapped at the shore.

Your friend was an eidolon, Daric. A soul. Such things happen to them.

He remembered how Penthesilia had cried out when Thola Nee Montyorn drew her purple cloak over and through her.

It doesn't help to brood.

In the center of the lake a spark ignited, brightening, growing longer, then broader, flooding the water with slate-colored light. The agitated shadow of a fish darted to the shore, while dark leaves and sediment heaved up from the widening brightness to reveal—most startling of all—his brother Jonas standing down there *below* the bottom of the lake. Jonas, garbed in a white suit, his nose winking as he glanced up, as he waved to Daric, then patted the pointed shape beside him—the nose of an ancient rocket.

Jonas will be draining the lake soon.

The lake was the top of the ship's bay, he realized. Jonas stood on a platform surrounding the ship.

Moving day, he thought.

The shore shuddered once more. The finger jumped in his hand as the last fish was caught, one with vague eyes and a green underbelly. He lifted it, watching the water harden around it with a gelatinous weave, then set it down carefully with the others. Ten cubes glimmering in the moonlight.

In the lake below, sediment slowly rained down, obscuring his view of Jonas and the rocket.

His heart began to pound.

We're really leaving, he thought. Into the starlines.

He put Grandpapa's finger in his pocket, lifted his jar in one hand, and stood up. The wall of pine flickered in the moonlight. He suddenly wished to roam his trails for a last time: the Blaze-bug Trail, leading through the rhododendron and hawthorn, where he had lain for hours some afternoons pretending he was the size of an insect, and the orchard a forest, as it had been in the ancient days; or the Blackberry Trail, one of his most cherished, protected by thorns; here he had spent most of the day following his return from Oppidum, while Jonas traveled into the city to retrieve—without success—the medallion.

Jonas's preparations to leave had begun soon after.

He had allowed Daric to help pack the vegetables and the parchment pages, and the rocks that Daric had enjoyed making his armies, laying them out in ranks on the floor of the workshop; the rough diamonds and trachzycs, emeralds and amethysts, and the rubies shaped for Grandpapa's eyes.

Appreciate this atmosphere. Remember it.

He thought, I'm going to walk.

With the jar flickering in his hand, he walked across the grass toward the pine.

Don't go far, Daric.

I'll go where I want, Shade.

He smelled wet stone and heard, from the open kitchen door, Grandpapa's trilling.

I'm going to ride my wheel.

Looking up, Daric wondered if the turret would stand here for another four hundred years. Day after day after day.

Like ancient clockwork.

He found his wheel canted in weeds near the rhododendron. Light fell on the wide yellow rim flecked with scratches and the blue hub that—as he neared it—unfolded into a seat.

"Wheel on," he said, dropping into it. The wheel hummed, spewing a faint geyser of dust, draping a harness across his chest, inflating, pedals beneath his boots. Daric set the jar beside him, made sure the seat had hold of it, then reached into the hand holes, which molded warmly to his hands; he squeezed with his right hand.

Wheezing, the wheel lifted from the grass, tilted left and right as he moved his left and right hands. He pressed the left pedal, setting the wheel in motion, then veered away from the house. The sudden breeze smelled of soil and damp grass.

I want to see the sunrise, Shade.

Branches brushed his head and neck, soaking them, as he moved between the outspread arms of the pine trees and down the Blazebug Trail. He stepped on the pedal, increasing speed, following the first curve—

Be careful, Daric.

—ducking another branch, gaining height to top a fallen tree trunk, whisking over the matted glistening grass now, with Phobos light shimmering through the canopy.

He thought, Shade, your memory of old Mars. I heard the ocean . . .

Yes.

Where was that?

On the shore of the sea Elysium.

Do you remember . . .

Do I remember being Darius? No, Daric. I was born of the Mind of Mars, of Grandpapa. Like you.

The ocean was burned away, wasn't it, Shade? In the Storm.

Yes. More than just the ocean. But Grandpapa saved the planet and the system. As I've told you before, he deserves our respect.

Beyond the rhododendron the trail began a wide curve, following the arc of the pine. Daric was watching the trail bracketed by his boots when a form darted out, scuttling now in front of him, to and fro on the path.

A red-and-gray-striped shell, with a hundred pale legs frantically treading the dirt.

A sandfink!

Grimacing, he jammed down the left pedal. The sandfink wasn't leaving the trail.

I'm going to catch it, Shade. We'll take it with us.

He leaned to the left as the trail bent right, ducked another branch, shut his eyes briefly as he passed through a scree of leaves, then saw pink light through branches ahead, morning light, as he broke through the last rank of trees onto the Ares plain.

Shade, it's heading for its warren! On the plain!

Free of the orchard, the sandfink began a broader weave through and around the spare scrub, heading to open land ahead, and the sun.

He thought, I've never seen one move so fast!

He pressed the pedal all the way; the wheel wouldn't go faster.

We shouldn't venture too far.

Thola's gone, Shade. Remember what Jonas said? She went offworld.

It won't tire, Daric. It'll just keep running.

I'm almost on it.

He bit his lower lip, aware of the orchard retreating at his back and the dry warmth of the plain enveloping him.

We're passing the perimeter line.

He barely glimpsed a marker—behind him now. They were

all the same, the bronze plaque reading: ARES HISTORICAL FOUN-
DATION SITE. ESTABLISHED A.E. 6773.

Then the sandfink disappeared.

Where is it?

He looked left, right, and saw only the dark plain, washed
with copper at the horizon, where the sun was now breaching
the hills.

Did it double back?

He looked over his shoulder.

Did it dig under?

Let's go back, Daric.

Grinning, he relaxed his foot, so the wheel began to decel-
erate, still moving forward, then gestured to start a rotation, the
turret and the orchard moving across his field of vision.

Jonas is busy beneath the lake, Shade. He won't care.

The wheel turned back to face the sun, slowing.

Daric, stop the wheel.

Why?

Stop the wheel and look there, beside the sun. Look closely.

He squeezed both hands, bringing the wheel to a halt.

A cloud of dust settled over him. The wheel sighed as it
dropped, with a bump, to the plain.

There. Look there.

He squinted.

To the left of the sun.

A blur against the pink sky.

A shimmer, like a heat wave or a trick of the light.

Insects, he thought. Metal insects.

A flurry, escaped from Oppidum.

He glanced down to check on the jar, his moth darting madly
against the glass.

Look at the shimmer.

He peered.

You think it's a flurry, Shade?

Don't look away.

Daric could make it out more clearly now, darker, closer. A dust dervish.

Let's return home.

He thought, But Jonas said we didn't have to worry about Thola. You were there, Shade. Jonas mentioned her bones. Glowing bones. How we could track her. You were there, but you didn't say anything.

Turn around. Let's go back. Quickly!

Daric swallowed, thrilled with the fear in Shade's voice.

Not a dervish, but something solid, flashing in the sunlight, in furious motion.

Daric felt a twinge between his shoulder blades.

A figure, with long loping legs and arms—like the creature from Oppidum.

The Grawl, right, Shade?

Aver.

What?

Daric focused on the Grawl, the long neck low to the ground, shoulders high.

Aver. Look left.

To his left lay the hawk, a black smudge on the rock, one wing jutting up. Blood all around, black on the rock.

Quickly! Back to the orchard!

Thunder rippled across the plain.

Daric grabbed the toggles—the wheel rising jerkily, wheezing—and jammed down the pedal, the sudden acceleration nearly tumbling his jar from the seat.

Quickly!

But the pedal was all the way down, and he risked one last glance—

Don't look. Ride!

—to see the Grawl—for surely it *was* the Grawl—lunging now across the red rock toward him.

Ride, Daric!

Thunder brushed his back.

This is as fast . . .

The toggles! He began to weave now like the sandfink, soaring over the rock, his eyes set on the distant turret, where Jonas and Grandpapa . . .

The wheel died beneath him, crashed, slid, scraping up a cloud of dust.

Get out! Run!

He yanked the harness from his chest, grabbed the jar, and struggled out of the wheel, onto the rock, began to run but caught his boot in a hole. He fell hard, twisting his right ankle, striking the rock with his chin. The jar shattered, the weeform flew off.

Daric!

He turned, stifling a scream, onto his back to stare up at the creature, its head whipping back and forth, braying mute to the sky.

Run, Daric.

The creature froze. High on the chest a figure wiggled out, with long arms and legs, the color of glazed sand, jumping free, floating slowly down. It crouched in midair, a dark face gazing at Daric, with winks of silver at its sides: long wires flailing in sunlight. As its boots touched the rock the figure dropped forward and scurried toward Daric.

He scrambled back, trying to get to his feet.

A dark face and wild gray hair, with the silver wires, and the arms reaching out.

"Stay, boy! Stay!"

A second figure appeared, tall and golden, floating slowly down.

"Stay! Stay!" cried the first figure, its face long and dour, with a twisted mouth and dark eyes. "Hold, boy!"

Reaching out for him.

"Leften said gentle," urged the second, striding up behind.

Daric tried to pull himself up, but the wires wrapped his boots, yanking him back. He cried out, tried to kick free.

"No damage," insisted the golden figure. "Gently there. Stand aside, Joom. Let me see." The golden face leaned close. "Are you the boy? Are you?" Dust swirled behind it.

"Looks the part, right?" said the other.

No good to struggle.

Shade, are they with Thola?

The golden figure pulled a string from its slender waist, shaking out a tent of fabric that winked in shadow. "Sleep beneath the elsewhen, boy."

As the fabric settled over Daric and extinguished his thoughts.

Yes, we're awake, Daric. Look around but say nothing.

He opened his eyes. His vision was blurry and grayed-out.

Nano-particles, he knew.

He thought, Where are we?

Blink, look around.

He did, apprehending glowing gray walls that curved toward him. He was sitting up, his legs stretched out in front of him. He blinked again.

We haven't left Mars. I can feel its line.

He tried to lift his arms, tried to move his legs.

I can't move, Shade.

His heart beat wildly in his throat.

Shade?

Listen.

I can't move at all.

Don't worry about that now. Listen.

Daric noticed a dark shape in the wall across from him—a shadow, as though of a human figure stretched out then forced back together, broken, with a long head leaning into the shoulder, arms impossibly long and bent inward, fingers curling out, pointed like claws.

Listen.

He heard voices. One high, the other low, gruff. He remembered the golden figure and—heart catching in his throat—the other with its dark face and writhing wires.

Are they with Thola?

These aren't Mori, and Mori don't employ others. Listen to the voices.

He tried to concentrate, to hear the words, which were coming closer.

Don't reveal me, for your own protection.

Beyond his boots the golden face, smooth and featureless, pushed up through the floor; not golden now, but gray. Gray arms and a gray torso and gray legs.

"The elsewhen has faded." The figure crouched beside him, head tipped. "Boy, do you understand me?"

Near the bright line of Mars was another, a red line, without numbers. Very near, somehow.

"Yes," he said.

"My name is Sisteel Nee Portia."

Say nothing.

"What's yours?"

"Daric."

The blank face regarded him. Blank, but not inanimate; the muscles pulled where the mouth would have been, suggesting a smile. "I knitted your ankle, Daric. It shouldn't hurt you."

"Please," Daric said. "I can't move."

Sisteel Nee Portia touched his forehead; his vision blurred and he fell forward. She helped him stand up, then let go.

Daric moved his arms, put weight on his ankle. No pain.

He reached into his pockets. They were empty.

Grandpapa's finger!

That's not important, now, Daric.

"Line is fabricated, Teely," said a gruff voice.

Wild gray hair breached the floor, then the narrow, dark face. "Let's be off, dispatch our 'fink," it said, climbing up, crouching, its wires flicking impatiently. Its eyes were level with Daric's, entirely dark and glistening. "Then on to the Scales, to redeem poor Quint, who surely despises his sleep of nothingness."

Daric tensed. He pressed against the wall.

"You're frightening the boy, Joom."

Daric, they're humans like you.

"Let it tremble!" said Joom, whose wires curled and uncurled beneath his face, maybe two dozen, some ending in pincers, some in sharp points.

The tendrils help him work, that's all.

"This is the one?"

"It is," Sisteel said.

Joom leaned close to Daric. "I am a lamb when compared to Quintillux Cunning Heart." He smiled, showing jagged yellow teeth. "Our Quint, there in the wall—our fierce Heart—nulled by a tender, may that man suffer the Scales! And now Leften leads us up . . ." Joom stood, unfolding his long lanky frame, and turned to Sisteel. "Teely, hear me—*raid the tower!* Think of what waits! Nothing better in the Wilderness, to be sure. All the prizes. The Pain Dragon, without doubt! The Pain Dragon!"

It's him.

What, Shade?

"If Leften considers it wise," said Sisteel Nee Portia.

"Is this . . ." Daric asked, pausing to swallow. He could not remember the name. "Are we inside the creature, from Oppidum?"

Sisteel might not have heard him. "Tell her the boy is awake, Joom."

"The boy, the 'fink!" Joom leaned low, and said, "One of the mint, from the old bones? Just like the songs? Wish to drown the planet away, cinder it like the home world, O Kral?" He laughed, a guttural sound.

Before the cry could leave Daric's lips, Joom climbed up into the ceiling, his legs kicking, disappearing.

Daric drew a deep breath. "Please, we're leaving today. It's moving day."

The blank gray face said, "Are they kind to you? Is that why you miss them?"

"Jonas and Grandpapa . . . they're my family."

"Have you lived there all your life? In that ruin?"

"It's a cenotaph," he said, proud to have remembered what Thola Nee Montyorn had called it. He swallowed, felt his heart calm.

From above: "Up, 'fink, Leften wants your company."

Hands reached down from above to draw him up, through a layer of light where hundreds of birds seemed to chirp, up into the Grawl's head, amid floating pictures of his house.

To his left, his right, above, the images gathered, compacted, with the orchard and lake pushed, glittering, against the turret's door.

Joom smiled, then disappeared down.

"Welcome, Daric," said a cold voice, higher than Thola Nee Montyorn's, but not as high as Sisteel's. "I am Leften Tine of the *Talus*."

He fought to see the woman reclining in the glowing wall.

"You look more frail than I expected."

He crawled toward her, passing through the images to find himself at the foot of a white pallet.

Leften Tine was clearly *raised*, similar to the Citizens of Oppidum with long limbs, a long neck, and a pale, smooth skull. Her eyes looked through him, as he had looked through the turrets. Her ears were nothing but soft, puckered holes.

Something crawled on the pallet by her hand, eight narrow, crooked legs like a crab.

"We're adventurers, Daric." Her eyes flashed. "We search for profit in the Wilderness of Ruin."

What's the Wilderness . . .

Our solar system, Daric.

Among the haze of turrets, something winked. Jonas, perhaps, appearing in the kitchen door, searching for him.

"We understand what you are. We understand where you come from. Look at me, Daric."

Leften Tine was smiling. Her smooth forehead, her cheeks and chin, somehow rippled. He thought of a thin mask, then of a mask floating on the surface of his lake.

"You really *are* just a boy, aren't you?" She stretched, her white robe rippling, too; her feet, with toes as long as his fingers, reaching for him, then relaxing.

"Please," he said softly. "Can I go home? My brother's waiting for me."

The crab-thing raised two legs, clicking them together. A watery image was cast between them, flickering, then gone. She took no notice.

"We have need of your help. Do you understand?"

This is betrayal, Daric. He's here . . .

Leften continued, "We wish to take you on a trip. And not entirely with strangers, no. With familiar company, whom we took from a tender in Oppidum. Ten eleven twelve, as he said." She reached into the wall and drew out a medallion shaped as the old Martian rosette. Once red, now gray. Then a voice, familiar—the calm voice of his pillow—said, "A trip home, Daric."

The medallion from Jonas's oak chest.

Betrayal.

Leften Tine smiled, made strange as it rippled across her face. The medallion pulsed. "To *Earth*."

Betrayal!

"To the Whirlwind Planet, Daric."

Leften Tine leaned forward, her long fingers suddenly at

Daric's forehead, as though to brush away his curls. "But first, boy, we must touch your shade."

Hands grabbed his ankles and pulled him down, into a blizzard of unseen birds and silver sky.

I've been asleep. Asleep in the elsewhen. Is that it, Shade?

His eyes were shut; he could not open them.

Shade, where are we?

Shade!

He was alone. The ever-present hand was gone from his shoulder.

And the weave of invisible lines had changed around him.

He reached out and found nothing, above or below.

He knuckled his eyes—they stung fiercely, were sticking, yet he was able to see now, better when he wiped them again, grimacing against the pain.

A pure darkness. Like gazing into the gendarme in Oppidum, gazing into a void. And as his eyes adjusted he recognized the countless stars revolving.

"Shade?"

No Dayblown Phobos: no Mars: no weight.

Crystal panels framed the stars. And the stars were not revolving around Daric; he was slowly spinning. The sun came into view, dimming as he stared to the color of an orange.

And his shade had been taken.

"Boy?" A remembered voice, nearby. Soft and cool, a woman's voice.

Someone touched his shoulder, enough to make the sun swing from view. Then a golden face, close up.

A numberless red line, suddenly bright among the others.

What was her name?

"Daric? How do you feel?"

He gulped air. Beyond the panels were narrow white branches stretching out, brittle against the dark, and a silver dot—a figure—drawing out folds of glinting silver, a huge half circle of sail.

Daric choked, coughed.

Her hand was at his mouth, wiping it, then giving him something to chew.

"You'll feel better," she said.

He shut his eyes, caught the starlines, apprehended the lines in all directions, brightest in front of him.

"Do you know what's happened, Daric?"

He swallowed hard, blinked.

"Look at me."

He did not want to. He reached for the lucid panels—which were farther away than he thought—and began to slowly drift toward them. But pain flared between his shoulders. He pulled his arm back, grimacing.

"What hurts?"

"My eyes . . . and my neck."

She touched his chin. "Look at me, Daric." The face floated close. He could see his own vague reflection there, black bangs floating above his head. "Look up." She pulled at the bottom of his eyelid. "Leften didn't wipe you clean, that's all." She touched his cheeks, traced under his eyes.

"My shade's gone."

The golden face was silent. Beyond, the silver figure dropped toward them through the masts.

"We removed it." Sisteel let go of him, and floated back. "Everyone gives up their shade, sooner or later."

Daric struggled for words, but felt tears welling up.

"Cry, if you wish. It will help your eyes."

He cried, unable to hold back, cupping his palms over his face, coughing. Soon he sensed lights blossoming around him, and heard a sucking sound nearby.

"Look. Look at me, Daric."

The golden mask was gone; she held it in her hand. Her face had wide, pale eyes—kind eyes.

Sisteel, he remembered.

Her scalp was circled with thin white stripes, continuing down behind her ears, and her neck. She smiled. "We wear sheens, of a sort. At least in the Wilderness, outside Triton."

Daric wiped his eyes, and teardrops broke away to float and tumble, until she reached up and drew them into her wrist. He looked around him. The clear panels had brightened to soft white, curving over him, meeting at the bottom. Some blinked with small characters or graphs, pale green and purple, flickering.

The colors, the silence, somehow soothed him.

"We're on the *Talus*. Do you remember?"

He nodded, though he knew this was not quite the same craft.

She reached for him, touching not his tunic but a blue suit, which rippled at her touch—not as Leften's face had rippled; this became hard, like shell, a blazebug's shell. On his chest was a gold crescent, with two marks below it. A circular line, and a white globe.

"This will give you gravity. We use a different sort, to help us down the well."

A voidsuit?

She touched the globe, and he moved irresistibly to the floor, though the floor seemed much like the ceiling. Unsure of balance, he felt the rest of him floating up while his boots remained on the panels below.

"When you want to swim, touch the other one. The circle. It's simple, right?"

"Yes."

He touched the circular line, floating up.

His hands were shaking. Noticing, she said, "The white tab on your sleeve, there, will give you nutrients. Push it."

He did, and felt a sudden warmth course through his body. He blinked against it, staring down at the two large symbols on his chest: a rock and an empty circle.

He thought, We're going to Earth. The Whirlwind Planet.

He shut his eyes and remembered Mars, and felt it, pulling at his stomach, along with numbers that meant nothing to him, that disappeared when he opened his eyes.

"You're not what I expected, Daric." A slight smile, made strange by her eyes, which were so light a blue they were almost gray. "You're not a monster. I was expecting a monster."

He struggled for a reply while she spun away, leaving him to stare at the stripes on her head and neck.

"Where's my sheen?"

She turned back, arms stretched out. "You have a new one. The resolution's better. Yours would gray out, wouldn't it? Do you know how old it was?"

He shook his head. He wiped his eyes and asked, "Why am I going to Earth?"

"It's your home world, isn't it? You're from the Earth, from long ago. You're Darius, the Leader."

"I'm not," he said softly.

She smiled. "You're *made* from him, the way this ship"—and here she glanced at the panels surrounding them—"the way this ship, the *Talus*, is made from the creature that chased you on Mars. Do you understand?"

He shook his head.

"I don't pretend to know everything, Daric. I'm not *raised*, I'm surely no Citizen. But I've heard legends about Darius, the *Leader*. One man who ruled for a millennia, ruled everything—nine millennia ago." She pointed at Daric with her free hand, and was suddenly at his shoulder. "How he started as a peaceful man, serving the world for a hundred years, you've heard it? And all the while making himself stronger with technologies. He forced the world into great developments. Mankind wouldn't have moved into space without his persuasion. And some say he discovered a magic algorithm, and used it to hold power. He built cusps to walk from world to world. He made the forests on Mars, and then the oceans, by releasing its ancient ice, drowning cities and his own castle. There are stories about that castle, and his ambry, and how he was turned into a tree but his followers rescued him. How he dismissed them, and disappeared. Though it's said bits of him are scattered in the outer realms. In chids, like you. And in things, like the medallion."

Daric wiped his eyes and blinked rapidly. "Not like me." He heard a rustling behind him, and turned in time to see the panels over his head bend inward and a dozen slender whips appear, undulating. Joom followed, kicking free to spin slowly before Daric.

He smiled, thin lips parting over sharp yellow teeth, and looked over Daric's shoulder, saying, "String's up, sails avasted."

"Excellent work, Joom," said Sisteel. "I'll tell Leften."

Don't leave me with him!

Sisteel called back. "She'll want to see you, Daric. Come along, to the Leften's chamber."

He tried to walk behind her, but finally pressed the circle, swallowing hard as he floated up.

"Point to where you wish to go, Daric, like this."

And pointing, Daric followed her around the bend and up a narrow tunnel, one not unlike the Grawl's neck, into a circular room not unlike the head, alive with visuals and ghostly images.

"We're lined up, Leften. Joom says full pulse on the sails."

"Hello, Daric."

It was not Leften Tine but the medallion who spoke, held by the reclining woman.

His eyes were drawn by hovering planets and a web of faint gold lines.

"Sit, boy," said Sisteel, touching his shoulder, guiding him toward the curving wall. She pressed the rock on his suit; Daric slowly dropped. Bowing to Leften Tine she floated down, disappearing.

Leften Tine did not move. Head tipped back, she stared at him. Her eyes were gold.

With a flick of her hand, she launched the medallion toward him. It slowly spun, the chain trailing after. Daric caught it. The rosette pattern flickered as it said, "You know by now who you are, Daric. And who I am."

"You're Darius."

"Yes. And so is Grandpapa, and Jonas, too. And so are you."

He let go of the medallion. It spun slowly in the air before him.

"Do you remember how Grandpapa would sometimes do nothing but hum old songs, Daric? How he would weep over the worlds he had lost? How Jonas would disappear for days, then come back without explanation, angry and withdrawn? Grandpapa and old Jonas were tired; they were, in a way, *broken down*."

"I love Jonas."

"As you should. As do I. Nevertheless, a breakdown occurred. Grandpapa especially. Eight thousand years had passed while he slept, hearing the treesong. He woke a confused soul, resurrected in a mechanical body. Worshiped by people he did not know. Grandpapa refused to be part of them, and with time they dismissed him. A favored few built him a hovel in the outbacks of ruined Mars, and gave a trinket to him for company—myself—but even I could not stir him. He mourned what was done to the worlds, what was lost. He covered the walls with paintings of his beloved worlds. And with help from me he raised another of us, a young Daric. Your shade.

"When the Storm was unleashed on Earth and came to Mars, Grandpapa saved us, yes, but only with the last remnants of his intellect and the help of another young Daric. The Mind of Mars was not much of a mind at all, after that. He raised another Daric and called him Jonas. He followed Grandpapa's plan, at first. He attempted to recover what remained of the Chryse castle, but ended up saving only a portion, which he cobbled together on dry land. Then Jonas spent years wandering across Mars, writing poetry—ancient wordplay—pursuing the love of a woman. For this he set sail to the stars. Ten years for him was a hundred for us! Grandpapa became all but a statue, locked in his century seat. Grandpapa and Jonas, they followed their whims. We are all allowed such indulgences. But now, at this late date, we cannot *afford* them. It is time to set ourselves back on the path. And the path leads to Earth. Our ancestral world. The heart of our empire."

Daric remembered what Penthesilia had said. "But . . . it's full of creatures. Whirlwind creatures, from the Storm."

"The world belongs to us, Daric. It grew from our technologies—our fingers. And now we must reclaim what is ours. I have struck a bargain with Leften Tine and her crew. They will give us the means, and will themselves profit by it."

He looked at Leften Tine. "She killed my shade."

Laughter rippled through her face. "Not killed, child," she said, drawing from the wall a century rose, which she launched across the cabin toward him.

He reached up and took it from the air, looking down into the petals to find his face reflected, six times. A face pinched with fear or anger that, looking up, urged him on to the Whirlwind Planet. Not to prove that he could survive there—the Leader returned—but to prove, by dying, that he was not one of them.

By dying, as Penthesilia had surely died.

Daric smiled, for these thoughts were his and his alone.

He learned to swim in weightlessness. "Heed the Voider's Creed, and float from Earthers freed!" cried Joom mysteriously, though

Sisteel told him it meant they *shunned* the artificiality of gravity. So Daric, too, shunned the rock. Floating, bounding, tumbling along the main compartment was more exciting even than his wheel.

Often those first few days he would shut his eyes and apprehend the starlines, always vivid, and try to find Mars, reduced now to a faint line and numbers. He would remember the Ares Plain, conjuring the land, the feel of gravity, the rock beneath his feet, the orchard and the orchard's rich smells, the clockwork of turret, sun, and Dayblown Phobos.

Daily (or as day and night, bright and dim, were measured aboard the ship) Leften Tine ordered him up to her chamber. She would say nothing to Daric, but motion him to the wall and let him sit there while—surrounded by the floating images—she guided the *Talus* on a wayward course through the system, from Mars to Mercury Scythe, out toward the asteroid belt and back, to Venus. Daric would try not to look at her feet with their fingerlike toes, or her face, undulating as she smiled and stared somberly at the glowing airborne dials.

It was to Joom, quite bravely, that he finally said, "Leften Tine is a *raised*, isn't she?"

"Aye, but of no World Prime." Joom turned away, then surprised Daric by adding, "She hates the Helio shine. Now off!"

"But, tell me, is she *here*?"

Joom smiled, showing his sharp teeth. "Is and is not, eh? In sweet, *doppeling* fashion." He floated up, pushing the boy out of his path.

Daric was allowed to wonder, somewhat happily, in ignorance.

When he slept he dreamed of Jonas and home, and of Penthesilia.

Once, he took a rose and planted it in the ship's translucent skin, and from this sprouted not his shade but Penthesilia, her entire form rising up, long red hair, purple dress, and bare feet.

She took his hand—in the dream she was not a soul or a ghostly ad—and led him through the ship's skin, into the void. The arcing bright lines of the stars, now visible, surrounded them. They returned to Mars, to Oppidum, and walked the Elysium Concourse with Phobos reeling overhead, trailing red and blue lines, trailing numbers, with Thola Nee Montyorn in its whirlwind wake floating down to the blue tiles of the plaza, smiling as she bound Daric's arms with coils of animate hair, a brilliant smile, as she drew her rippling cloak over Penthesilia, who, crying out, became a silent century rose once more, tucked into his breast pocket by Thola's long fingers.

"Joom, why do we use sails?"

Joom was floating in the ship's central chamber, some wires drawn close, others nudging him along a bank of instruments.

"Away, 'fink!"

Daric ducked the tentacles. "I mean, my pillow was old, but it said sailing ships haven't been used since this was the frontier, back before the Heliocracy."

Joom moved to a crystal, which showed the huge circular sail glinting with laser pulse, and other, small sails trailing like water weeds. "A ploy, to fool the gens and the KayTees." He licked his teeth. "We're an old ship, one of many slouching around the Wilderness—a frontier if ever there was. Pay us no mind, no. Let us stagger close to the Whirlwind Planet and—lo—while they look away discharge a sleek invisible tear that holds you, 'fink. All under their noses. Now find and follow Sis—you star-juice swampies."

Daric touched the circle on his chest and floated down deck by deck through the *Talus*, past the shadow of Quintillux Cunning Heart (the limbs seeming to twitch if Daric looked long enough, as though the creature sensed that he was responsible for sending it to the tender in Oppidum, and its death).

He found Sisteel in the lowest deck, where she worked on a silver boat tapered at the end and rounded at the back; indeed, very much like a tear, Daric thought. Tumbling nearby was the crab-thing, with images flickering among its legs. It was called an *auchtille*. Joom was always knocking it aside. Sisteel and Leften Tine ignored it.

"Sisteel?"

She straightened, touching the side of the boat, which poured away to reveal an interior couch.

"Sisteel, have you had the drink, too? The star drink? You've heard the voices?"

She stepped back, nodding, and watched him for a long moment before she spoke. "That's the litany. It's from the spore. Don't you know?"

He shook his head.

"Most are older, before they take it. Most want to be mariners. I was twice your age. I didn't hear voices, but I suddenly knew things. Everything I needed to know to sail the void. Understand?"

"Yes." He pushed against a panel and began to slowly spin. "I can feel your line, but not Leften's. Because she's not really here. Right?"

Sisteel nodded. "Let's test you. Shut your eyes. Tell me the first thing that comes to you. And think of . . . Dombus."

He chewed his lower lip, thinking "Dombus," appraising the bright green line that appeared.

He said, "Dombus, three-eight-eight, seven-two, three-five-zero."

He opened his eyes.

"Those are coordinates, good. What else?"

He shut them again, and focused on the green line. On distant Dombus with its glittering seas. "It's far from here. I can see oceans. Something warning me, about the water. About *toxicity*."

He opened his eyes.

"Good, Daric. I think it's all there. You'll just have to practice it."

He shut his eyes again, and this time apprehended a forest, with purple foliage spreading above, like countless domical vaults.

He described this to Sisteel, adding, "I've dreamed of it before."

"And I, too. That's *Myiepa*."

He spoke the name to himself. "Why do we dream of it?"

"The liquid you drank contained a spore from Myiepa. There's a story told about it, like the stories of the Leader. Would you like to hear it?"

"Yes."

"Long ago a ship called the *Beneficent Argonaut* was marooned there, on the forest planet with its high purple canopies. It wasn't a harsh place, no predators, just fauna, plant life, and a good portion of it was edible. The crew survived for three years until a ship rescued them, all in good health but for a strange feeling, a *presence*. They called it a connection with the land, with Myiepa. Not a bad presence. It didn't ask for anything. It didn't tax their body's energy. But when they left and went their separate ways, they found that connection telling them about new places, places they'd never been, sensed as lines and colors. All the fauna on Myiepa was a single telepathic organism. Do you know what telepathic means?"

He nodded. "They talk with their minds."

"Although the Myiepan never seemed to talk as much as *connect*. Even across the void. What the survivors experienced was the spore they'd ingested and absorbed on the planet, searching and connecting to other spores, in search of its body: the planet Myiepa."

"But I know numbers, and names of stars . . ."

"The captain of the *Argonaut*, Alissia Gra'Hague, became obsessed with this spore, its structure, its effects on the mind. She became the planet's missionary, and the first and greatest void mariner. She designed an *information*, a drink, that incorporated the Myiepan spore. It uses the spore as its engine, and the drink carries all the things a traveler would need to know, coordinates, facts, and figures. And she removed portions of Myiepa to every faraway world—a monumental task—but now most worlds can be felt on the lines."

"I saw a shrine. In Oppidum." Daric recalled the black pedestal and the gnarled thing on top.

Sisteel nodded. "All this became part of the Creed, like shunning the rock. A mariner could hold their people, their universe, inside themselves. When you took the drink the spore woke up inside you, and began to search for home, reaching out, from shrine to shrine, from person to person, encountering all the other spores throughout the Heliocracy. And your small portion became part of a large one. Does that make sense?"

"Yes." He swallowed, thought he tasted it, something metallic.

"But always within us, Daric, is this urge to go to Myiepa. All of us. We resist, it's not too hard—though if we were to shut our eyes and swim through the stars without conscious thought, we would find ourselves there. It's happened before."

He nodded, remembering his walk beneath the high purple canopies.

"Think of the Earth. What do you see?"

The line was easily held. He apprehended warnings and darkness, then an image: not the world but its moon, a bone-white orb, one half of it etched with dark stars.

He told her, and she nodded, and would say no more about it.

The image stayed with him, became part of his dreams with Penthesilia and the purple forest. When word came from Leften Tine that they were nearing Earth, he followed Sisteel and Joom up to Leften's chamber, to find his vision manifested in the air beyond his outstretched hand: the bony moon etched with dark, starlike spots.

He pulled back his hand, and stopped.

Leften Tine regarded him through half-closed eyes.

He found another image, closer. The dots were really hexagons, each hexagon made up of black rectangles, thousands of them. He knew what they were.

He felt a stomachache, the beginning of fear.

"Sisteel, take Daric below," Leften Tine said. "Prepare the boat."

"Yes, Leften."

She took his hand and led him down the passage.

"Those are gendarme, right, Sisteel?"

She nodded. "But they won't bother us, Daric. They watch the Storm."

"How many?"

"Maybe a million."

In the main compartment he pulled free and pointed to one of the lucid panels. It looked upon the Earth, a world banded in dark cloud, purple and black, with slender rust-red threads, swirls of bright blue.

Home, he thought.

And beyond, ducking out of view, the dead moon and its million gendarme.

Silent now, Sisteel placed an emerald ring around his neck for air, and also the medallion, slipping the century rose into a link on its chain. She helped Daric into the boat.

Her eyes were lost behind the golden mask as he settled into the soft couch, heart thudding against his suit. He wanted to ask how they would find him again, but then the door sealed, and Daric was alone in the shining interior.

He looked down at the medallion. "What now?"

"Sisteel Nee Portia has programmed the boat," it said. "We simply ask to be taken to the target. When our task is done, we ask to be taken to the ship. Touch your throat—the recirculator. It activates your air supply."

He touched the emerald ring, felt a cool draft over his face.

"Boat, main view."

An image appeared before him: Sisteel standing in the *Talus*'s lower bay.

"Boat, sound," continued the medallion. "Confirm exterior sound, Sisteel Nee Portia."

She raised her hand.

"Boat, view and sound off. Daric, we're ready. Settle into the seat, let it fold around you." He did, feeling the fabric of the couch roll over his legs. "Touch the second tab on your sleeve."

He touched it and felt heat rushing through his muscles, his fingers spasming, his lips twitching. Then calm and clarity.

"Boat, begin trip."

The silver walls sang with bird chirps, then the craft shook, plummeting for a long moment before the pressure eased.

He clutched the medallion tighter.

"Our destination is our capital—or its former location. We should land within a quarter."

"Can I see out? Can I see Earth?"

"Boat, viewer ahead."

The planet loomed, half in shadow, rotating against a swath of space. The moon was hidden.

"Viewer, stabilize image."

While he studied the clouds, a strange sound came from the medallion, sonorous and scratchy, reminding Daric of—he shut his eyes to concentrate—of a tree's voice.

A second, similar voice joined the first, then a third, lower than the first two, akin to how Jonas's voice compared to his own. A fourth was deeper still: Grandpapa's reverie.

He opened his eyes.

"Is this music?"

The voices sang a peculiar four-part melody.

"We wrote it, Daric, some ten thousand years ago, in Alexandria by the sea."

The deepest tree-voice ran unending, while the others skirted and darted, in and around.

"We called it *String Quartet Primus*."

Darting like birds in the orchard.

"We also played the cello—not very well, though ours was the only dissenting opinion at the time."

Daric listened, following the music, which began to sound familiar.

How did he know the smallest bird would swoop here, and the largest would follow?

"It's our passport, Daric. The key to breaching the Ceres Storm."

The Earth was clearer now, wide purple bands made of smaller clouds and spirals, brightening in places—Tyrian purple, he recalled—lit now with veins of fire.

Lightning?

If he ignored the music and stared, concentrated, he could see the smaller clouds were made up of smaller clouds still.

"You witness the twilight of the Ceres Storm."

"My shade remembered it."

"He remembers it on Mars. Even then I was where you found me. In the oaken chest, hidden away. Not trusted for centuries, nearly forgotten. Woken by the Mind of Mars, new name on an old face. But the world down there was once mine. Strange now, but familiar. I am going home."

They were close enough for him to see the storm clouds churning, inky depths disintegrating and re-forming. All of which reminded him of decay and, somehow, of death.

Death as he'd found it in the orchard, where creatures had died and festered in the summer heat, in shadow, to be discovered by him on his excursions. Mold and bone-white in the darkness, disintegration and death smells that now seemed linked with the exuberant music, over which the medallion sang:

"From pole to pole and planets wide,
'Cross warp and weft of stellar tide,
From Earthly dust to Time's Divide,
Our Leader proves the faithful guide."

A patch of clouds lightened, shadows gathering around shallow mountains, becoming clearer. What he apprehended was no longer the face of a planet, but a distant *landscape*.

He recalled the dirigere trip, how he had looked down on the Ares plain. Now he was a thousand times higher, his boat no longer sailing in space, but dropping like a rock.

He smiled, his eyes fierce and fixed, as the visuals faded and the couch held him tight, and the boat shuddered into the atmosphere.

But soon after, the boat was plucked up, no longer being pummeled by the air. It was being held.

"Boat, main visual!" he said.

A dark, glistening shape materialized, too close.

Daric recoiled. "What is it?"

The medallion said nothing, absorbed by the *String Quartet Primus*. With a jolt, the dark shape fled. The craft began to plummet.

Daric bit his lower lip.

The tree-voices threaded and darted.

Soon the pressure eased, and the boat rode smoother air,

banking, dropping in jerks to finally, with a gentle bump, touch down. The interior dimmed as the couch unfolded around him, and a wall poured away to steam and odd noises—what might have been water in his pond, rippling against the shore; and a high keening cry, distant, lost now as the medallion increased the music's volume.

The steam faded, revealing high dark hills.

He pushed himself up and struggled to his knees.

The boat lay at the end of a long, perfectly straight trench, capped with red clouds. The walls were steep and smooth, pure black with sparks of yellow, and purple tones seen in the corner of his eyes.

"Leave the boat. Quickly, Daric."

He tried to stand but his thighs were shaking; he fell against the chair. He sought the tab on his sleeve, pushed it, then, muscles burning with energy, heart thudding, he sprang up, out of the portal.

Unexpectedly, the ground was like sand; he stumbled, then straightened, squinting up at the high ridges. How far up?

Turning, he examined the boat, whose silver skin was torn on top and along the tapered sides: claw marks.

"What should I do?" He glanced around, stepped toward the closer ridge—he would try to climb.

"We won't be returning to the *Talus*."

"What?"

"Leften Tine and her crew are the KayTee. They had no intention of keeping a bargain with me, nor I with them."

Daric tripped, fell forward, onto what felt like sand, then was glassy smooth, black, streaked with yellow. He pulled back to find the glowing outlines of his hands, bleeding away to a faint luminous cloud.

From all around: a rippling sound.

Daric struggled to his feet.

Nano, he thought. Ancient nano, little machines.

"What should I do?"

Behind the medallion's music, the rippling sound grew louder. Then motion from above, the black ridge undulating, rising like waves on water.

"Daric, you must call out, 'I am Darius! I have returned to my world!' "

Suddenly, shapes lifted from the ridge, stunted heads with long, sharp beaks, great wings shrugging free.

"Now, Daric!"

He turned, and turned again. All along the trench wall birds were rising, leaning forward.

Daric forced the words, "I'm Darius!"

The birds, a tangle of necks and beaks, with wings beating against the red sky, cried out now in high, piercing voices.

An awful sound, like an animal's death cry, lingering.

He called out, "I'm Darius! I'm Darius! I've returned to my world!"

He clutched the medallion, holding it up now, turning round—"I'm Darius! I've returned to my world!"—and soon the birds settled, quieted, gazing down at him, each with a plumage of white hair winking in the skylight.

"I'm Darius! I've returned to my world!"

Behind him, the sound of boots pulling free of wet mud. He turned to find the boat tipping, the ground reaching myriad sharp fingers to caress the silver skin, melting it to form a silver pool into which the boat quickly sank.

"I'm Darius!" He looked up, held the medallion as high as he could, so that the chain cut into the back of his neck. "I've returned to my world!"

In the corner of his eye, among the purple tones, a last wink as the boat sank out of sight. Above, the birds shrugged, beating the air, craning forward, stitching their beaks.

Sparks fell, all around.

The medallion cried, "The skein! They're weaving our judgment! Hold me higher!"

He shrugged free of the chain and held it as high as he could, blocking the sparks and a sudden brilliance.

Another bird. Made of light.

He blinked, tried to hide it behind the medallion—sharp luminous wings against the sky, folding back.

He managed, "I ... Darius ..."

Then the thing dropped in a thrust of brilliant light.

Was inside him, burning, as he fell to the ground. Crying out now in his own voice, matching the bird's cries. Thinking Daric's thoughts, reaching back to Mars, to the turret, the orchard. Farther.

From somewhere, "Ahh-awk ... ahh-awk ... toc ... toc ..."

Grandpapa the metal man afloat, paint-spattered, his ruby eyes lowered, despondent.

"Awk ... toc ... toc ..." The birds spoke overhead, in caws, in wing beats and beak rattles. "Toc ... toc ..."

While the thing reached back to Daric, the other Daric surrounded by painted planets, with Grandpapa looming above.

"Tok ... awn ... Ahh ... tok ..."

He screamed. He shook his head, tried to pull away, to scream aloud, "I am Darius! I am Darius!" The words circling in his thoughts, while the thing withdrew.

He sank to the ground.

Looking up, he found it wavering on the ridge: It had rejoined its voice.

He gripped the medallion in both hands.

"Good, Daric, good."

"It ... wanted to know ... about old Mars."

The ridge of birds now stirred, peering down.

"We've passed the test, I think."

"Something my shade gave me," Daric said. "A memory."

A faint ripple above as the sides of the ridge sank.

The floor began to rise, while the edges flattened out, glistening a dull purple beneath the red sky.

Daric stood up, legs braced.

Above him the sky darkened to purple, then dissipated, brightening to blue.

"What's happening?"

Around him a field rippled green, spreading outward. And the light, which had seemed mournful, now glowed, vibrant, alive with motes, as though the bird had spread its luminous wings through the air.

"Look, Daric, the *ground note* of the Ceres Storm!"

Green shoots lifted from the field swelling into trunks that sprouted branches and bright leaves. To his left, pine trees crested the turf, gathering shadow, while to his right a slender stream threaded poplar and oak.

He stood now in a forest that might have been Old Mars or something older: Earth of the *ancient ancient*.

"This is our work, Daric. Our ideas made manifest."

Then something gleamed amid the trees, a vague fire through the branches, darkening from bright orange to the red of Penthesilia's hair.

The figure, with Penthesilia's pale face and the same purple dress, stepped carefully from the trees, as if it, as if *she*, had never walked before.

But it can't be, he thought. It isn't.

Arms held out, she stopped a few paces away. Her eyes, the bright red he remembered, met his own with the force of her personality, and she smiled, the same comfortable smile—though she could not possibly be Penthesilia—and offered her hand.

He stepped forward and took it, and found it real and warm, as it gripped his own.

He pulled back. "You're not Pen."

Trying to affect an anger he could not properly summon, he said, "You're pretending to be Pen."

She clasped her hands in front of her. "I am the Autochthon," she said, in Penthesilia's bright voice.

The medallion spoke, "We have returned to our world, Autochthon, to search for our Machineries, left ten thousand years ago."

Penthesilia was watching Daric.

He said, "I'm not Darius."

"You know of Starstrider. This intrigues us. Please, Daric. Tell me."

Daric struggled for words. "Starstrider? I . . ."

"Your thoughts were of Starstrider."

Shade's memory! Of the Storm.

"Those weren't mine. They're from my shade." Here he lifted the rose from the medallion's chain. "He was changed into this. A century rose."

Daric held it up.

Penthesilia might have never seen one before. She took the crystal stem.

"Shade was once me, on Mars. He lived with the Mind of Mars, who was my Grandpapa, and . . . and who was Darius, too."

Penthesilia studied the rose.

"Autochthon," said the medallion. "I am Darius Prime. I lived here ten thousand years ago. I walked the cusps from world to world. I cultivated the Ceres Storm."

Penthesilia held out her free hand. Daric gave her the medallion. She shut her eyes briefly. "These are thought matrix. We will grow them, and ask them of Starstrider."

Grow them?

"They've tried . . . Would they be able to hurt me, ever?"

Penthesilia slowly shook her head. "No, Daric. You are living substance of Darius. Nothing will be allowed to hurt you." She moved back three paces and knelt, laying rose and medallion on the grass to either side, then stood and spread her arms.

Silence. Then the forest trembled, birds scattered above, soundlessly. For a moment the truth of this artifice staggered Daric; he remembered his view from the *Talus*, of the Whirlwind Planet, the purple and black bands, red swirls; all of it watched by the moon with its million gendarme.

Penthesilia smiled, while below her the artifacts melted into the grass only to sprout, an instant later, as crowns of loose black hair.

Feeling detached, Daric watched the upturned faces thrust from the grass, shut eyes and crimped mouths, followed by slender, armor-clad shoulders, torsos, hips, legs.

As the soil pushed them up the boys curled forward, slouching, moaning.

Lastly their boots, free of the ground now.

Daric leaned close. The boy on the left was marked on his forehead with a yellow rosette; the boy on the right—Shade—a black rosette. Otherwise they were exactly the same, moaning now, blinking furiously, fists uncurling.

They looked up at the same time, their eyes locking on him.

Daric recognized his own face.

His voice, in great pain, coming from behind those clenched teeth.

The Autochthon, kneeling between them—Yellow and Black—folded her hands on her knees and said, "Tell us of Starstrider."

Black tried to speak. He gasped, choking.

"Please, they're in pain . . ."

She looked up at Daric. "We must know."

Yellow was staring at his hands, clenching and unclenching his fingers.

I looked like this in Oppidum, thought Daric. When the smoke got me.

Before she could ask them again, he said, "They'll need some time." He paused. "We . . . I was sent down to get the Machineries. Have you heard of them?"

Penthesilia studied him, while the other two struggled to their knees.

He added, "The Machineries once belonged to Darius, long ago. They're supposed to be under the earth here."

She clasped her hands in front of her. "Everything still belongs to Darius. They are his, to do with as he pleases."

"Then I'd . . . I'd like to see the Machineries."

She shook her head. "They belong to Darius—the Darius who has *always* lived here. This is his land. You are his guests. You will have to ask him."

Him?

The Autochthon gestured, drawing his attention across rolling hills, toward a shadow on the horizon. The others saw it, too. Black moaned, Yellow struggled to his feet, while the shadow billowed upward, with red and gold sparks sketching arches, rolling lines, rising to form five towers, broad and strangely scalloped, darkening against the sky.

The Autochthon turned back to him, smiling; Pen's familiar smile.

Black was struggling to his knees, staring down at his hands, flexing the fingers. Daric knelt beside him. "Shade?" Does he have bones? Little machines pretending to be bones. Pretending to be my bones.

"Shade?"

Black nodded, grimacing, blinking. He looked up at the castle, which was now surrounded by small lakes spanned by narrow white bridges; a white path had stretched along the rolling hills toward them, ending behind the Autochthon; grass rooted in the slabs of white rock, as though it had been there for ages.

Daric helped Black to stand up.

"Shall we?" the Autochthon asked, as Pen would have asked it.

Yellow stood up, working his mouth, smiling. He breathed deeply. "Our castle . . . at Chryse." Another smile, straightening.

"This way." She began walking along the stone path.

Yellow stumbled after her. "Autochthon . . ." Black followed. Daric walked behind them both, observing while, step by step, they gained control of their bodies. *My body*, he thought, studying their narrow shoulders and blown black hair, their faces made strange in profile, ashen foreheads, penetrating blue eyes, sharp noses, dour mouths.

His face, yet not his face.

With each step the castle became clearer; perhaps it was made of birds, the hundreds winging overhead, flecks of ash caught in clear water, drifting down toward the castle, darkening the red and gold into a hue called Tyrian purple, into black etched with silver, the small arches of windows gleaming like inset jewels, thousands of them ranked up the edifice.

As the party reached the first bridge, Yellow moved in front of Penthesilia. She stopped.

"Autochthon, answer me this. The castle is ours from Chryse, on Mars. It marks the constellation Scorpio at the summer equinox. So why is it here?"

"I found it in all your minds."

"Tell me, then. The entrance to our Machineries. It originally lay below the Citadel, protected from the Storm. Does it still exist?"

But she walked past him, up the bridge.

Yellow squinted, then smiled.

Daric followed Black. At the top he approached the side, with his elbows boosting himself up to look over the wide rail. Water.

Machines pretending to be water. Below the surface tattered green leaves dimly turning, twisting. But no fish.

His own reflected face, looking up.

"See what our infernal machines have done."

Hopping down, he found himself—found Yellow—smiling, shifting his weight from boot to boot, saying to Black, "Don't you understand, old Shade? We're young!"

Yellow walked backward, then jogged away, running down the bridge.

Black remained by Daric's side, watching the boy diminish along the path, accompanied by a slow shrug in the hills to either side, thousands of small birdlike heads lifting as though disturbed from sleep, soon dipping back down, becoming earth once more.

The last lake was largest of all. Beyond it was ground of glass, carved with white lines and yellow circles that angled out from the towers of the castle. The arching entrance was flanked by two towers of white stone. They struck Daric as familiar: The flat tops were like home, on Mars.

Black understood what he was thinking. "I helped Jonas raise one from the ocean floor. After Darius drowned them."

"The original was veiled in ash-light, of course," said Yellow to the Autochthon, gesturing to the entrance. "Otherwise a perfect replica."

Daric squinted up at the windows, the tiered towers rising, stacked smaller and smaller, to where huge yellow and black flags shivered in a breeze.

"Autochthon," Yellow was saying, "you tell us Darius is here. Which Darius?"

"The one who built the castle."

A faint red light stirred in the archway.

"The firebirds. As on a wintry Martian night." Stepping through, Yellow spread his arms and gazed up at the orbs of fire floating here and there, tossing a quivering glow into the high vaults, lighting long yellow and black flags.

Pen followed, then Daric, with Black beside him.

In the distance a voice, strained by age or acoustics, said, "*Bonjour.*" At the far end a shape appeared from the shadows, a white form slipping free, stepping now onto the tiles, uncertain in the light.

"*Bonjour,* my friends."

None replied.

Daric blinked once and found the shape had jumped closer, still approaching, with a rasping step. He blinked again and saw it more clearly: an old man wearing a long white robe. Or perhaps a statue of an old man, made of marble come alive.

It raised an arm, shrouded in white.

Yellow walked toward it, with Black and Daric close behind.

An old man, older than Jonas.

He wore a robe patterned with swirls of pale blue, his sandals scraping the tile as he walked, carrying faint sounds, what might have been wood voices.

"Music," said Yellow.

Closer, Daric could see a lined face, white hair and eyebrows, and familiar blue eyes. The old man halted, and so did they, a dozen tiles between them. "Yes, a sarabande, cast in the form of a modest processional. I've gotten better, over the years." The voice was hushed, but carried an undercurrent of familiar humor. "Less sardonic, more refined. Perhaps as good now as I thought I was back then, so long ago." His eyes sparkled as he smiled; a smile that said not to take him seriously, one that reminded Daric of Jonas, how he would say something outlandish and hold your gaze for an instant longer than he should, and smile, as the old man had just smiled.

In a voice that rose and fell from a whisper, the old man said, "Long ago, I postulated the arrival of others." He drew his robe close around him, his eyes roaming their faces. "I'd stopped hoping. You are me, I see. You, too. And you."

Daric nodded.

"Interesting."

Yellow spoke up. "I once lived here, on this land. Ten thousand years ago."

"Yes," said Darius, looking up and around. "All three of you have lived here, in one way or another." Again, he smiled. "You have a mark, do you not? Let me see." He approached Yellow—it was now clear that he was three heads taller—and brushed aside the dark locks of hair, revealing the rosette. Daric studied it, too, and the eyes that were his own, and were not.

"The Martian insignia, I think."

Yellow touched his forehead. "In our colors."

"You have a black one." Darius shuffled over to Shade, and gently touched the mark. "Interesting. And over here, a smooth, youthful forehead."

Daric felt the old man's cool, rough finger on the skin above his eyes.

Is he alive? Is he the Autochthon?

"So, we are all distinguished visibly, but we'll need to distinguish ourselves with names, too. I am Darius, and you"—this to Daric—"are . . ."

"I'm Daric."

"Appropriate. And you?"

Black gave a shallow bow. "Darius."

"And lastly?"

"Darius, of course."

The old man shook his head. "Hmmm. That would lead to much confusion. You are obviously of a sort with our Daric, here. So I shall call you Yellow Daric. And you . . . you shall be Black

Daric." His voice was louder now, awaking echoes far above. "This makes perfect sense, I think."

Grudgingly, they nodded.

Darius smiled, glancing up. "Shall we retire to more comfortable surroundings?" He turned and walked back the way he had come.

Following Yellow and Black, Daric wondered if the old man was simply a part of the planet, like Penthesilia—the Autochthon.

He noticed the pattern on the floor, faint gold lines engraved, straight and circular, a star chart into the distance, all around. Daric stumbled, dizzy. The stimulants were wearing off.

"This way, this way." Darius ushered them into a smaller room, lit with stationary lamps. A small wooden table and chairs occupied the center. Daric felt more comfortable.

"Here we are . . ."

Daric pulled back a chair and sat heavily, with Yellow and Black on either side; Darius opposite, his back to the hills. His eyes lingered on Daric; sad eyes, in spite of the smile. "You have a question."

Daric tried to think of the right words. "Are you real, like I'm real?"

"Or am I like your brothers, here? Grown to order?" Darius laid his large hands on the table. "I *exist*, Daric. I have counted a thousand orbits of the sun." He smiled, as if this amused him. "I am the only such inhabitant of this planet."

Daric nodded.

Yellow suddenly stood and walked to the open wall, clasping his hands behind his back. "Darius," he said, trying to make his thin voice resound. "We come for the Machineries." He turned back to them. "Is the term familiar to you?"

Darius spoke the word silently: Machineries.

"They lie far below the surface," Yellow continued, "and can be of no use to you. They are not of the Storm. They were built to survive it, in case I wished to return."

Darius nodded, regarding his hands, which he now held fingertip to fingertip. "I will have to consider it."

Yellow nodded, shutting his eyes briefly. "Very well."

"Please, sit."

Yellow complied.

"And now," Darius said, straightening in his chair, looking from Yellow to Black to Daric. "May I ask a question. To this one, to Black Daric."

Black glanced up, his eyes fierce, leveled at Darius.

"What was Starstrider's fate?"

Black said nothing.

Daric leaned forward. "Please, tell me . . ." This to Darius. "Who's Starstrider?"

Darius looked at Black, then to Daric said, "The Storm's ultimate expression."

Yellow smiled. "Grandpapa's nemesis."

"Created at the peak of our energies, sent up and out to the next world, to continue the Storm. We received the burst confirming planetfall, but then never felt its presence again."

Black nodded, straightening in the chair. Softly, he said, "I helped defeat it."

Darius watched without expression.

"I was a boy then," Black continued, looking down, his voice strengthening. "I served the Mind of Mars. He hated much of what we'd done, especially the Storm, though we hadn't deployed it, of course. Not even when the empire fell, and Darius was transfigured. Eight thousand years passed before it was used, by others. When it had finished with Earth, and headed toward Mars . . ."

Black was momentarily distracted: Through the open wall the hills rippled, full of rustling shadows. "It couldn't be destroyed, but it could be *contained*. I helped Grandpapa imprison it, using its own energy." Looking up from his fingers, Black said, "On Phobos. It's the second Martian sun, now."

Dayblown Phobos!

As Daric tried to understand, the golden floor stirred like water, and hundreds of tiny eyes winked open.

Behind them, soft footfalls.

The old man opened his eyes, gesturing to the door, and the rose-colored shadow of the Autochthon. "You must be tired. The Autochthon will take you to your chambers."

The grand Architrave. The lapidary pond with its iron dolphins. The Chamber of Audiences. During the long walk up winding stairs, Yellow named each room, as though making them his own. But Daric could tell he was not entirely comfortable. Daric could read his own face, the furrowed brow when Yellow thought they weren't looking, the fleeting scowl, while the Autochthon climbed and climbed, and the three of them followed up to what must be the highest part of the castle.

The Autochthon stopped before a small door. Yellow pushed it open, stepping into a small room furnished in wood, with three beds looking opposite a wide window. "Autochthon." Yellow stepped close to her. "The walk was surely meant to tire us out. Yet I feel no need to rest. How long precisely must we wait?"

Its face impassive—not like Pen's at all—the Autochthon said simply, " 'Til it's time." With a gesture of her white hand drawing shut the tall door.

Black, his shoulders rising and falling as he caught his breath, sat on the edge of one of the beds, hands on his knees, and stared at the floor.

"You were a boy, then, Black. Under the tutelage of Grand-papa. We cannot blame you."

Black ignored Yellow.

Daric went to the window. The two smaller towers were below, with the land stretching out to a dim horizon.

Yellow approached.

"There used to be an ocean outside, Daric. I could watch the sailing ships."

Daric looked at the familiar profile, made strange by the half smile, the upper lip curling over a gleaming eyetooth.

"Of course, our Citadel stood here. Not the Chryse castle. I must admit to liking the former. The dark rock, which suited the sea and the coastline. A hundred towers, each flying our yellow-and-black gonfalon. During a brisk breeze one could hear the snapping. I was often told it broke the nerves of visitors." Looking over at Daric, Yellow added, "And of course we were never called the Leader back then. Never."

Daric ignored him. He yawned. He was exhausted. He trudged to the pallet farthest from the window, kicked off his bulky boots, and lay down, trying to ignore the others' voices.

He shut his eyes.

Where are Jonas and Grandpapa? he wondered.

I don't think they came after me. How could they have followed the *Talus*?

Yellow and Black talked for a time, in voices that became more quiet, and more similar—suddenly strange all over again. Then one announced, "Daric, we're going to explore."

Black, he decided.

"For Machineries, Black. As though we could keep secrets from Darius. We will return."

The door opening, footsteps shuffling out; the door shut. Daric felt immediately relieved. He relaxed his shoulders.

Try to sleep, he thought.

He thought of home. Was it empty? Remembering his room, his pallet. The bedside table. The stairs winding down and around, past the Actuality gauges. Try to sleep.

The lower levels, thrumming with sound of gears grinding. Jonas . . . where was he right now, in the ship? He pictured Grandpapa installed before a window, looking out at the stars.

Try to sleep.

What about my fish. Did they take them with them?

The moth. Gone, too.

Won't see them again.

But I'll find Jonas. Somehow.

Aware of the utter silence in the room, he thought of Jonas, and how he might follow the bright starlines from planet to planet, in search of him.

He dreamed of a forest. The same forest as before, he realized, with ranks of trees on all sides, marching into the hazy distance, and overhead the high purple treetops, like endless domical vaults.

Walking, he stared down into the ivy, sensing numbers in the leaves, counting the Wilderness all around.

"Is he awake?" This was later.

Someone leaned close.

Another voice—the same voice—whispering, "He dreams."

Daric's voice.

He remembered exactly where he was, a realization seen as a flicker of motion beneath his eyelids, a tightening of his mouth.

"No doubt of Myiepa." The first was trying to whisper, but doing badly. "He will yearn to leave. We can thank Grandpapa for that, at least. What do you see out there?"

"Just the trees, the garden. The clouds are lower than before, getting darker."

"Darius has decided. It wouldn't take him long, of course."

"Whisper."

"Ah, there we see it."

"What?"

"The shade's imperative. You try to deny it, this unbidden

urge to help your charge. Sometimes it just runs wild."

"I have a memory. Surely you have it, too. I was young, in the garden catching insects. Butterflies, bees, wasps. We liked to put them in the freezer, all sorts, but mostly bees and wasps. Some we'd add to our collection, and some we'd mark with a number, and let them thaw out on the picnic table. We'd wait for them to wake up—they always did—and fly off. But once, I remember, we were marking a wasp and it came to life in my fingers, twisted itself. I've never forgotten that sting. When I disobey the imperative, something very much like that happens. Come look at this—more birds."

"Can you read our fate in their numbers?"

"You're right. He's decided."

Daric waited a few minutes before stirring, sitting up, his muscles aching.

He rubbed his eyes.

"Rested?"

He found his own face on the next pallet over. Yellow.

"Yes."

Black stood beside the window. "Good morning, Daric."

"Good morning."

Yellow stretched. "We are waiting for Penthesilia. The door is now locked. As Black will no doubt tell you, we failed to find any Machineries last night. In fact, we found ourselves here, at this door, without ever meaning to return."

"She's not Pen," Daric said. "The creature. It isn't Penthesilia."

"Good, you retain your senses."

Daric felt a sudden annoyance welling up, bit it back.

"You can help us," said Yellow. "Ask to see the Machineries. If we can reach the *Pyre*, we can leave Earth."

After a pause, Daric said, "I've already decided what I'm going to do."

Yellow's eyebrows jumped. "Really, Daric? What?"

"I'm going to ask for the boat back. For myself."

The look in Yellow's eyes pleased Daric.

"To the *Talus*? It would, of course. And from there you would be delivered to the KayTee Clan, and then to the Scales. Is that what you want?"

"I'll go back to Leften Tine, and Sisteel. I'll tell her—Sisteel—I'll tell her about Darius, and that he wouldn't let me take anything, and that it's useless to get to the Machineries."

Yellow shook his head, leaned forward. "Daric. Sisteel may have seemed kind, but she was simply working for Leften—the *real* Leften, doppeling from some luxurious egg on Triton, you can be sure."

Daric looked to Black.

"Daric, you certainly don't deny that all of this"—here Yellow gestured at the room, though Daric knew he meant the castle and the garden, and the cloud creatures—"was started by us."

Daric said nothing.

"Ideas and motivation. A seed we planted ten thousand years ago, from which grew the Machineries, and things like century roses—we *planted* them, Daric. Without our guidance they led to the Storm and the sedate, metal-minded worlds of the Heliocracy. Those who serve the singing suns. But down below this castle there lie Machineries unknown to the rabble, safeguarded by the Storm. Marvels made *by* us, *for* us."

Daric looked to Black, who said, "It's true."

"Yes, it *is* true. And our ship waits for us below. I was sure of this, and so had no intention of returning to Leften Tine. Our ship will get us away from Earth, from the Wilderness, if you desire. We can obtain more information, like the drink you consumed in the Heliotrope. The asteroid belt is a frontier to the KayTee, a zone they have no interest in. Certain establishments exist for the mariners. And we will be free to go wherever we want to go. Wherever *you* want to go."

Daric met Yellow's intense eyes, and tried to ignore the faint smile, the gleaming eyetooth. "Grandpapa told me a story about the Leader. About how he was turned into a tree. An oak. And how he stood there for a thousand years thinking, crying sometimes, wishing he hadn't done all the things he'd done. Grandpapa had you defeat the Storm, because he was sorry for what he'd done."

Yellow shook his head and smiled. "Yes, Daric, he was turned into a tree, and yes, he wept. But not for what he'd done—for everything he'd *lost*. For everything he'd left behind. *Here*, on Earth. I'm sorry you don't remember that."

Daric said nothing.

"We had another name then, Daric. Did Jonas ever tell you?"

He shook his head.

"Black, do you remember?"

"Jim," Black said.

"Yes. That was one of them."

Jim.

"Darics, Yellow and Black."

Darius beckoned from the table and chairs. The room looked nearly the same as it had the day before, though the columns were made of white birds, sluggishly moving and preening.

Penthesilia remained behind, by the stairs, while Daric followed Yellow and Black. As they seated themselves, Daric walked past them, toward the columns, where eyes winked open; and framed between, the white stone towers that were like home on Mars. Beyond, at the edge of the forest, were dark clouds. Black birds, winging.

He stopped, leaning over the edge.

Far below was the arching bridge and the pools, and within the limpid water shadows moved as the clouds moved on the horizon. Something surging up, glinting.

Gone, now.

Behind him, Darius said, "Let us talk of ancient times."

What should I do?

Yesterday, the solution had seemed obvious. He would ask for his boat back. But Yellow was right, he understood that now. Sisteel was kind, was perhaps the kindest person he had met since Penthesilia, but she had often donned a faceless suit, and worked for Leften, who, it seemed, worked for the KayTee Clan.

His own voice: "Do you remember the Traitor Planets, Darius? A dire campaign, and a great triumph."

Who can I trust?

"We dealt with them, did we not?"

Once, he would have said his shade.

Jonas. He could trust Jonas. Jonas was different from the others, from Grandpapa, from Yellow and Black.

"Yes, Darius, we *dealt* with them. The triumph. They fell to their knees and whispered our name, and we could hear it from our ship, the shudder of it."

But Jonas's far away, now.

Daric leaned forward, looking down.

How far down? Would the trees catch me?

To his left a bird flapped up, dark wings folding as it settled on the edge. It shook its head, a beak as long as Daric's forearm glinting in the light.

The bird hopped closer. Daric studied its feathers; each one was subtly moving. Was every feather a bird? Ready to fly apart, a cloud of birds ready to pluck him up should he fall.

"All of that, Yellow Daric, and still we failed. Until others awakened the Ceres Storm—another processional of ours—to reach out and take the other worlds."

Daric stepped back.

Yellow and Black now sat on the chairs before the throne. They were watching Daric. And after a moment, Darius, too, turned and watched. He smiled, cleared his throat, and said,

"Daric, you are a true boy. A wandering mind—how I admire that. Forgive me, please, and allow Penthesilia to show you the garden." Darius gestured.

Daric looked to the distant arched door, and the shadow that was the Autochthon.

He nodded and walked toward her. Only when he left the room did he hear their voices—*his own* voice, "Ah, it's love."

Yellow, he knew.

To which his shade replied, "He dreams of her, I know. Of Penthesilia. He yearns for companionship. Perhaps one day he'll find her, and restore her."

"And grow to love her, no doubt."

"Love," said Darius. "We loved humanity, there's a truth."

She led him not to the garden but down flights of stairs, to the lowest level of the castle and a dull gray door that might have once been polished, reflecting a pale brilliance where the Autochthon stood—still Penthesilia to his eyes.

She said, "This leads to your Machineries, Daric. Our world has no touch down there. We cannot say whether they are still alive. Do you understand?"

Yes, he understood, now.

Darius had already decided.

"Yes."

"In Yellow Daric's mind there's the image of a ship. The ship should exist with Machineries. You must find it, Daric, so you can leave this world."

Daric nodded. "I understand."

"Ask it to open."

Doubtful it would work, he said, "I'm Daric. Open."

Nothing. He said it again, louder, then, when nothing happened, said, "I'm . . . Darius. Open."

But the door remained shut.

The Machineries were dead. Was this so surprising, after so long?

Spotting a faint gray rectangle beside the door, set about level with his eyes, he remembered how Jonas's box had once opened to his touch. He reached out and placed his palm against warm metal.

The door slid back, revealing a small, gray room.

"You must descend alone. I remain here," the Autochthon said.

Daric nodded. He wanted to ask what he should seek. He would have asked Pen. Instead he stepped inside, finding the room more narrow than he thought. He might stretch out his arms and touch the walls on either side.

He heard the door slide shut, and turned in time to glimpse the Autochthon's raised hand.

The walls brightened.

The sheen relaxed against his skin. This room was *real*, was old enough to have been used by the original Darius....

"I want to descend," he said.

With the sound of air being expelled through a vent, the room dropped. He swallowed hard, then reached out and braced himself against the walls.

How far down? he wondered.

Biting his lower lip, he thought of the Autochthon waiting at the door; far above, now.

All of it distant.

I'm alone.

The room fell, faster, farther than Daric had anticipated, might have been heading for the planetary core, melting the rock as would a gendarme.

Then deceleration jolted his ankles and calves, and he crouched, braced against the walls as the room slowed, and—his stomach lurching—stopped.

Daric straightened. He blinked furiously, waiting for the dizziness to pass.

What if it's all dead here? Should I get out?

He opened his eyes.

The air shuddered, the walls brightened for an instant.

The door slid back, revealing darkness.

A sound like distant horns playing two slow notes, each horn out of sync with the others.

I'm alone, he thought.

He stepped forward, his boot clicking on a hard surface, while he apprehended huge shapes crouching on either side of a bare path.

I'm alone.

Another step, and this time it echoed crazily around him, kindling a dozen blue lights high above.

He called out, "I am Darius."

More blue lights winked on.

He stomped the ground. The shapes around him intensified, limned with yellow light. Towering, sharp-edged. Nearby, an object resembling a pin-struck crystal globe. Beyond it a giant stone hand, grasping.

He stood still, listened. He smelled *real* things; mildew, oil, the burnt odor of electricity.

Nothing nano, he realized.

Even on Mars—at home—there had been nano.

He began to walk down this wide aisle, gazing up at the blue and yellow lights, and a shape that floated between. Glimmers of red branches, like a giant thornbush suspended in midair. Daric squinted, but it was too hard to make out.

All this has been here longer than the Whirlwinds, he thought. Longer than the Darius above.

Yellow might have walked here. *Did* walk here.

Something brushed his sheen, a rasp as he stepped through invisible fields, similar to those that protected the engines at home. The distant horn tones quickened, jumping up to higher notes, dropping down to lower ones, though all of it easily ignored.

From the corner of his eye: motion, something in red, moving between the Machineries. Gone now.

I can run back to the room. I can fight it.

He stopped. "Hello?"

Motion from the other direction. His heart quickening, Daric turned to face the aisle, and found a figure clothed in red standing in the middle distance.

He squinted, unsure. "Hello?"

A vibrant voice: "*Bonjour,* My Glory."

A tall figure in red robes, a square red hat settled atop a long face. "You have returned." The figure spoke without surprise. It approached, making no sound. A long, pale face with white eyebrows. Daric could not see the eyes. "From Parson's Planet, I presume. A stupendous renewal, My Glory."

Daric nodded, bewildered. Though each step brought the figure closer, it grew no larger. Four paces away, it was no taller than Daric.

"You might be a boy again. I recall an old holo, of you as a child, My Glory, wandering the tarmacs of Europe. Really, you now compare quite favorably."

The figure stopped, observing Daric with narrowed eyes that nonetheless gleamed brightly.

A miniature man.

Daric said, "Who are you?"

"The Curator, My Glory." The figure bowed, so that its face was lost beneath the square red hat.

"You were taller . . . when you were farther away."

The Curator straightened, smiled; he was not fazed by Daric's confusion, rather, he seemed to expect it. "I compensated. I do not wish to tower over My Glory."

"Please, don't compensate."

Nodding, the Curator clasped his hands and appeared to slide closer to Daric, though he did not move; he was taller now, as tall as Darius, meeting Daric's eyes, yet giving the impression he looked at the floor. "You no longer wear your Defenses, My Glory. I shall fit another for your . . . renewed form?"

Daric could not reply.

"Is there something you wish, My Glory?"

He nodded. "I need a ship. I need to leave this planet."

"You'll want the *Starswarm Pyre*, My Glory?"

The ship Yellow mentioned?

"Could I see it? Could I take it to the surface?"

Nodding, the Curator lifted a hand.

Something eclipsed the yellow lights above—a square shape, tall on one side. A large black and yellow chair settling down beside them.

The Curator gestured. Daric climbed in, gripped the arms, as the chair arose smoothly, while alongside the Curator floated up to slowly sail with it along the aisle of Machineries.

"According to my inner dials," the Curator said, laying a hand casually on the arm of the chair, "it has been some time since your last visit. I mistrust them—my inner dials. But could I hazard to ask, My Glory, has it been close to a thousand years?"

At least, thought Daric.

"I think so, yes."

The Curator nodded. Sparse white hair beneath the red cap, bushy white brows. The eyes stared ahead but were clearly aware of Daric.

Beyond, another red-robed and hatted man floated in midair.

They're *souls*, he thought, like Penthesilia. *Eidolons.* The Curator and all the mirror forms lurking in the aisles.

"The Machineries have maintained themselves excellently, My Glory. All are excited, may I say, by your arrival. To your right, if you'll notice, the Cyclones, taken from the Plutonian Rebels, beside them cases of your manuscript pages in mint condition. And your instruments, violin and theremin."

Another distant figure in red, dropping slowly to the aisle.

Daric's suit glittered suddenly: a bar of light streaming from his chest to his boots.

The Curator explained in a low voice, "Measurements for your Defenses, My Glory."

He nodded, uncomfortable with the Curator's gray eyes, which held an implicit understanding lost to Daric. "A cloak has now been placed in your cabin aboard the *Pyre*. It provides, if you will remember, My Glory, total personal protection up to a force ten attack."

Daric looked away—simply to look away—back at the Cyclones, which were almost behind them.

Straight down, the aisle was imprinted with long gray scars. They had been invisible from below, but stretched along most of this wide aisle.

Tracks, he realized. Tracks from ancient wheels. Wheels like my wheel set on end. Wheels that rolled and carried a burden on their backs.

"Your new Defenses have been stored aboard the ship, My Glory."

Daric nodded. He looked at the shapes on either side. To his left crouched a giant mechanical spider, its skin glinting. To his right, a tower shaped like a pyramid, shimmering with faint lightning.

Leften Tine wants these things, he thought; not for herself, Sisteel, or Joom—for the KayTee Clan.

The Curator gestured at something stretching overhead. Silhouetted against the distant lights, the shape suggested a wing. Daric squinted up.

Beside him, the Curator's hat winked, projected a narrow beam up on spangled green scales.

Yes, a wing. An enormous wing carved from jade.

"The Pain Dragon slumbers, My Glory."

Pain Dragon, he thought. Joom mentioned a Pain Dragon.

Daric followed the wing into shadow, where a great bulk spread in the darkness, its silhouette jagged on top.

"It dreams of times long past." The Curator leaned closer, clearly moved by the sight. "Oh, I've sifted them, My Glory. Memories of the Traitor Planets, how it brooded down upon them, planet after planet, Coeus Alpha and Malachite and Pirie. How it fed on their minds and wove a skein of agony, then observed from afar—with a sort of *saturnine* ecstasy—as they succumbed. Ecstasy, My Glory. I often wonder if there was ever anything else as sated."

A sound shuddered through the air, echoing wildly, kindling hundreds of lights in the distance.

A growl, dying away now to silence. From a different direction than the dragon.

"Your ship prepares itself. We can walk from here."

The Chariot slowly dropped, touched down with a slight scrape. Daric stood. "Is it far?"

"I can feel its breath, My Glory." The Curator beckoned, leading Daric down a narrow aisle that ended in a silver haze. "Supplies are now fully loaded, My Glory, and waiting for your inspection."

Another growl. Daric slowed, staring at the haze.

"It lies beyond the ash-light, My Glory."

With the Curator floating beside him, Daric stepped through and found himself in darkness. As his eyes adjusted, and the faint lights above brightened to red and yellow stars, he discerned the dark floor and the darker shape waiting beyond, crouched low like an animal ready to pounce.

Black, like a gendarme.

"My Glory, your *Starswarm Pyre*." The Curator floated

past—a vague red shadow—to shine his light across the low-slung head, the narrow shoulders, and the powerful, folded hind legs of the ship.

"The sound . . ." Daric said, feeling the air shudder.

"Its panther brain is still sharp, My Glory." The Curator smiled. "Many years have passed since Starswarm was your pet—I'm afraid my dials won't render the exact datum. But be assured, it still yearns to *hunt* for your enemies."

From under the ship's nose, a stairwell descended, black with silvery rails.

Daric approached.

"Curator, I have to leave. I have to go back to the surface. Is that possible?"

"We simply await your orders, My Glory."

Daric began climbing. Ten steps up the Curator said, "My Glory."

He stopped, turned. A red-robed crowd had gathered.

"My Glory," said the Curator, front and center. "We wish to pledge our everlasting allegiance and admiration to you on this momentous day. Your memory will be kept alive until your eventual victorious return." The Curator smiled his strange smile, then bowed, his face lost behind the square top of his hat.

Daric was unable to reply. He climbed the stairs into sudden warmth and silence. A wide, comfortable room paneled in wood. "Hello?"

Behind him, the staircase withdrew; the outer door shut with a *whump*. While a voice spoke from the walls, the voice of his pillow. "You are Darius, you are authorized."

"Ship, I want to go to the surface, directly overhead. Is that possible?"

"The access is open. Yes, My Glory."

Daric felt a subtle pressure beneath his shoes.

"We are there, My Glory."

. . .

The world was now a black plain to the horizon.

A figure in white robes stood just below the ship. Darius.

Climbing down the stairs, Daric detected movement in the plain, undulations nearby becoming black bird necks and wings, bright eyes opening, drowsily blinking.

As Daric stopped before him, Darius said, "My boy, I am glad you've returned."

The old man gazed up at the ship. "This is ours, I think. I feel it in my bones." He smiled. "While you slept last night, I pondered the bloodline—you and I, Yellow and Black, and so many others, the chain stretching back to the old, tired Earth." The voice was calm, but carried echoes in the ground around them, in rustles and sleepy caws. "I thought much about the *abominations* we had allowed, the cruelties encouraged. Redemption was required, but what that should be I could not say, cannot say—yes, I realized that, Daric. But here is what I *knew*. We had created the Storm and thereby Starstrider. We had launched it, we entombed it, and so I knew that we could also set it free." As Darius fell quiet for a moment, his voice lingered in the birds. "No doubt your companions above, your Sisteel Nee Portia and Leften Tine, wondered at the brooding clouds that darkened our face, and later, the golden traceries that signaled our success." When he smiled, his eyes flashed like the sun. "I found the *key*."

The sun winked into view overhead. Not the sun, but a bird made of light—the Autochthon—winging circles above them.

"Daric, you are to be our emissary."

Daric swallowed, tasting copper. "But I don't . . ."

"I ask for nothing now. I am going to allow you to leave, Daric. And you owe me nothing until you're ready to give—though you need give nothing but this *promise*: Throughout your life, you will work toward a decision. Shall the Storm slumber in the moon of Mars, or shall it wake?"

On the horizon the merging of black and gray continued. Closer, the ground was buckling, the entire earth heaving: birds taking flight.

"I cannot say which is right or which is wrong, nor can you, at this time. But I think, at some point, you'll find the answer. Perhaps you'll choose to let it sleep. So be it. But if you so desire, you may reach for the key which I will hide deep inside you, and renew the Storm."

Darius gestured, and the Autochthon was suddenly at Daric's shoulder, wrapping luminous wings around him, a soft voice whispering—

. . . *Plexus Foley oh Iridani oh Triton Two oh Coeus Alpha* . . .

—the words of the Myiepan spore, into the starlines, which took them, spinning tight, fading.

Daric sank to his knees, aware of the thrumming beneath his hands. He gained his feet and saw—through the scattering shadows all around—a century rose lying on the ground before him. Shade.

Daric hesitated, then lifted it. You've helped me before, Shade.

From everywhere, Darius said, "I've arranged quite a diversion for the *Talus*. . . ."

Daric listened, then bowed low, and stumbled back up the stairs, into the *Pyre*.

The door shut; the floor shuddered beneath his shoes.

"Ship?"

The voice, his pillow's voice, from all around: "Yes, My Glory."

"We need to leave Earth, right away. And avoid anything you might . . . run into."

"Yes, My Glory. Please, sit down."

Across the room, a door opened. Daric walked through to find himself in a larger room nearly filled by a great black table and chairs.

He sat. "Ship, the storm will . . . move aside for us."

"I shall be prepared, My Glory."

Transparent squares winked into the air around him, some with ancient writing, some with graphs.

"Call me Daric."

Staring at an image would bring it forward, until it filled his sight; columns of numbers now, updating wildly.

"I am called *Starswarm*."

He tried to settle, and drew a deep breath. "Thank you, Starswarm."

"You're welcome, Daric."

Motion—the ship rising, a calm ascension, the pictures showing a tunnel of birds, streaking past, then darkness.

The stars.

Surprised, Daric said, "Could I look back?"

All the squares winked with new images. Framed with numbers, with symbols, flecks of blackness launching from the moon, thousands and thousands of gens; the surface of Earth boiling with silver and red fire; gens dropping amid numbers and symbols, into clouds, into fire; the Earth swelling and flashing, the images one by one lurching at his eyes until he looked down at the table, at his clenched hands.

He thought, We're leaving.

To find Jonas.

Behind him a voice said, "Dearest?"

IXION AND THE SCALES

The ship was full of ghosts.

They roamed the corridors and the sixty-six chambers, transparent people in a bewildering array of uniforms, lavish suits and gowns, decrepit rags. Most were worshipful, some merely courteous, others indifferent, though the majority would at least bow to Daric and wait for orders that never came.

The only relief was found in the music dome, high on the *Pyre*'s back. Not even Starswarm, so often prowling the lower decks, came up here inside the dome, seemingly open to the stars. Days ago, Daric had carried up black cushions from the couch in his cabin and piled them where the floor met the edge of the invisible field. They were the only furnishings but for the theremin and a box that held his meager possessions: the rose, and the seven strips from the Heliotrope on Mars.

Now he sat as he often did, legs crossed on the matted floor, elbows on his knees, palms cupping his chin. Were he to command it, an ecliptic web would appear, transposed on the dome to mark the local worlds. But what he liked most of all was to simply sit and stare, and feel the lines inside him inform the darkness all around.

He had been aboard for eleven days. The *Pyre* roamed the edge of the system; the line of Pluto was strongest. To his eyes the sun was remote, nearly indistinct among the stars—strange, since everything he felt on the lines indicated local disaster, warnings that scurried like white spiders, trailing strings of numbers behind. No doubt they referred to Earth and the newly resurgent Storm, but trying to apprehend more, beyond a basic impulse *avoid*, was like trying to see something that forever stayed in the corner of his eye.

Behind him, someone sighed.

He knew who it was without looking, the floating woman, the only ghost who came up into the music dome. An ancient, like the rest. She had said this was her favorite place.

"Dearest."

As before her strange motions caught his eye: a flash of her white arm against the stars.

"I've no luck with this."

He turned, found her floating over the theremin's black globe, attempting to grasp one of the handles. She smiled, her head slightly inclined. Her dark hair was pulled back, emphasizing the curve of her forehead, her sly blue eyes and dark lashes.

Like the other ghosts she only seemed alive when she spoke or smiled.

"Sculpting the air, that's the key."

Her hair was bound with silver wire into a tail that now curled up, over her left shoulder. Her other arm, her legs, floated upward, too, as though she were anchored to the ship only by her hand, and playing at losing her grip.

Today she wore a dress more transparent than the rest of her, in ripples of bright yellow and red.

"You tried to teach me once, remember?"

She raised her hand higher, fingers splayed. As she did her chest lifted, the tips wide and dark against a pale swell—not like Leften Tine's, but a conical shape, the ancient shape.

Daric looked up to find her smiling.

"You *do* remember," she said.

He turned away, and she laughed, quietly. He felt a clotted heat in his chest—anger at himself, he knew, for giving in to a ghost.

She's not a person, he told himself, not even a soul. Though he could not entirely believe it.

He looked out at the *Pyre*, at the shoulders directly ahead under the pointed ears. Scattered windows shone, opened by Daric while exploring the ship, in rooms he had not visited since: the court of black marble, with tier on tier of somber, expectant ghosts; the octagonal chamber ranked with roses; or the mirrory garden, where a dozen wandering Darics had searched, wide-eyed, for the exit.

Some of the windows winked with distant ghosts, looking out.

"You once loved nothing more than standing here, a con-jurer." He looked back to find her slowly spinning, her arms brought up close to her chest, legs together. "You would stir the air, and the music would shimmer around us . . . you once wrote of it, in verse. Something about starlight given voice."

She was the only ghost who floated.

Maybe this was why he didn't order her away, for she *would* go. All of them, even the indifferent ghosts, if nearby, would vanish at his command, reappearing at some other part of the ship, never leaving entirely.

He had tested it those first few days, then begun to simply walk away from them. But soon, even that seemed a chore, and he began spending most of his time in the music dome, which was open like the *Talus* to the stars, and where none came but this floating woman, whose name he had never asked.

Daric cupped his chin, shut his eyes. He tried to ignore her, wondering, Where's Leften Tine? Joom and Sisteel?

If they find me, what will Starswarm do?

Soon after departing Earth, the ship had swept the system, noting all the deviations from a familiar empire—moons missing, moons where no moons should be, strange ring-ships departing Triton. It had brooded, there was no other word. Its eidolon had slipped from the shadows, a panther, dark but for the yellow eyes, padding sullenly past Daric out into the corridor; and he, following a few paces behind, had suggested they wander the edge of the system.

With a flick of its tail, Starswarm had agreed.

Yesterday, Daric had told it they should get information, drinks or matrix, at a place out of the way, and Starswarm promised to search the areas sparse with *occupation forces*, and had lain down at Daric's feet and calmly licked its broad paws.

Behind him the woman said, "A disembodied head and hands."

Daric looked over his shoulder. Her blue eyes were smiling as much as her mouth.

Who was she?

"You can change the color," she said.

He stood up, keenly aware of her eyes as they roamed his pleated black suit. "Remember? The tab, feel there, on the inner sleeve, the right-hand sleeve." She reached out, then pulled back. "Press it."

When he said nothing she added, "Blue was always your favorite. Like the cooling suns, you'd say."

He almost responded, then walked through her floating arm, to the gray disk that shuddered beneath his boots and dropped slowly into the ship.

He stood now in a corridor whose walls angled to a point overhead. There were no ghosts nearby, though in the distance, where the corridor curved from sight, the old woman stood weaving her basket of straw. She looked up. From here Daric could not see her eyes. He presumed them to be widening in surprise, as they always did. The basket fell from her fingers; she caught it, and stooped, nodding slowly, said, "Good midmorning, My Glory."

Still nodding, she hobbled out of sight.

Why do ghosts drop baskets?

Starswarm had found it impossible to explain the ghosts, saying they were simply a part of the ship, doing what ghosts did, had always done, aboard the *Pyre*.

Daric looked at his sleeve, reached in to find a rough patch in the otherwise smooth fabric. At his touch the suit brightened to a russet tone, like rock from home. Curious, he applied various pressures, the suit changing to purple, aqua, leaf green; but black seemed the best, the least distracting when he was watching the stars.

He walked down the corridor to the bathroom, and afterward returned to the disk, and was carried up once more into the dome.

She was gone.

The theremin stood by itself, a black globe atop its twisted metal stand. His first time up here it had activated, crying out at his approach. Now it was silent, turned off.

He walked to the cushions and sat down.

When will Starswarm have the answer?

He lay down, shut his eyes. The familiar lines aglow with numbers and images, just out of reach. The warning, like spiders.

He dreamed, as he often had these last six days, of Myiepa.

Each tree with its high arching branches formed four distinct vaults, joining end to end with the others, blocking the sky with the strange regularity of its foliage.

Daric turned in place, looking down the rows of trunks, the avenues footed with flowing ivy, dotted with white flowers. The dreams always started here: The rows, the trunks a mottled green near the ivy, lightening to silvery brown high overhead. Sometimes it changed, sometimes clearly a dream with Jonas or Penthesilia stepping from the trees, and the trees becoming his garden, full of shadows.

But often the dreams were just of the forest, and the forest never changed.

He began to walk, looking down into the ivy. He wore the pleated suit from the *Pyre*. The leaves whisked across his black boots, edged with fine yellow hair.

There was always a pang of familiarity. As though home was somehow here, lost from sight but nearby. As though Jonas or Grandpapa were in the shadows.

"Jonas?" Aloud, to summon him, within the dream. "Jonas? Grandpapa?"

All the shadows fled.

He looked up into a burst of light, distant through the trees; a soundless sphere of white light expanding, rank by rank through the trunks to engulf Daric, a white roar quickly fading, gone but for an umbral glow in the ivy, heralding thunder.

It echoed down, tremendous.

A voice said, "Dearest?"

Daric opened his eyes to the stars.

"Are you awake?"

She floated back, arms outspread. "Starswarm asks to see you. Something about a question you had."

He blinked, sitting up.

The light, the thunder, were still vivid. But then the dream began to fade, as dreams do.

"When you come back you could tell me what it's about, if you feel like talking. You used to love telling me things."

Resisting the urge to reply, Daric stood, stretched. He walked to the disk and was carried down among several ghosts—the fat man who always grunted and blinked at the sight of him; the gaunt soldier with a pocked face and silver smile; again, the old woman with her basket, looking up, her eyes widening in surprise. He passed through them all, down the corridor to where it branched, then turned left, up a flight of stairs. Here was the aft kitchen. He opened the tall wooden cabinets, trying to decide over hot plates of ham, turkey, steak, bowls of applesauce and vanilla pudding, finally settling on chocolate biscuits, warm from the oven.

"Starswarm!" he called out. "Did you want to see me? I'm in the kitchen."

The *Pyre* did not reply; a newfound habit. The ship now communicated only through its eidolon. The panther would be slinking through the corridors toward him.

Daric took up the biscuits and headed back down the stairs, deciding to wait for Starswarm in the Wood Room, where he could eat his biscuits in silence, if not solitude.

On either side of him the ghosts bowed, smiled. "My Glory."

"Praise and terror, My Glory."

He looked down at his boots.

Since coming aboard, he had done much walking; it helped him to think, to place his thoughts in order and follow them, as his boots would follow the ship's passageways from the black grating of the lower decks to the decorated tile up top. Those first few days he had pondered Darius's instructions, and tried to feel the key the Autochthon had placed inside him, remembering what Darius had said—about how Daric would have to make a decision one day. One day. Not now. Not anytime soon.

Trying to ignore the ghosts on either side, the soft-spoken pleas or praise, he thought, Starswarm's found somewhere.

I can leave the ship. Alone. I can take Shade. Try to find a way to change him back, into something. Ask him where Jonas maybe went. Shade should know.

Briefly, Daric smiled.

He reached a door that automatically swung inward, ushering him into the dim glory of the main hall, with its burnished copper walls and burgundy carpet.

I can take the seven strips with me, to buy information. A drink. Something to tell me all about the planets. So *I* can guide the ship.

Halfway down he passed one of the worshipful ghosts, an old woman with short blue hair. Averting her eyes she croaked, "My Glory. Praise to you, for saving my family and all those loyal on Cerberus Nine. Praise . . ."

The door was twice as tall as Daric. He twisted a gold handle and stepped inside, pushing it shut behind him.

Silence.

Directly ahead were two chairs and a table, set below an oval window, the tabletop reflecting an oval of stars. Shelves began on either side, twenty rows in all. The books were made of ancient trees. Daric liked that they never spoke aloud to him, never changed in his hands or gave him what he asked for. Each was a mystery until it was opened. The best were full of pictures.

Setting the biscuits on the table, Daric walked down the aisle to his right. He'd already looked through the first two rows—those books were shelved on their spines. He stopped halfway down the third. The last book had been a history of Mars, pictures of the ancient rock plains, pink and white skies, then the first buildings, blocky domes, the land becoming yellow and green; then mansions made of glass rising into blue sky; a dirigere, yellow and black, reflected in the elaborate ponds before the Chryse castle; low shining cities and rolling hills of forest; an ocean with sailing ships; the two moons taking turns in the sky, though toward the end of the book—as he expected—there was only one, gray Phobos.

Panic.

He pulled out the next book, lugged it to the table and sat down, put his boots on the second chair, then tipped back. He flipped past the first few pages filled with characters and symbols—including the familiar eight-pointed star—to find images of people laid out on white pallets in a white room. Many images, pages of them.

One person whose arms were replaced with long appendages, ending in tendrils. One with wings, gray sad wings that drooped on either side of the pallet. Another with legs fused together, forming a fleshy fin, its ashen torso cut open and folded back.

He began turning the pages more quickly, allowing the images to barely register. Dead faces with eyes that nonetheless seemed alive, looking out.

Then a flock of winged people, like his pilots.

All staring out, smiling ecstatically.

Daric closed the book. He wondered, Did Darius make the pilots?

A ghost rat appeared beneath the table, sniffing the carpet. It froze, staring up.

Watching it, Daric ate a biscuit and remembered how his pilots had appeared, fluttering down from the ship beyond the garden, moments later half flying, half walking out of the rhododendrons, against a billowing white cloud in the sky beyond. Did Jonas know them? Jonas had traveled the stars, too. Yellow and Black had said so, on Earth.

The rat jumped, squeaked, and scuttled off, while behind Daric a shadow moved with a rolling gait into the room.

"I can report success, Daric."

Starswarm stood at his elbow, not a ghost but a solid, cold creature, shiny black but for the yellow eyes peering up, and the glistening white smile.

Not an eidolon, as Daric understood it, though Starswarm insisted this was the proper term.

It sat, perked its sharp ears, and said, "I have found an ideal port. The asteroid, *Ixion*."

"Ixion," Daric muttered.

"Excavated in the *ancient* days by the Hephaestus Doge Conglomeration, converted into an offensive platform during the Wars." Starswarm's voice was his pillow's voice, metallic in its incisored smile. "Ixion had eighty levels of living quarters, twenty-five berthing bays connected with two central dropshafts, a skein of plasma taps across the surface." The construct tilted its head, eyes widening. "Following your glorious victory, Ixion was allowed to remain operational. However, during the Fifth Cycle its officers became corrupt. An example was made of them. One of your experimental storms. The population was transmuted to low-grade crystal and the station decommissioned, obsolete."

Starswarm peered beneath the table. "Much time has elapsed since then." The eyes, with their slitted pupils, darted back. "The very stars have changed. Yet Ixion is rudimentarily operative. I find slight energies below the crust—two hundred three inhabitants. Ships approach in a furtive manner, skirting the ecliptic. Those docked on the surface do not match the prevailing designs, suggesting they are not the principle *Occupation* population." The panther fell silent for a moment, as it often did when mentioning the Krater-Tromon.

"If this is a place of illegal commerce, then *information*, as I understand your meaning of it, would no doubt be a commodity there." Its smile broadened, baring the larger, blunter teeth toward the back.

"Good, Starswarm."

The panther bowed. "I am worried, however, about you going without escort. Your renewal . . ."

Daric interrupted: "I found a defense cloak in my quarters." He suppressed a sudden smile at the thought of leaving the ship.

"Perhaps we could consider an alternative—neutralization of the inhabitants, allowing a journey down without danger."

Daric shook his head.

The panther looked up, head inclined. "I assure you, Daric, that I will not let anything harm you." It seemed to nod, then once more bravely met his eyes. "I was born into this second body, long ago, with that supreme purpose."

Daric opened the book on his lap. "Tell me when we arrive."

"Yes, Daric."

The *Pyre* shuddered.

Around him the books rattled in their shelves, while the stars, in the oval window, began to rise.

9847329147 Ixion Beta-nine-nine-five 2313792875498.

The asteroid slowly tumbled in the distance, bone-white, dull green, and gray. If it weren't for a faint *presence* on the starlines, Daric would have presumed it dead, like all the others. But Ixion's line was *alive*, somehow carrying other lines with it.

Closer, becoming clearer to his eyes, a patchwork of white, green, and gray fields.

Crouching in the transparent dome on the *Pyre*'s front paw, Daric thought, How many mariners?

"Praise to you, My Glory," said a ghost, behind him. "From those who died on Pluto's frosty plains . . ."

He gathered the heavy black cloak about his shoulders. It was too large, nearly down to the ground, but the inner pocket was the perfect size for Shade and the Heliotrope strips. And after its initial greeting, the cloak had promised not to talk further, as Daric ordered.

He fastened a white ring around his neck.

Behind him, the ghosts . . .

"Is he going to leave the ship?"

"He's putting on an *airlace*, I think."

"My Glory, may I inquire, are you going to leave the ship?"

"To visit his troops on that platform."

Daric clutched the sides of the cloak, hands shaking.

Behind him a hoarse voice said, "I would recommend a security detail, My Glory."

It was the soldier, his silver smile lost in concern. Daric looked past him to the others, dim faces overlapping into the shadows, hopeful, fearful, each with eyes that shone.

Then she appeared, floating up through them. "You found it," she said.

Daric let a moment pass. "Found what?"

"The cloak."

The asteroid was shrouded here and there with low twisted structures, charcoal shadows. Daric squinted.

Ruins.

"Starswarm would like you to look for *bilobyte* ingots."

Ruins . . . and crystal people inside.

"Are you listening, Daric?"

He nodded. "Bilobyte ingots," he said.

"They were quite common once. They might still exist. But if not, any kind of contemporary charts."

The asteroid's rotation slowed, while the backdrop of stars began to revolve.

She said, "We hope to update the *Pyre*'s navigation system."

If mariners are here, maybe they have drinks. The spore. Information on the local worlds. I can take us where we need to go.

She gestured. "See the white circle, there? With the ramp in the center? Starswarm says it's the least active ramp with people nearby. Eight ships are docked. An atmosphere cap lies just below. Starswarm reports activity under the surface."

He found the circle, then the ramp, just before a marker shone on the bubble. The ramp was darker at one end, but near the top were gray blots—ships. Only four were visible.

"We'll drop you beyond the perimeter, the white, there, on the green field."

How far from the edge of the field to the ramp? Would the tenders be nearby?

He caught Ixion's line, tried to read the numbers.

"We'll withdraw, and pick you up in two hours."

He said, "I won't know how long."

"Your cloak will give you a chime. In two hours. Understand that, cloak?"

"I told it not to talk."

"If you get lost the cloak can guide you back to the ramp, or broadcast a signal to Starswarm. Just ask it."

How far away were the mariners?

He touched his necklace, found the inset stone, and pressed it. The air became cool and close, the sound of his breathing loud in his ears.

How many levels did Starswarm say?

"You never changed the color."

Eighty?

"The color, of your costume," she said.

Daric withdrew the invisible gloves from his pocket—gray rings he pulled over his hands, to his cuffs. He flexed his fingers. "Black," he said, looking up. "Like the void mariners."

She gave what seemed the most genuine smile yet. "You *are* remembering."

"I'm not Darius." He gathered in the cloak, checked the seal on the inner pocket.

"Not entirely. You're the best of him." Eyes widening, she exclaimed, "Starswarm says jump, Daric! Jump!"

While behind her the ghosts cried, "Victory, My Glory! Victory! Victory!"

Daric turned, hesitating, then leapt from the *Pyre*'s paw.

·   ·   ·

For an instant he thought himself adrift, caught by the wheeling stars.

Too exhilarated to panic, he looked past his boots and the frozen folds of his cloak, at the vast fields, green and gray, and the white circle, the ramp with its four ships rising, becoming clearer, his own vague shadow flying across the mottled green toward him.

His boots struck, the cloak slowly spreading out as he fell forward.

Silence but for his excited breath as he straightened.

Daric looked up, then around, searching for a shadow, but the *Pyre* was gone. Emptiness stretched on all sides.

No more ghosts.

To his right, the sun dropped into the notched horizon.

He found the ramp, caught Ixion's line, bright with numbers, with fainter lines, red and blue—void mariners—then set off toward it. His first step was too strong: His boots left the surface entirely. He struggled for a moment, the cloak undulating across his shoulders, then came down in a crouch, arms out. He started again, slower, more careful, soon settling into long floating strides.

His footfalls left a haze of green dust behind.

As he approached, the first ship seemed to rise into view, hunched with four legs folded on the ramp, its sharp snout jutting down, all of it dulled under ice.

Daric slowed.

On the side of the first ship was a faint star, yellow and gray, once yellow and black. Darius's star.

Old ships.

Starswarm's wrong, he thought. These aren't visitors.

Eight of them. Dead.

To his left the sun broke from the horizon, climbing, casting across the fields toward him, down the ramp on the ships one by one, glittering the hulls, to a haze at the bottom that caught the light a vivid blue—the atmosphere cap.

But mariners *are* here, somewhere below. I can still try to get information.

He started down, careful, his boots raising plumes of ice and dust, around the first ship, a gash in its hull opening on a dim, ice-stilled interior and emerald shadows.

I won't call Starswarm, he thought as the sun vanished, gone over the wall to his right.

With every step he took, gravity tugged harder. The fifth ship was shattered on the ramp, the last three partly dismantled.

Reaching the atmosphere cap he paused, drew a deep breath (holding the red and blue lines, the numbers), then stepped down, into the blue light that crackled around his boots and upward, climbing his legs, his cloak, his chest and shoulders and face, closing with a faint *pop* over the top of his head.

24 553 23586832 146590672095

The starlines—the mariners—swarming with numbers . . .

23 621 90462105623 4248223676237250

Somehow indicating: downward.

His necklace ceased. Stale air wisped away.

He stopped, listening, but heard only the icy rustle of his cloak, and his own breathing. The ramp ended not far below.

People stood there, staring up.

They said nothing, did nothing.

He called out, "Who are you?"

They were gray. Entirely gray. Six of them, no taller than Daric.

Chids.

Behind them a portal opened on a dim bay.

He walked slowly down the ramp, searching their faces, their eyes, blank and gray. All of them were scowling. Statues, dressed like the chids on Mars, in boots and tunics and loose pants. There were footprints in the dust around them, small ones.

Daric touched a shoulder—rough stone—then jerked back at a sudden sound, what seemed a *voice*, warped, coming from ahead.

He stepped around the statues, into the bay, listening. On the far end were five large ships, the scattered lightlines striping them like wasps.

"You a monkey?" To his right, a figure scurried sideways out of the shadows, pointing at Daric. "You a monkey!? Monkey from Green!?" A boy with messy blond hair, younger than Daric, hunching forward, grinning. "You!"

In the distance, near the ships, movement: a gold shape, stretching, streaming back and forth.

"You a monkey?" Behind the boy a second appeared. "You a monkey!? Monkey from Green!?" A similar boy with short blond hair, grinning. "You?"

98127 791823981717 19283719287391287391827739817

He caught the lines—three blue, one red, farther on, *downward*. But nothing nearby.

Both boys wore tattered white and blue shirts, gray pants, black boots.

"You!" the first boy cried, crouching. "Talking to you! Monkey? From Green? Huh?" He grabbed something on the ground, then tossed. It struck the wall above Daric, clattered down. A bit of dark glass. "Huh?!"

"You!" cried the second boy, crouching. A reflection. "Talking to you! Monkey? From Green? Huh?" Grabbing and tossing something, too, but nothing struck the wall, nothing clattered down.

While the gold shape streamed closer.

"Huh?!"

Seeing it, the boy yelled, "Pog! Slow down!" He turned back

to Daric and pointed, again and again. "Spy! Look—spy from Green! Slow down!"

The reflection: "Pog! Slow down!"

"You're a spy!" the boy yelled at Daric.

The shape streamed toward them (as the cloak rippled across Daric's shoulders), then shattered to gold mist, and a large boy stumbling forward, a pale, stunned face.

"There! Right there, Pog! Spy from Mister Green!" The first boy threw more glass, hit the wall behind Daric.

The other shook his head, looking at nothing in particular. His face looked pressed-in, glassy. A clear mask of some sort.

"There! Right there, Pog! Spy from Mister Green!"

"Look at him!" The first boy jabbed his hand in Daric's direction. "Say it! You're a spy!"

The other—Pog—blinked. His eyes were small and black. He touched his throat and the mask poured from his face into his palm, a clear disk. "That seem fast?"

The reflection: "Say it! You're a spy!"

"Sure felt fast." Pog took notice of the other boy and his reflection, who was crouching, leering. "You gotta calm down, Chev." Pog slipped the disk into his breast pocket. "He's just a chid." To Daric: "Right?"

Daric nodded.

"Brought the monkeys! 'N' hounds!" Chev tipped back his head and howled, piercingly.

"Chev!" Another voice, from the ships. "What now? Pog?"

"Brought the monkeys! 'N' hounds!"

First Pog, then Chev, turned to the ships; after howling, so did the reflection.

A figure was walking toward them, an older girl, tall, with brown hair. "Who's that?" She wore a gray short-sleeved shirt and black pants.

Pog lowered himself wearily to the floor, legs half-crossed.

"Found a spy!" Chev called out. "Sneaking down the ramp! Right there! Spy from Mister Green!"

She ignored Chev.

The reflection: "Found a spy!"

Closer, she put her hands on her hips.

Pog shook his head. "Nah, just a chid, Mila. Renegade, maybe." He squinted up at Daric. "If you're trying to get out with the ships, you're on the wrong side. Shut down, south ten to one. We're clear."

Chev picked up another bit of glass.

Pog said, "The robes won't take you. We all tried."

The girl: "Put it down, Chev!" Her upper left arm was circled with red diamonds.

"There's only one way off," Pog said. "Right, Mila?"

Chev dropped the glass, kicked it away, glowering at Daric. "He's a spy!"

The older girl looked closely at Daric, his cloak. The diamonds on her arm were moving.

"I'm not," he said to her, ignoring the others.

She nodded with wide brown eyes. "My name's Mila."

"He's a spy!"

Daric faltered, then told her, "I'm Jim."

"Monkey Jim!" Chev grabbed a bit of glass, lobbed it straight up, stumbling backward. "Monkey Jim!"

"Chev!" She lunged for him.

"Monkey Jim!"

Pog said, "He's sugared up, Mila. Way up."

"Monkey Jim!"

"You didn't stop him?"

Pog shrugged.

To Daric's left, a delicate voice asserted, "It's likely he stole the cloak." A young girl with limp white hair seemed to float out of the shadows. "I've not seen chidders in such clothes." She walked toward them with arms held out, smiling.

Mila said, "Nap time, Sofie."

"She's not Sofie now," said Pog, heaving himself to his feet.

"Sofie!" Chev ran to the girl, yelling in her ear. "What does *Sofie* think!?"

She gave no reaction, did not look away from Daric.

"Sofie!"

Mila grabbed for Chev.

"What does *Sofie* think!?"

"Try and take it!" Chev crouched, circling outside Mila's reach; then his reflection, too.

"Try and take it!"

Daric said forcefully, "I'm going to the blackrobes."

Mila lunged at Chev, caught his shirt. "You're on the wrong side, Jim."

Chev yanked free, cackling, then touched his neck—another Chev appeared, and another, five, six, each cackling after the other, a crowd.

"Death to Green!" Chev grabbed a rock and flung it up, the motion echoed to either side.

The rock struck the ground beside Daric, and scurried away.

"Death to Green!" cried the reflections as Chev chased the rock—which was not a rock—crying, "Broochek! Broochek!" waving his arms.

An insect. A black beetle.

"Broochek! Broochek! Broochek! Broochek!" cried the reflections, chasing the empty floor all around, while the beetle doubled back.

Daric looked across the bay, and felt confirmation in the starlines, signaling *below*.

"Broochek! Broochek!"

As Chev came close, Pog grabbed his arm, dragged him in, yanking a shiny square from his neck. The reflections popped out.

Mila said, "Good work, Pog."

Pog shoved him away, but Chev ducked and dove toward him, grabbing for the square locked tight in Pog's hand.

"Mine now, Chev. It was broke anyway."

Sofie, whose eyes had not left Daric's, said, "He doesn't wear the clothes a chidder would wear, does he?" She cupped something in her hand—the beetle. She tossed it at Daric—but it struck the empty air in front of him, was knocked away in a flash of blue light, falling behind Chev and Pog.

His cloak rippled, then was still.

Chev froze, gaping at Daric.

Sofie smiled. "Intriguing."

Mila was walking around Daric. "You get that on Ix?"

"The other cache, I bet," said Pog. "Told you, Mila. The eye—remember?—said the spiders found another load, old weapons. Soldier stuff. Stuff Green didn't want."

Sofie nodded.

Catching Ixion's line, from beyond the derelicts and *downward*, Daric began to walk. Behind him, a scuffle. Mila appeared on his left. "Jim, can you find Taverners?"

Could he? He might return to the surface, call Starswarm, and have the ship take him to the other side. But the lines drew him on.

"Let's take him!" cried Chev, somewhere behind. "Ride the fall!"

Sofie trotted on his right side. "Why give a defense cloak to a chidder?" She reached out to touch the cloak, then pulled back. "I suspect you are an instrument. But whose? And why?"

The ships loomed against the lightlines, sweeping hulls pitted and chalked.

The middle ship had a portal gaping in its belly; five overstuffed chairs in five sizes were laid out below.

Chev was beside Mila, jabbing her arm. "I get to go!"

"If Jim wants us to take him, Chev. Maybe he knows the way himself."

Daric hesitated, then shook his head.

"We're taking you!" Chev cried.

"Not me," said Pog.

A beetle scuttled past, black like the other one. Mila scooped it up easily; it scrambled around her palm onto the back of her hand, up her wrist. She straightened, caught it with her other hand, raised it to her eyes. "We race them every Tuesday," she told Daric.

"Broochek," cried Chev. He tugged Sofie's hair and ran past. "Broochek! Broochek!"

It walked nimbly across her fingers, tiny mandibles flexing, eyes twinkling—not a beetle, but a mechanism made to look like one.

Mila said, "Don't know what it's like where you come from, Jim. But *they* serve *us* here. Part of their sentence. Right, broochek?"

At his other side, Sofie demanded, "Are you with the Sifters?"

"He's a first!" cried Chev, doubling back. "An ugly first!"

Sofie brushed limp white hair from her eyes. "The firsts are extinct, chidder. Except in the heart of Mister Green." She smiled up at Daric, showing tiny teeth.

"Broochek!" Chev was chasing another, which scuttled back and forth—faster than Daric expected—into shadows.

Mila said, "Have dinner ready when we get back."

Shambling over to the largest chair, Pog replied under his breath, then sank down into the cushion.

"Couldn't hear you, Pog."

"Said I'm taking it easy, *Mila*."

Sofie had moved in front of Daric, walking backward, smiling up. A beetle scurried past her.

"And keep Sofie occupied." Mila marched the girl over to the smallest chair, pointing, but she sat in the next one over, the second-largest. "When she's back, put her to bed."

"Yeah, right."

"Chev?"

He appeared, scrambling from the shadows, leering at Daric.

"You can come along, but only if you calm down."

"I'm calm," Chev said. "See?" He grinned with half his mouth. "Calm."

Mila returned to Daric, waving him on. "Can you believe it? We're the last of the south-ten chids."

Chev ran ahead, into the bay beyond the ships, among crude stacks of rock and metal. "See this? This one?" He pointed. "Jim! This one? See it? Monkeys, came through! Mister Green sent 'em—chased down the renegades! This claw right here—I tore it off one! Tell him about the monkeys, Mila!"

She shook her head. "I'm sure we've all heard it."

"These're melts from blackie." Calmer, Chev pointed to a pile of black rock mixed with dull crystal. "This piece there, that's really old and might be an ear. One of the soldiers', I'm not sure. See? I got it and Green didn't." He lifted a shard. "Death to Green!" He pitched it at Daric: It was struck away in a flash of blue light. Chev cackled.

"Do that again and you don't ride! Hear me, Chev?"

He returned to her side.

"Turn out your pockets. And walk right in front of me. Don't run."

He did.

The doorway led onto a ramp, angling down; the walls were scarred, gray and black. Chev hunched forward, letting his arms hang, and hooted, shambling a zigzag path.

Daric tried to concentrate on the starlines, the insistent numbers, the red and blue lines. A red one felt closer than the others. Soon there was light ahead, the boy's shadow shivering up the ramp, his voice echoing wide, "Mila!" They followed him into a broad, low-ceilinged room. "Look, Mila! Cubes!" He crouched beside them, three blue and yellow cubes, similar to those Daric had made with Grandpapa's fingers, at home.

"Don't touch, Chev."

"They forgot 'em!"

The cubes caught light from ahead, the far wall shimmering entire.

"If they left them, then they're nothing good." Mila pulled him to his feet.

"*Lemme* look!"

Daric discerned downward motion to the light. He walked toward it, and found it filling a wide shaft.

The floor simply ended.

A drop.

"We're going, Chev."

72 4692375 37508508576320 5748793936596762546046

Radiant motes spun down and around from a gray ceiling, the current tugging warmly on his face and hands, as the starlines were tugging.

How far down?

Below and across from this platform was another; the motes, as they fell past it, became dim orange. And below that, to its left, another—vague orange. Then the brilliance swallowed everything up.

"Tora tora!" cried Chev, running past Daric, leaping out head over heels into the motes, a surging bright cloud over and around, and settling, slowly falling.

"Ready, Jim?" Mila stood beside him. "Just like the ancients." Then she stepped out, the motes swirling around her as she fell forward, easily, upside down and around. "Come on!" Her hands making bright curls as she gestured.

Ixion itself, the line of it, the numbers, drew him in. He stepped into warmth, into brilliance, the motes against his face, his eyes, as he fell headfirst, more slowly than he expected, around and down, struggling—the cloak whipping darkly—moving on his back with the platform overhead, rising out of reach, into brilliance; the motes settling.

The second platform, with its frontage of orange light, climbing past.

He struggled with the cloak.

"Easy." Mila was sprawled beside him. "Relax, Jim." Her voice tickled his ear.

Daric focused through the motes. Behind him, another ramp was rising into view—empty. How far apart were the walls? he wondered. A stone's throw?

Far below his boots, Chev cackled.

"You're not from Ix, are you, Jim?"

He shook his head.

"There're two Falls, straight through, each way. They were off for the longest time, then Mister Green figured out how to work them, to carry out the history. I guess they'll be on 'til the tenders go."

He made an effort to relax, breathing deeply, feeling warmth in his chest.

Below, Chev was a shadow, wildly somersaulting.

Daric caught the lines, two blue and one red, and maybe more. On the other side of Ixion, but closer.

"You get used to it." Mila stroked the air. Her palms, coming close to his eyes, were vividly pink, a rush of diamonds beyond. "So where are you from, Jim?"

The lie came easily, from the starlines. "Dombus."

"Where's that?"

"It orbits Cyril's star," he said, catching its line. "In the Pelagic system. Its moon . . . its moon is called *Heron Platte*."

213090980 28340928 09238423749162398164175038459828 76

Mila kicked slowly, waving her arms, turning in place. Motes tangling in her hair. "You hear anything about the storm?"

After a moment he said, "Only a warning. To avoid the inner planets."

With the motes suspended, and Mila now settling, staring up, they might not have been moving at all, but for the platforms rising past her shoulder. "Sofie's eye says it's coming here. That's why they're clearing all the history out. And that's why all the tenders are leaving."

Daric squinted at the platforms, down dim halls. "It's not coming here."

"The eye—it likes getting Chev worked up, then Chev gets Pog worked up. The real truth is, Mister Green's finished. Done with Ix. He has all the history, or pretty much. All the crystal soldiers. His spiders are digging up the last bits."

"Mila, who's Mister Green?"

"He owns this. All of Ix, the history. Everything." She smiled. "Us."

"Is he here?"

She shook her head. "He hasn't visited since last year, right before the Kay chids were turned into statues. You saw them on the ramp—that was the last of the Kraters. But Peer Tromon's his benefactor, and we're Tromon chids. That's why he left us alone, I think."

KayTee.

"At least south-ten to one," she added.

Daric forced his eyes down, thinking, This is a KayTee base.

"Maybe he just forgot us. He took the gen—the blackie—back to Triton."

He remembered Sofie grinning, tossing the beetle at him.

"There's only one way off for us, Jim. I'm sure of it."

Sofie had said that *his clothes were not the sort a chidder would wear.*

"Dizzy?"

"No." Daric wrestled back the edges of his cloak. "Could the eye—could Sofie's eye get me into trouble?"

Kicking, stroking, Mila swam upside down, smiling easily. "It's a tourist. From Coeus Alpha. Mister Green hated having the eyes around, so he never listened to their complaints. Some of the chids—on the other ramps—they'd lock an eye up, put it to bed early, so it couldn't have any fun. We're halfway there, Jim." She tugged at his boot, until he got the idea and began awkwardly flapping his arms, moving upside down, rising now.

Chev somersaulting high overhead.

The mariners *are* here, he told himself, catching Ixion's line, and the others.

He reached into his cloak and touched the inner pocket: The rose and the seven strips were still there. He checked the seal, then straightened his legs, looked up.

And I can get out. It won't take me long. And the gens are gone.

"See, Jim, you get used to it."

He nodded, wondering how long he'd been gone from the *Pyre*. The cloak would sound a chime, he remembered.

Stretching, he looked up at Chev, then down, focusing through the motes. A dark speck. How far away? He couldn't tell at first, then ... "Mila ..."

"I see it." She whistled. When Chev looked down she made a sort of signal with her left hand, then pointed.

Grinning, Chev swam to the wall and slapped it with his palm, halting, as though stepping out of the river of motes.

"Fetch," Mila said as they passed by, and Chev nodded, leering at the thing. He crouched, then kicked off, dove, motes scattering, reached out: He snatched it up.

Mila and Daric waited at the wall, then pushed off, alongside him.

"Broochek!" Chev opened his palm. The beetle floated up. "Not mine, Mila! I swear!"

Mila pinched the shell, bringing it to her eyes: The little legs flailed. "Who sent you?"

Chev yelled, "Sofie, I bet! Mila—Sofie!"

"Who? Broochek? Tell me!" Light flared on the back of its shell. "You're not going anywhere." She pinched it tighter. "Answer me. You're for Sofie's eye, right?"

"Death to Sofie! Lemme step on it, Mila!"

"Who, broochek? We're the Scales now, remember. I'm the Scales for you."

"Death to Sofie!" yelled Chev, upside down above them.

"Who?" She lifted it closer.

"Banzai, broochek!"

As Chev cackled, Mila tightened her grip, twisted, and the broochek came apart in her hands. She flung the pieces in opposite directions.

"Stupid thing. I warned it."

Before long the current brightened overhead: a ceiling, an end to the fall, drawing them toward the last platform. Chev was first, up and out.

Daric tensed, readied his arms and legs.

Mila was next, stepping out—a sudden shadow—then Daric, up and out, coolness on his face, motes trailing away, the floor beneath his boots. His knees buckled.

Daric straightened, blinking. In the dimness on either side were stacks of cubes, ten, twenty, with a straight path ahead.

"Bull's-eye!" Chev had broken into three cubes already, and now clutched a black weapon as long as his arm.

"Chev!"

"Sofie! Where are you?!"

"Put it down, now, Chev!" Mila squinted into the dimness. He did.

"Don't touch anything!" She peered into the nearest cubes, wiping them with her palm. "Spiders probably left them."

"Spiders don't care! Spiders're dumb! Look, there's doppels, Mila! Ones that really work! Geysers! And air necklaces! I was right!"

"Calm down."

Ixion's line drew his eyes to the ramp ahead, angling up. One of the lines—the red one—brightened. Nearby.

"Don't worry about the broochek, Jim. We got it before it could talk." Mila was peeling back a cube, reaching in to withdraw a silver crescent. As she gripped it, yellow light pulsed along its edge. "Your cloak can probably take care of you. But just in case, you could take one of these. It's old. Still works." She offered it.

After a pause, he shook his head. "Taverners—it's at the top?" Though he could feel it, might have walked there with his eyes closed.

"Yeah. Turn right, all the way to the end. And you shouldn't ride the Fall back, Jim. Call your ship. Have them pick you up on this side."

Distracted by the red line—growing brighter still—he nodded, saying, "Thank you," as Mila said, "Just in case."

Chev had begun tearing into the cubes, and Mila dashed over to stop him. Daric hesitated, then turned away, stalking up the ramp, more quickly, aware of their diminishing voices, and the line brightening again as he reached the top. An empty corridor, lit with zigzagging lightlines curved off to either side. There were sounds to his right, clangs and shuffles, and voices.

I just need to buy information, he thought. How long did it take, in Oppidum?

While the line signaled to his left, numbers quickening—

0823 4662198 37928390823 43376298723473209847092873497 349 5098032485 20938409283409283409248450236408723 6462

—heralding the black-robed mariner who appeared around the bend, a blue face turning left, right, left . . .

6650665328413418398008834383 83

Closer, Daric discerned her strange robe, sharp like petals of a black flower folded tight across her shoulders, around her waist, down to ice glistening at the hem.

The side-to-side motion ceased, her eyes narrowing, settling with visible surprise, on Daric.

She slowed, stopped beside him, looking down.

9837 3681125875 98298734601872630273234987234098324

"Your signature is strange." Yellow eyes, with pale red pupils.

Farther down the corridor, a faint metallic voice cried, "Broochek, broochek!"

Daric said, "I need to buy a drink. A matrix drink."

"You'll find them in Taverners. You can feel the shrine? The *heart*?"

He nodded.

"Broochek, broochek!"

"Shall we attend together? This way." She continued on, with Daric hurrying beside her. She nearly floated.

To either side were cubbyholes with low ceilings, small shops, the tenders calling out hopelessly. One, a heavy man with gray hair, offered up a desperate smile and the creature called *auchtille*, its legs spinning images between. "Look at my auchtilles, Mariner! The classics of Baron Prazeel! Think of the clarity they offer!"

"I can't read your name," she said, looking down at Daric.

He faltered, then told her, "Jim."

Another tender: "Mariner, I'm here at the mercy of the Clan! Sure to go to the Scales without your purchase! Think of Alissia's blessing."

"What's your name, madame?" Daric asked.

"I am Bele Gra'Vize of the *Celestes Aura*."

"Broochek, broochek!"

To his left, nestled in a small alcove, was a stunted tree covered by broocheks, blue, green, and black, milling on the gnarled branches. Three silver birds with lime-green eyes were perched on the highest branch, just below the curved ceiling. Clacking their wings, they cried, "Broochek! Broochek!" gazing down upon the tender, who worked over a tree stump and a broochek flipped on its shell.

Daric slowed to watch him work: the fat hands poised, the broochek's tiny legs twitching, innards boiling with light under the tender's fingers.

"Child." Bele Gra'Vize gestured, and continued on.

At the corridor's end was a golden wall, and floating before it a blue globe with many silver eyes. Sighting Bele Gra'Vize, the eyes dilated and a mouth appeared, widening into a smile. "You've reached Taverners, Mariner! Step in! Step in! Forgive the shabbiness of the hall." Noticing Daric, the globe dropped, the eyes narrowing. In a cold voice it said, "No thieving chidders here! No theater!"

"My guest holds Myiepa," Bele said. "He can feel the shrine. Can *you*, thing?"

Daric looked past the wall, at Ixion's brilliant line.

The globe floated up higher. In a more reasonable tone it said, "Our gen has gone back to Triton, Mariner. The chidders take advantage, grow more bold."

"This boy is no native. He's my *guest*."

A pause. Then the mouth trembled into a half smile. "I am required to warn. You've reached Taverners."

Bele Gra'Vize passed through the wall; Daric followed, into a room dense with dim blue light, with tables stationed at intervals, each with a robot torso sprouting from its center—narrow shoulders, long silvery faces, twinkling eyes. All but one were empty.

Ixion Beta Nine-Nine-Five . . .

The line was like sunlight.

To his left, the source. Daric squinted into the gloom.

"The planet heart," said Bele, beside him.

Like the shrine in Oppidum, it resided on a black pedestal, a snarl of leafless branches, blue-green and gold, singing the brilliant line and numbers of Ixion.

"Jim. We must sit."

The other tables had turned to watch, their faces aglow, smiling; all but the last, across the room, where three mariners were leaning back in tall chairs, vague with blue fog.

Bele Gra'Vize approached the nearest table, and the high-backed chairs surrounding it.

"Welcome, gallant starfarer, to this dreary rock!" the table said, its face dimming as they climbed up, though the smile remained. The eyes widened. "Excellent informations include Heliocratic patterns at galactic plane V minus five, the swath of empire holding the opportune Keledan Five. And an easy-to-absorb evacuation source, for those unfortunate enough to be tied to the Krater-Tromon declaration. What informations do you require?"

"Amalthea current," she said. "Minus five."

"A bold choice. Three cornets."

Cornets?

She reached into her sleeve and drew out three narrow strips—patterned like his own with white stripes—then offered them to the table, which plucked them up in one hand.

"Agreed," it said, and ate the strips. "Amalthea current, minus five." It turned to Daric and said coldly, "I allow *no* theater, chidder."

Bele Gra'Vize tossed back her cowl. Her white hair was cut close and curling to her skull. She glared up at the table. "What of communion? Do you allow that?"

"Of course, of course." It smiled again. "We serve the planet heart and the hearts of mariners! We serve the singing suns," said the table, struggling for cheer. "I will take the chid's order, whenever it's ready."

Across the room one of the mariners lifted a bulb and drank

down the contents, then leaned back into his chair.

Blue fog seeped from his face.

"Your line is strange to me, Jim. Not fully formed." Bele leaned toward Daric. "You've had the drinks before, but how many? What were they called?"

"I only had one. It was called"—he bit his lower lip, trying to remember—"it was called . . . *Solus Alpha*."

"You had no primer?"

He shook his head.

Two bulbs of liquid climbed through the tabletop before Bele Gra'Vize.

"Amalthea current," said the table. "Minus five, as ordered."

"Ludicrous!" Across the room, one of the mariners had roused himself, raising the empty bulb to the table's eyes. "A nano-storm on the third planet—what's the *vintage* on that?"

Some of the tables turned to watch.

"Order please, chidder!" His own table glared down.

Daric began to reach into his cloak, then hesitated. He pulled out five of the strips and laid them down. A beam of pink light shot from the table's eyes, touching each strip. Bele raised her fingers; the table straightened. "Three will buy you a drink, though the price is exorbitant."

The table said, "We are forced to charge, Mariner, on behalf of the dread Krater-Tromon Clan! We gain nothing but the purity of the shrine and the heart."

Across the room the mariner was arguing: "The storm and their Scales—the Earth be buried!"

Another replied, "Peace. It was Alissia's world. Remember that."

"Order or depart, chidder," said the table.

Bele Gra'Vize took three of Daric's strips from his hand and offered them up. "A zero primer for him."

The table ate them, and a moment later said, "Agreed, zero primer."

Daric leaned toward Bele. "I need a drink to tell me about this system. As much as possible."

"Table, how much for a local cantos?"

"One cornet, madame."

She fed another two strips to the table. "Current contemporary, plus-ex."

"Splendid. Current contemporary, plus-ex cantos."

Remembering Starswarm's request, he said to Bele, "Could I purchase . . . bilobyte ingots here?"

"Why?"

"For my ship."

She smiled gently. "Your ship should never know more than you, Mariner."

"Is it possible to get . . ."

"Not here," she said. "Taverners is for people. It's the only place on Ixion."

Daric nodded. After a glance at the other tables, he drew out the century rose. He held it close to his chest. "Is there anywhere I could change this back?"

"A vessel?"

Two bulbs appeared in front of Daric.

"Zero primer, current contemporary, plus-ex cantos," said the table.

Daric ignored the drinks. "I need to speak with it."

"Change back, as in renew?"

Daric shrugged. "Whatever I need to do, so I can ask it some questions." He tucked the rose back into his inside pocket.

"Renewal's only available on Parson's Planet. The tier of worlds, the winding river. But if you only need to talk you can load it into a broochek. Outside, remember? At *Osud's*? You were watching the broochek tender work. You could always load it back into a vessel later."

Daric nodded.

One of the empty tables had turned to watch.

"Beware his prices. It shouldn't cost more than two strips, including download. Even for their best model."

He nodded, then looked down at the bulbs, his throat clenching. "Does it matter which I drink first?"

Bele shook her head. "Though it's tradition to drink from the Myiepan side. That one. Now, I must finish my own drink and return to my ship." She saluted him, touching first and second fingers to her forehead. "With the suns."

Feeling suddenly adult, Daric returned the salute. Bele Gra'Vize downed the contents in two gulps, set the empty bulb on the table, and leaned back in her chair. Blue fog seeped from her forehead, her cheeks. She shut her eyes.

The other table had looked away.

Daric lifted the first bulb.

For Jonas, he thought. Holding his breath he gulped the liquid down. He swallowed, tasting sourness, and coughed, then grabbed the other, draining it in four gulps.

Coughing, he leaned back in the chair.

Should I have taken off my sheen?

His lips tingled; his shoulders shook.

Bracing himself in the chair for the remembered flood of light, the voices, he found—

—tall trees surrounding him in ordered rows, rising to purple foliage, endless domical vaults.

Daric blinked.

Myiepa. The dream forest.

How?

He coughed, swallowed.

Around him the ivy rustled, shadows and bright leaves.

Mariners wandered in the distance, three of them.

This isn't a dream, he thought. Never was.

A fourth mariner appeared closer, walking slowly with hands

clasped, narrow face downturned, long yellow eyes darting, active, as she rounded a tree.

"Bele?"

She looked up, startled. She seemed to have trouble focusing, then walked toward him through the ivy, past a single white flower. "Jim."

"Where are we?"

She knelt. Her eyes were bright, jumping. "You've been here before, surely."

"I thought I was dreaming."

She shook her head. "Not you. The spore. We're inside *its* dream, of *Myiepa*." Her eyes darted left, right. A moment later she said, "This is an idealization. I've been to Myiepa, and the trees are not so ordered there, so regular. Understand?"

Daric nodded.

"You're young. Perhaps the transition can only be made near sleep for you. But when you get older, you'll choose communion at will."

Daric looked at the mariners. "Those are the other customers?"

She nodded. "You see them because they're physically nearby, with the shrine. When you grow older, more experienced, you should be able to see others who aren't." She stood up, looking over his head. "I see my last lover. There. He's on the fourth ring of Plexus Foley."

She pointed; Daric saw nobody.

"But the important thing is the spore. You should know things, now. About the system. Look into the heart. Into the ivy. It's all there. Isn't it."

He looked, and found the voices, the remembered voices—

. . . mercury scythe one one five seven tethys oh one two seven three mars five one seven three . . .

—dormant in the ivy like shadows, jumping out as his eyes found them, subsiding as he looked away.

. . . oh ixion krater-tromon general mandate oh all mariners may be used to help evacuate historical objects from the path of storm oh . . .

Voices mingling as leaf shadow, tones singing between, and colors.

He looked up.

"How did you get the primer, Jim? Did you take it yourself?"

"My Grandpapa . . ." he said, then faltered.

Behind Bele, a flash of white light had appeared in the distance.

He pointed. "Can you see that? There."

She looked.

"A flash," he said. "It's still there."

A white cloud, slowly fading.

"I see nothing where you're pointing. But that's not unusual."

He stared at the distant trees but became distracted by the information all around, leaping in the shadows. He looked back at Bele. Her eyes too were darting among the ivy. "The evacuation mandate, the restrictions—you feel them? I'm bound for Amalthea. I can't risk being compelled to stay and help." She looked up at Daric. "I must leave, Mariner."

He nodded.

Bele touched his shoulder. "With the forest suns."

She was gone. Daric looked down into the ivy, then, remembering his dream—the burst of white light through the forest—squinted at where the light had been, began to walk toward it, distracted by the ivy, by another shape within, formed by shadows, by shapes and colors and numbers—the Wilderness, all around. Daric stopped, kneeling, reaching down. Ixion was here, somehow in the soil, and the other asteroids scattered nearby, while in the distance were Venus and Mercury Scythe and Earth.

And directly ahead, where the light had been—still was—was Mars.

Home.

"Chidder!"

He struggled up, opened his eyes, dizzy: The table was leaning over him, prodding his shoulder. "Chidder!"

Daric coughed.

Bele Gra'Vize had gone. The other mariners—

... oh Gid Sha'Meed oh Portra Voltray oh Castalline Drex ...

—whose lines were brighter than before, were still at their table, heads tipped back.

"Chidder! Absorption time has passed!"

Daric coughed a sweet-smelling mist that stung his eyes.

He blinked it away.

... oh present location ixion krater-tromon hall section four bee oh taverners oh ...

Strands of voices one on the next, separated with strange music that was also colors.

He coughed again, wiping his mouth. A blue stain dissipated on the back of his hand.

... oh Currency dot cornet standard oh ...

I'm okay.

Sternly: "Absorption is complete, chidder."

How long? he wondered, stirring.

... oh taverners absorption period one quarter standard ixion krater-tromon ...

Daric said, "But I haven't been here long."

"A quarter has passed. Depart, chidder."

A quarter, he thought.

... oh 14 23 01 03 local time ...

And I have the information. I can find Jonas. All I need to do is talk to Shade. Buy a broochek, get to the surface.

Daric reached into his inner pocket; the rose and two strips were there.

Buy a broochek, get to the surface—

...oh evacuation source ixion krater-tromon hall taverners...

—ask the cloak to call Starswarm.

The nearest table was watching him.

Daric climbed off the chair, assuming his cloak about him, wondrous at the lines and voices, layered in his eyes and ears.

...vector three three present location ixion krater-tromon hall section four bee oh taverners oh...

He found he could look through them to utter clarity, around the vivid room to the other mariners—

...oh Gid Sha'Meed oh Portra Voltray oh Castalline Drex...

—beyond the motion of Ixion, the planets, and suns. Focusing now, drawing everything aside. A hum behind his eyes.

Daric walked toward the wall, pausing at the planet heart, the singing line clouded with numbers. He blinked, and continued into the hall.

...oh vessel BRIGHT SYREEN dock three two departure 13 43 oh CELESTIS AURA dock three one departure imminent bound amalthea...

The line of Bele Gra'Vize was nearby—

...oh M Bele Gra'Vize destination Amalthea present location vector docking bee two...

—he could *feel* her on the surface of Ixion.

At his side, the globe was watching with narrowed eyes. Daric coughed, tasting sweet liquid, then forced himself on, down the corridor to the broochek shop, and the gnarled tree covered with broocheks.

The tender had quitted his meticulous repair work and now napped against the trunk. A gold broochek was perched on his shoulder. Overhead, the broocheks and silver birds made soft hoots and clicks.

... oh ixion krater-tromon hall level 06545236 three section oh Osud's Emporium oh currency 06546526 cornets oh ...

As Daric stepped into the shop, the birds beat their wings and cried, "Broochek! Broochek!"

The tender stirred, grumbling. His eyes popped open, black and bloodshot in a wide pink face. He set about straightening his plentiful robes; the broochek struggled to keep purchase on his shoulder.

"I'd like to buy one," Daric said. "A broochek."

... oh BROOCHEK current trade ...

The tender's eyes narrowed. He looked up. "You? *Buy?*"

... one cornet strip local currency ...

Concentrating, he discovered how to *look away* from the information, and felt the voices calm.

He pulled out a single cornet, then the century rose. "I need this loaded into it."

The tender straightened, grunted, and laid his thick hands on the silver-topped tree stump. His fingers were wrapped with gold wire. "I don't serve renegades, bless the Scales."

... oh ixion krater-tromon colloquial renegade native child fleeing krater-tromon indenture oh avoid contact ...

Daric *looked away.* "I'm a mariner."

"A chidder who's a mariner?"

"I can pay."

The tender took the rose, squinting at the petals. "Will cost you three cornets for the broochek, one for the transfer."

"It should cost one for the broochek."

"One! Bah."

Daric pulled out his last cornet, and said more firmly, "The starlines tell me one will buy a broochek." He laid the strips on the stump.

The tender squinted at Daric, then plucked them up, lifting them to the broochek on his shoulder; the broochek whistled.

"Nearly not," said the tender. With great, grunting effort, he turned and set the cornets on a branch behind him, where a larger broochek plucked them up, carrying them into the tree. Overhead, the birds flapped their wings of beaten silver, chirping loudly. With further effort, the tender lunged for a broochek on the lowest branch. He set it on the stump.

"There. Your broochek."

A black one with eight legs ending in silver points.

Daric leaned closer, discerning drops of silver for the eyes. "Will it be able to talk? Could it hear me?"

"If the transfer works. Risk is yours."

. . . Osud's Emporium one three three broochek transfer rate . . .

"Will I be able to hear it?"

"Loud as a broochek can talk. Loud enough held to the ear."

Daric nodded. "I'll do it, then."

"Fine, you'll do it." The tender lifted the rose, rotating it beneath his eyes, then set it on the stump. Laying the broochek beside it on its shell, he placed his hands over both; the wire on his fingers glowing, tendrils of light jumping from his fingertips.

The rose faded to gray while the broochek stirred its tiny legs.

Soon the rose was white.

The tender flipped the broochek over. At first it made no movement, then each of the eight legs twitched in turn, and it began hobbling.

The tiny eyes were shining.

"Might be quiet for a while," said the tender.

"How long?"

The tender straightened, then said expansively, with glowing gestures, "Imagine for yourself. You get put into one of these—right now—into oblivion, might be. You're awakened by us looming folk, find what were hands are claws, what were eyes are crystals, what was mouth are mandibles. Time must pass."

Daric reached for the broochek, gently lifting it by the shell. The legs plucked at the air.

"Some never want to talk, though."

He dropped it on his palm.

"Never do anything, some. So be it. Judgments been passed. I simply give them better shells."

The broochek stumbled, righted itself, struggled up the hillock of Daric's thumb.

"Shade."

Daric raised his palm to his eyes, while the dealer crumbled the rose to dust, and blew the dust from his stump.

"Shade?"

The tender sagged back against his tree and shut his eyes.

Daric held the broochek to his ear, heard nothing.

The birds began to chirp quietly.

Carefully cupping the broochek, he walked back into the corridor, staying near the wall, out of the way.

... oh ixion krater-tromon hall level 06545236 three section oh Osud's Emporium ...

He thought: I need to get to the surface.

... oh edict 2277 triton requests all local mariner vessels aid in evacuation of krater-tromon facilities 34 244687 3567788 sol system ...

Daric slowed, and *felt* for an exit, a way to the surface, and another line pulled at him, from farther along the corridor. He hurried after it.

Nearing the ramp that led to the Fall.

... oh dropshaft 56485 colloquial fall warning avoid indenture to krater-tromon ...

... oh BELE GRA'VIZE vector 4583 3432 2917 tangent dee destination amalthea ...

She was on the surface, above.

He walked faster, following the corridor around a slight curve, toward the elevators that were ahead.

The broochek pinched his palm.

Daric opened his hand, raised it to his chin as he walked. "Shade?"

The broochek made a small noise, scrambling awkwardly.

The corridor was nearly empty here. Daric stopped, held the broochek to his ear. It was crying out, an insect's whine.

"Shade," he said softly. "You're with me. Daric. On Ixion. An asteroid."

. . . local time 14:30:01 oh 00:07:03 calibration . . .

"Shade, it's a KayTee base, but I'm taking us to the surface. We're getting out on the *Pyre*."

His shade moved one leg after another.

"I had to put you in a broochek, Shade."

The wide silver eyes seemed dazed.

. . . oh ixion krater-tromon hall one level three section three one dee oh . . .

. . . 92 482372 42789318723 . . .

. . . oh Bele Gra'Vize departure oh Amalthea . . .

. . . 38 836333 83833287388 . . .

He stepped to the wall, blinked. Bele Gra'Vize's line had vanished into numbers, into the starlines, though he could reach for it still, could feel the distance—beyond the asteroids, then beyond the system.

He let go the line, opened his eyes.

"Shade, I'm taking us to the surface. Starswarm'll be looking for us."

The line directed him to a door on his right, which slid back, revealing a small gray room. Daric stepped inside; the doors closed.

"I want to go to the surface," he said, not sure if he should say anything. The room lit up with yellow stripes, then lurched into motion.

I could've gone with Bele, he thought.

He lifted his palm to his eyes, uncurled his fingers.

"Shade, where's Jonas?"

The broochek turned circles, stumbling, its eyes dimming, then brightening.

"Shade?"

Faintly, it cried, "Why?"

The room lurched, traveling sideways now.

... 239084 oh landing fields ×5 oh landing fields ×7 oh landing fields ×9 943857 ...

"Shade? Can you hear me?"

A tiny voice. "Why ... here?"

"Shade! I'm taking us off Ixion!"

"Why ... this body?"

"Shade, it's just temporary. Shade?"

But the broochek said nothing more. The room stopped, then began to rise.

... 098237 oh CURLEW oh Mariner, activate your personal atmosphere 493737 373743754 ...

Daric touched his throat. The necklace activated, cooling his face.

... CURLEW 398773 oh warning zero atmosphere ...

The doors parted on a small room. A crystal window looked onto the surface of Ixion. Once inside, Daric heard the door shut behind him. The room popped against his ears; the door opened. He stepped out in a whirl of dust, onto a chalky path, a gray field out to the curved horizon, each star fixed with a brilliant line, and numbers.

He began to walk, looking up, searching for Bele Gra'Vize among the wheeling stars, finding her distant, hard to hold.

Daric blinked it away.

To his left were ruins, tumbled broken stone, heaps of melted metal, what might have once been ships. Four spires jutted up, canted, beyond. Somehow familiar.

He would move farther away, into the field, to call Starswarm.

He walked slowly around the ruins. The spires climbed into view, and a fifth was revealed, shorter than the others, at an angle.

A huge stone hand, clutching. He'd seen one like it in the Machineries, on Earth. He thought, Tell me about this.

Focusing back through the lines and voices and colors.

Tell me.

. . . 98723974 Ixion Historical Foundation Site 023984793274 . . .

Daric reached into his pocket and fumbled out the broochek. The legs poked his palm as the broochek righted itself, turning toward the stone hand. Daric lifted it close to his ears, into the pocket of air, and heard the high keening cry. "Cusp!"

"Shade. I saw one like it on Earth!"

"Our cusp! One on every world! None on Mars! The Mind destroyed . . . The rest remain!"

Daric stepped closer. The fingers of cracked green stone, blocky at the tip; the palm a nest of angles upon which was imprinted a rectangle, the size of a door.

He lifted the broochek. "Shade, do you think it still works? Do you know how to use it?"

Pressure began building on his ears.

Then the stars blurred. He stared, dumbfounded, the cloak rippling across his shoulders.

The starlines vanished. Numbers and lines, gone.

Impossible silence.

He worked his jaw, tried to clear his ears.

A calm voice said, "My Glory." The cloak. "You ordered me not to talk. Yet I must report the appearance of a containment field."

Daric turned in place, reaching, encountering it, all around. "Cloak . . . is the cusp doing this?"

"No, My Glory. It emanates from *behind* the cusp."

He fumbled the broochek into his pocket. "Cloak, call Starswarm!"

"I'm afraid the fields prevent transmission, My Glory. Without my countermeasures, it would have stunned your encephalonic levels."

The pressure in his ears became a tightness in his throat.

"My Glory, there is the source."

From behind the cusp a figure had stepped out, entirely black, unfolding slowly, as though from a crouch. Impossibly tall now, taller than the stone wrist, with long, gaunt arms, and long, curving fingers. Within a helmet of pale blue air a long white face watched him.

The cloak: "My Glory, we are receiving a transmission."

A second voice spoke, close to his ear. *"Leften Tine thought you would return to Mars."* A cold voice, a shadow's voice, as the eyes narrowed, and the face brittled into a cruel smile. *"But the Scales have blessed my trap, it seems."*

Daric stepped back, his cloak rising against the field, sparking.

"The station carried you to your cusp. I am Quintillux Cunning Heart, from the Talus.*"*

The figure, the shadow from the *Talus*'s wall, looked up. *"There will be a moment of disorientation."*

The stars winked out.

Pure blackness overhead, and Daric felt panic rising up his throat. In silence—too much to bear—he groped inwardly for the lines, the numbers.

The figure now a shadow on the gray, twilight plain of Ixion.

Then the stars reappeared, wheeling. Daric looked up and around, found the sun—what must be the sun—smaller than before, mute, dropping into the horizon.

"Your ship has been left behind, Darius. We are now in Triton orbit." Smiling, Quintillux looked down at Daric, then turned to the cusp. *"A boat will arrive shortly."* He kicked soil at the cusp. *"And you, thing . . ."*

From behind it, something crawled into view, low, familiar

as the dust scattered, with a red-and-gray-striped shell. Impossibly, a *sandfink*, from Mars.

With the point of his boot, Quintillux nudged it over, onto its shell, then stood watching—its hundred white legs flailing, the head within the bony shell moving back and forth.

He flipped it upright.

The cloak: "My Glory, I apologize, my defenses . . . are collapsing."

A brilliance stabbed at Daric's eyes. He slowly fell—it seemed to take forever—landing on his right shoulder, unable to move. Unable to see for a moment, blinking, pain along his shoulder and side.

"Chidder, it wishes to speak with you." The long face smiled down.

A sandfink, but not a sandfink, not possibly a sandfink.

"I'll grant it this. And the roses as well. The renegades. As a gift."

Quintillux dropped two century roses into the dust before Daric, then turned away, scanning the skies.

While the 'fink awkwardly approached, eyes glinting.

It stopped beside the first rose, nuzzling the petals, as though sniffing. The face beneath a sweeping vertebra of shell not quite a sandfink's.

Looking up, it found Daric and continued on, crawling up to Daric's chest, pushing into the pocket of air at Daric's chin, to Daric's ear.

An eye, black and wet, narrowed craftily, peering. A *human* eye. A small voice said, "Seven. A fine vessel it is."

Daric cringed at the cold breath on his neck.

"We meet again, chidder."

The tender, from Oppidum.

"My establishment taken, eaten entire for the want of a single chid, eight. For a rose rightfully mine, three, you'll agree. I defended my wares. The Krater-Tromon gets nothing but praise from me." The eye blinked. It looked away, then back. "I answered to the Scales, as you shall, nine. Was made to serve the corpse of him I killed. My only pleasure knowing that you, chidder, have been found. To be delivered to Green, who sits at the right hand of Peer Tromon, blessed are the Scales, ten."

4

THALMAS GREEN

Daric leaned back against the maple tree and shut his eyes. He was drowsy, but not enough to sleep.

At the corner of the Estate's crescent-shaped grounds, he shifted his shoulders and settled in the grass, listening. A sparrow, maybe a robin, was singing on the mansion's roof high to his right. In the pine island the crows were cawing back and forth. Directly ahead, the fountain splashed, swelling and fading almost imperceptibly; all of it with the slightest of echoes, from the shell.

The Estate had seemed unbearably quiet at first. It was really the starlines' fault—they were gone, either dead inside him, or blocked by the shell and the worldglass beyond. Those first days, whenever he was alone, he'd dwelled on their absence, recalling the lines and numbers, the voices leaping in the ivy shadows; and this new, utter silence, this *deadness*, had started expanding, forcing him to move, stand up, wander his bedroom or the mansion's marble halls, or the grounds.

He breathed deeply, let his shoulders drop.

It was Friday. Twenty-seven days had passed since his arrival on Triton, and it all seemed normal enough; while his capture, his time on Earth, in Oppidum, seemed distant, like a dream. And the days before that . . .

The afternoon dwindled to a vague silver-blue on his eyelids, to the specks of dust floating in his tears, brittle and translucent, twitching as he turned his eyes left and right, settling for a time while the silver-blue deepened, gained dimension.

Drowsy, staring into it, he thought of home, the red rock and the open sky, the rustle of leaves in the orchard, the copper smell of the air, and how it changed at irrigation time. Home, with Jonas and Grandpapa, and Shade. A normal day. A normal morning.

What had it been like?

Daric remembered.

Waking to the turret's curved wall, the circle of fish bones tacked above his pallet: how the slanted morning light would strike them, in the otherwise dim room. How he'd sit up, aware of Shade waking, too, and it was always his pillow that said good morning first, brightening as he stood up, barefoot on the cold floor in the cold blue light. "Good morning, Daric. The hour is . . ." Its voice was also the medallion's voice, and Starswarm's voice.

Sometimes he'd wake too early and have the pleasure of going back to sleep, tucking himself in the warm blankets as the pillow darkened, tiredness overtaking him, to rise later in the morning, with sunlight on his face. The smell of pancakes from the kitchen.

"Good morning, Daric. The hour is ten o'clock."

Daric would mutter, "Morning," and get clean clothes from the chest of drawers—the short-sleeved shirt and tan pants, the rust-colored tunic that was the most comfortable, or the blue long-sleeved shirt that had once been Jonas's. Toss his pajamas on the floor. Shade would complain about that later. Jonas making breakfast downstairs: the sound of a fork scratching a metal bowl.

The smell of pancakes making him hungry.

You missed the nine o'clock visit, Daric, Shade would say. *You should go see Grandpapa before breakfast.* And Daric would climb the stairs, hands on his thighs, up and up, doing his duty, paying respect to Grandpapa as Jonas had done when he was little, up and up, past the other artifacts—the ceremonial urn with the Martian rosette on the side, the lightning rod twice as tall as Daric—hearing Grandpapa's chirps, then his voice calling out, "Ah, my boy, good morning," the echo of it on the stone, like the gears grinding in the basement.

Grandpapa's silver stand, showing scrapes and dents. Grandpapa gazing down, golden against the fresco of stars.

"Good morning, Grandpapa," Daric would say, and dutifully tell of the day outside, whether there were clouds, or what the Actuality instruments had read, even if he hadn't done them yet.

"Another day, young Daric!" Grandpapa's voice would become more energetic, more spiky. He would sometimes sing old songs, or talk of Mars when it had forests, or what Earth was like in the *ancient ancient*.

Stomach growling, Daric would wait for a break in Grandpapa's story, then say good-bye 'til later (Grandpapa raising and lowering his right hand) and climb down, around and down. Around and down.

And down.

Daric?

There at the corner of the Estate, beneath the maple tree, Daric had fallen asleep, and now dreamed of climbing down the winding stairs to Jonas in the kitchen, who was at the griddle, singing under his breath as was his habit.

Daric, you should feed the fish before breakfast.

"Ah, there he is, up and about." Jonas looked over, his silver nose winking, his eyes smiling a moment before his mouth did.

Daric wanted to rush over and hug him, but resisted, suddenly aware that this was a dream.

"I've fed your fish already, young sir." Jonas flipped the pancakes with an ease Daric had always envied. They were thin and golden brown with bubbles at the edge. They smelled wonderful.

I'm on Triton, he thought.

"Breakfast in a quarter. With hot maple syrup, if your luck holds out."

Where are you now, Jonas?

A strange question, Daric.

Daric turned away and walked through the open kitchen door, feeling the static of the house field against his sheen, squinting at the morning sun. The sky was copper washed with yellow at the horizon, and the orchard wet with shadows. A cool breeze ruffled his hair.

As he walked toward the lake Aver wheeled overhead, crying hello.

He thought, There's a ship down there, Shade.

What do you mean, Daric?

And you're going to be turned into a beetle.

Daric picked up a rock and knelt on the shore.

What?

You're here, too, Shade. Somewhere. On the Estate.

The Estate?

Merode went to look for you.

He tossed the rock into the water, peering through leaps of wiry sunlight, at his fish lazing over the plum algae.

We should go inside now, Daric, and help Jonas set the table.

This's a dream, Shade. I was thinking about being here and I fell asleep. I'm in the Estate, by the maple tree.

As he stood up, Merode's voice, surprisingly close and clear, startled the morning to silver: "The sun's a thief, Daric, and with his great attraction robs the vast sea."

.   .   .

Daric opened his eyes, blinking at the branches of the maple tree and the silver-blue shell beyond.

"Look what I found."

Merode was kneeling beside him, holding a book on her lap. "The one I told you about. The ancient poems."

He sat up, stretched. The dream faded but for Jonas. Jonas standing at the griddle. Jonas smiling kindly.

"Father had it on his desk, in case the lords and ladies drop by."

Where is Jonas, right now?

"Daric?"

If I could reach the starlines again . . .

"You awake?"

He nodded, blinking.

Merode's long blond hair, straight behind her long neck and rounded shoulders, was silver in this light.

"How long was I asleep?"

"Long enough for me to commit my crime. Longer, really. I didn't wake you at first. I watched you sleeping."

Her eyes were green and flecked with gold.

"Really?" He looked down at his white cotton shirt that buttoned down the front, the suspenders holding up baggy brown trousers, the muddy shoes.

"Remember yesterday, when I had to wake Father up. He was in his bed with a sleep cap on, and his face looked empty. Absolutely empty. Off in the worldglass, communing." She shook her head while idly scratching her ankle. "But when you sleep, your face isn't empty. You're watching your dream. Does that make sense?"

He nodded. Relaxing against the tree, he wondered what his face had shown.

"I was reading you a poem. Want to hear it?"

"Yes."

"It was one he had marked. Father knows they might ask him to recite, and he wants a good one ready." She opened the book, leafed through the pages. "Let's make sure I have it down." Brushing the back of her hand on the grass, she silently read the poem in preparation.

Merode was so often active that she seemed a different girl when sitting still, bored, even sad when her eyes looked down and lost their color. For an instant she became that first girl, the one he'd seen from his window, walking gloomily along the stone path.

"Ready, Daric?"

He nodded.

" 'The sun's a thief, and with his great attraction robs the vast sea,' " she began, with admirable assurance. " 'The moon's an errant thief, and her pale fire she snatches from the sun. The sea's a thief, whose liquid surge resolves the moon into salt tears . . . ' "

Daric remembered the white light in Myiepa, how it rushed through the trees when he spoke Grandpapa's name.

Like a signal.

If I could get outside, past the shell, to the starlines, I could talk to Grandpapa, have him tell Jonas where I am. Or Bele Gra'Vize . . .

"Daric?" The poem had ended. She closed the book, and tugged the hem of her white, short-sleeved blouse. "Well? What did you think?" With her left hand, she tucked her bangs behind her ear.

He nodded. "I like it."

"Are you in a mood?"

He shook his head.

"There's some easier ones in here. We'll let you read after dinner." She fell silent, brushing her hand along the grass.

Somewhere on the pine island, a crow was cawing. Another on the roof of the mansion replied. At dusk all the birds—the crows, sparrows, robins—would fly to their roosts, scattering up from the trees, sharp-winged against the scarlet strands of the evening shell.

Strange, but nothing compared to what was outside.

While he watched Merode's hand, his thoughts turned back to his arrival: Quintillux Cunning Heart floating him to a window to watch the slow fall, their ship cutting through currents of worldglass into a world like Oppidum without its fundamental, a crystal garden gone wild, writhing, where once outside, Daric was watched by tier on tier of figures, shimmering ranks of green and gold, and closer by Citizens in crystal eggs, who leaned forward to watch with wide, fearful eyes, smiles tugging at their lips; and all of it—the Citizens, the surging buildings, the escort of six-legged hounds ambling on either side, muttering at the glassy ground—all of it vanishing like one of Jonas's magic tricks, in the time it took to step through the entrance of the Estate, where Thalmas Green, archaeologist of Triton, extended his hand in the ancient custom, saying, "Welcome to my world, Daric."

That first morning, he awoke on a huge bed, in a huge, quiet room.

Terrible memories crowded in. The sandfink with the tender's voice nosing in beside him. Quintillux Cunning Heart throwing down the roses—Mila and Chev. The descent to Triton.

And the starlines were gone completely. The silence was numbing. He stared blankly at a box on the small bedside table, some moments later realizing it was a clock, the tiniest hand jerking around, making the faint *tick-tick-tick* that had been in the room all along.

He sat up, grimacing. All his muscles were sore.

Along the wall to his left was a tall window with many panes, full of yellow light. The walls were dark paneled wood halfway up, becoming paper stamped with purple crescents. The ceiling had a square lamp in the center.

The bedside table was wood, too, and the desk, and the doors. It had all barely registered before he'd collapsed, exhausted, into bed. Now, with the window light, and the purple crescents above and around, the room seemed wider, the ceiling higher than the night before.

Daric flung back the blankets.

He was facing the door with a gold handle: It led onto the hall, he remembered. To his right were two doors, standing open on a closet and a small bathroom. To his left, beside the bed, was the table with the clock on top. Beyond it a desk and chair, and farther along the window full with yellow light.

He struggled out of bed, wincing, unsteady, dizzy for a moment. He looked down at his white short-sleeved shirt and white shorts, which he'd changed into the night before, and walked to the window, leaning his elbows on the sill. A low yellow sky, a wide lawn curving off to either side, a fountain tossing water ahead, and far to the right a clump of pine trees.

Flat stones made a path across the lawn.

Daric pressed his forehead to the pane. To his left a white wall curved out, with tall windows—five rows, five floors. He was on the uppermost floor, the building curving away from him, against the larger grounds, which curved toward him.

And the sky not far overhead was solid, down to the brick wall beyond the fountain.

How much do they know about me? he wondered. About Starswarm? About Earth?

Did they find Shade?

Squinting, he realized the sky was made of strands, yellow and silver, becoming a pure silver near the walls. And the strands were vaguely swaying.

He walked to the closet. An assortment of shirts and pants hung from hooks. None seemed as comfortable as his old clothes, but his old clothes were gone.

His leg muscles gave out. He barely made it back to bed and pulled up the covers, calves aching.

How much does Thalmas Green know? he wondered. He owns the chids on Ixion. Maybe on Mars, too.

Sometime later, footsteps approached the door; there came two light knocks. "Daric?" The voice resonated through the wood.

Shoulders stiffening, Daric said, "Yes."

The knob was turned, the door pushed open. The archaeologist of Triton stepped sideways into the room, clutching a tray. He was large, as Daric remembered, with sloping shoulders, a gray cloth suit that rustled as he crossed the floor, the wings of a black tie tight against his throat. "I hope you're feeling better this morning."

His voice was low and careful, and somehow like the long curls of dark polished wood above the door.

Daric nodded.

"You certainly look much better. Now, I've brought you soup, toast, and juice for starters." He set down the tray with arms extended, and knocked a corner: Soup spilled over the china bowl, and the wrinkles deepened on his forehead.

Strangely, he was only half bald, with wiry dark hair at the back of his head.

His eyes, pale blue and dry, moved from the spill to Daric. "My daughter's more skillful at this." He dabbed with a napkin, then lifted a tub of butter to one side of the plate, put a spoon on the napkins. "You've had quite a journey. I expect you have questions. I expect we both do. But we'll talk only if you feel up to it." Straightening, Thalmas slipped his hands into his coat pockets. "Think of this Estate as apart from Triton. We're our own sovereign nation, my daughter Merode and I. A rather quiet nation, usually." He looked from Daric to the food. "Lunch is at noon and dinner at six. Breakfast we tend to eat on our own, whenever we feel like it, though Merode sleeps much later than me." The eyes returned to Daric. "Tell me, have you experienced any dizziness?"

Daric shook his head.

"Aches?"

Daric nodded. "My shoulder. My neck."

"They were rough, the *Talus* crew." From his waistcoat pocket, Thalmas Green withdrew a narrow tube. "I want to check . . . if you'd allow . . ." Leaning close he shone the light into Daric's eyes, flicked it away, then back. There was dirt under his fingernails. "Yes, that's good. Quite good." He slipped the light into the pocket and reached for Daric's neck, probing gently the bones behind his ears. "The aches should go away. I can give you something for the pain if it persists. There's a chance you may have dizziness, with some ringing in your ears. Gone by tomorrow, in any case."

Thalmas straightened and looked around the room. "You have new clothes in the closet. If you don't like them we can find you some others. You don't need a sheen, of course. I believe you were told to leave yours on the boat?"

Daric nodded.

"I'll drop by before six, and see if you're feeling up to dinner." At the door he hesitated. "We go by the ancient calendar here, Daric. It's Saturday." He left the room, softly shutting the door behind him.

Daric sat for a time, staring at the tray, listening to the silence, the *deadness*, then noticed the food: it smelled wonderful. He was wary but saw no other option but to eat, and the soup scorched his tongue and was delicious. He slurped from the edge of the bowl, finishing it quickly, then the buttered toast, washing it down with orange juice that was sweet and coldly satisfying. Afterward, feeling better, he went to the bathroom, then changed into a shirt that buttoned down the front, undershorts, trousers, and canvas shoes.

He opened his bedroom door and leaned out. His room was at the end of a high-ceilinged hall. A short distance away was a skylight full of yellow light, and beyond, as the corridor curved from sight, a second. To his left a stairway leading down. Silence and stillness, pricking at his ears. Daric stepped back inside, shut the door, remembering the starlines, the voices in the shadows— how Ixion had been beneath his boots in the ivy, and Mars directly ahead, marked by the white light. Like a signal, he thought, when I said Grandpapa's name.

He went to the window. The shell had changed slightly, becoming more silver than yellow, the strands sluggishly moving. How high is it? Daric found it hard to judge close by, but in the distance it looked three times as tall as the pine trees.

And was Triton just outside? The swaying city?

There came movement in the pine, a figure stepping from the trees, down the incline. A girl with straight blond hair to her shoulders, walking slowly with her arms behind her back, hands grasping her elbows, her face downturned. She wore a white short-sleeved shirt and faded red trousers that were wider near the bottom. She was slightly taller than Pen, with narrower shoulders, but similar long hair.

As she passed the fountain she glanced up at his window: Daric stepped back. When he looked again, heart pounding, she was past the far edge of the mansion, then gone.

He returned to the bed. Thalmas's daughter. He tried to remember her name. He stared at the clock, stood up and paced the room, then lay down, thinking of the questions to come— about Ixion, and Starswarm, and Earth. He tried to sleep but the nightmare memories and the silence made him panic, sit up.

He thought of the Scales.

When the clock hands were straight up and down, footsteps approached his door, and there were two light knocks. Through the wood: "Daric, are you feeling well enough to eat?"

Daric stepped into the hall. Thalmas Green gave something between a nod and a slight bow—he wore the same heavy suit—and descended the stairs. Daric followed, holding on to the wide wood rail, becoming aware of the smell of spices and baking bread.

"Do you like your new clothes?" Thalmas said over his shoulder.

Daric barely nodded, then, more faint than he intended, asked, "Where are my old ones?"

"Stored, for safety reasons. But we can easily acquire some in the same style."

They reached the first floor and walked along a marble hall. Thalmas told him of each room as they passed—a library with books Daric could read if he wished, a parlor with sofas and overstuffed chairs, a music room with a piano.

Thalmas slowed, gesturing to the left. "This was originally the pantry, but it's a smaller space, and more comfortable, really. We use it as a sort of informal dining room."

The room was small, with paintings of trees and flowers; three lamps provided a soft light. A table occupied the center, draped in white cloth, laid out with silverware. The girl sat opposite the door, in the same short-sleeved shirt, staring down at her fingers hooked on the edge of the table.

"My daughter Merode. Merode, this is Daric."

She looked up briefly—long green eyes. She rearranged her fork and spoon. With first and second fingers tucking long bangs behind her ear.

Daric had nodded, seating himself opposite her, feeling suddenly awkward, vaguely frightened. He let Thalmas serve him—rolls from a big plate, a bowl of steaming vegetables, slices of white meat glazed with honey. "Merode prepared the meal tonight. She's an excellent cook."

The girl said nothing.

While they ate, Thalmas talked about his own family history, which he had traced back to the *ancient ancient*, and about Merode's mother, who was now on the Heliocratic capital, Plexus Foley, as a seneschal for the KayTee. And how the Estate had been built fourteen years earlier when Peer Tromon *gained primacy* in the worldglass.

"Did your guardian ever teach you of the worldglass, Daric?"

Daric shook his head, and was glad when Thalmas continued talking.

"For our Citizens, it is language and art and politics in one. It encases Triton and mirrors the flux below, for the city is always in flux, floating much as ancient continents would float on currents of deep lava. You sit in its only unchanging portion, Daric. Around you the world is continually re-formed by the *raised*. They live mostly in the worldglass and look down, yet they also look outward, watching the stars. And for their portion, they live in the world itself, almost like the tourists on our wilder worlds. And the glass mirrors this flux, evolved into something that is art, and politics, and language."

Daric stole glances. The girl's attention was on her food. Did she resent his presence, or just not care? She didn't look up until she was done, her eyes glinting green and gold as she turned to Thalmas and said quietly, "May I be excused, Father?"

"Daric, you haven't asked about your broochek."

He sat up against the maple tree, stretching his shoulders. "Did you find it?"

She set the book of poems on the grass beside her. "Of course. My crime, remember? It was in the seventh chamber, in the Sanctuary. With your old boots and your necklace. So I timed out the field, stole it back." She added, "They're so common, broocheks. He probably thinks it caught a ride on your cuffs. They do that."

"Where is it?"

"I hid it in my city."

He nodded, remembering the huge eggs in her room, how the silver egg contained the city, and the gold egg held Merode while she *communed*.

"He'd never think to look there. If he notices it missing, that is, which of course he won't." She leaned back, staring up at the shell. "And my Citizens are absolutely loyal. Absolutely."

A bell tolled in the branches above him, three times; another, more faint, tolled in the pine island, and a third near the opposite side of the crescent-shaped grounds, in the swingset arbor, visible by the tops of its poplar trees above the pine.

"Thank you, Merode."

"C'mon." She grabbed the book and leapt up, brushing grass from her yellow-and-white-striped trousers. "Father says it's my fault we're always late."

Daric stood and stretched again, then followed her across the lawn.

"You'll have to go in with me tonight, Daric."

"Can it work with two?"

"Two chids it can."

I can try to talk to Shade, he thought. Find out where Grandpapa went. And Jonas.

They were nearing the fountain, a bowl of white rock shooting founts of clear, cold water; its pings and plashes were always gratifying for Daric. Then the path narrowed as they rounded the pine, close to the shell.

"Merode." Daric moved closer, so that their shoulders brushed. "Did it talk? My broochek?"

"No. But I tried. I complimented it, said it looked classic, very retro-ancient. Nothing worked, Daric. It just walked around in circles." On their right the swingset appeared, backed by the half circle of poplar trees. "So I turned its legs off and put it in the Old Empire Park. Really, it works well. I've told my Citizens it's an oracle. Something to add a bit of mystery to their lives."

They were approaching the arched façade that marked the other end of the grounds, the mossy stone capping a downward flight of stairs; the entrance to what Merode called a *sepulcher*.

"Thank you, Merode."

"I'm sure it'll talk to you. But if it doesn't, you can leave the city, Daric. You can watch me while I commune." She was the first to reach the sagging stone stairs, and looked back, over her shoulder. "I'll look empty, Daric. I promise. Just like the real raised. A peaceful face, with nothing behind it, nothing." Then she was dropping into the shadows of the narrow hall, rounding the corner. Daric followed, coming upon her stopped before a bookshelf. She hefted the volume of poems onto the second shelf. "Father!" There were no lightlines. Globes floated here and there, giving white light and a faint yellow flicker, most apparent on the ceiling and in Merode's hair.

On their left were high tables with stacks of brushes, the sonic picks, jars of cleaning fluid, rags. Ahead, a doorway led farther into the Sanctuary, seven rooms each larger than the last, where glass capsules held what Thalmas called the treasures of time.

Daric had often wondered if Mila was here, too; the century rose she had become.

Or had she gone to the Scales?

"Father, it's three o'clock! Where are you?"

Those first few days, Daric had learned the halls and the grounds, walking away from nightmares.

From the patio around the edge of the mansion, to the maple tree alone in its corner, where he liked to sit and watch the shell, the mingling, swaying strands; or across the lawn to the path of stones, to the fountain, the rippling water; to the pine island, climbing the slope into the trees, shouldering through branches, with soft needles underfoot and the smell of pine sap. At the island's center, standing with trees close around, and flecks of silvery shell high overhead.

The bells would ring hourly, first at the far end near the maple tree, then the mansion, then the nearby swingset.

Daric quickly figured out how to ride the swings, kicking off, pulling on the chains, watching the ground sweep past his shoes, pulling harder, seeing how high he could go, high as he dared— the chains slack at the peak, then taut—flying forward, at the end leaping off, out and over, onto gravel.

At night he dreamed of Ixion, and Mila's smile. She wanted to be turned into a rose, he'd think. The only way off. That was what she meant, the only way off Ix, being turned into a vessel, taken away.

Thalmas, apart from meals, was usually occupied with his studies in the Sanctuary or his third-floor suite of rooms. He asked no questions of Daric—at least not the questions that Daric feared. At dinner, Thalmas would do most of the talking, of the wonders he'd uncovered on Neptune's moon Miranda, or among the Onomule Glass colonies. Usually, Merode said nothing; she sulked, even outside of dinner. Whenever he came across her during the day, she was busy, reading a book, or working in the garden, or the lab. She would barely acknowledge him with a glance, and usually ignored him completely. At meals she responded to Thalmas when he asked her questions, but always succinctly, and always asking to be excused as soon as possible; though on the second night, after answering one of Thalmas's calm questions (about her horticulture studies) Merode had rolled her eyes. Thalmas hadn't seen her do it, but Daric had, and Merode *had seen* him see it. Daric thought it might signal a change. But afterward, when they found themselves alone in the hall, she went on her way without comment.

The fourth day, a Sunday, Thalmas approached Daric in the swingset arbor. "Would you join me, please, Daric?"

Daric had jumped off the swing, followed Thalmas along the gravel path, trying not to panic but sure that the questions would come now, about Earth and Darius, about the Storm, and Shade.

But as they rounded the pine island, Thalmas chatted about the swingset, how it was a design from the *ancient ancient*, and of the varieties of birds inhabiting the Estate, sparrows, robins, thrushes; leading Daric across the lawn to the central patio, along the mansion's side hall, and under the skylight marking the intersection with the main hall, which curved off to either side.

Thalmas had fallen silent.

Throughout the house, clocks chimed two o'clock.

Directly ahead were black double doors that led—as he vaguely remembered, with renewed nervousness—through a series of chambers to the outside.

But Thalmas turned left at the last moment, into the study.

The walls were lined with bookcases like those aboard the *Pyre*, a dozen tinted-glass lamps; at night a dim blue fire in the brick fireplace.

"Would you like some apple cider, Daric?"

Daric shook his head.

Thalmas approached the fireplace, and the plush chairs around it. "Sit down." He gestured with an open palm.

Daric sat. He willed his shoulders to relax, while Thalmas lifted a ceramic mug, then poured hot water from a pot on the sofa's end table, adding a cinnamon stick. A brief, intense smell of apples reached Daric as Thalmas sat across.

"How are you and Merode getting along, Daric?" Thalmas sipped his cider. He blew on the surface, blinking dry eyes against the steam.

"All right."

"She hasn't been too friendly, has she."

Daric said nothing.

"She's not used to guests. You'll have to give her time."

While Thalmas sipped again, Daric looked at the dark fire-place.

"But you seem to be getting used to these new surroundings. How are you feeling? Have the headaches subsided?"

"Yes."

Thalmas leaned back slightly, looking from Daric to his cider. "Darius was a historian of sorts. Did your guardian ever teach you Earth history—the *ancient ancient*?"

Daric shook his head. "He said I had to be older."

"There was a time called the Renaissance, and a family called the Medici-Triune. The KayTee is much like that, Daric. Your ancestor once made a great study of them. His history of the time is the primary text on the subject."

Daric said nothing, while Thalmas's eyes lingered at his cider. "Daric, you should be aware that I have considerable weight with the Families, especially the primes, the Tromons."

From his coat pocket, Thalmas withdrew a metal flower. Its petals were black, the stem forming a three-pronged stand. He set it on the table beside his chair. "This is a recording device, Daric."

Heart suddenly in his throat, Daric nodded.

"You needn't worry about Leften Tine and the others— Cunning Heart—they won't be bothering you here." He crooked his head at an angle to his shoulders. "But formality requires me to ask you several questions. Simple questions, really."

Daric nodded.

"Did you return home to Mars, Daric, after your escape from Earth?"

"No."

Thalmas sipped, then sipped again. "Have you seen your guardian Jonas since then?"

Daric shook his head. "No."

"Do you know where he is right now, or where he was plan-ning to go?"

Looking at the metal flower, Daric said, "I haven't seen him since . . . since the *Talus* took me away."

"Did you know of any plans to relocate?"

"No."

"Hmmm. Your brother never talked of travel?"

"He did."

"Where to, Daric?"

"He never said. Just talked of leaving Mars."

Thalmas was silent. He nodded, as though to himself. "Your old home is abandoned. The sensor equipment was destroyed. It appears a ship was once docked beside it, but the KayTee haven't had any luck finding it." Thalmas lifted his mug. While he sipped, Daric pictured, with painful clarity, the empty home, the drained lake.

"Did anyone ever visit you there, on Mars?"

Daric was about to shake his head, then said, "The foundation people once a year. And sometimes some farmers."

"All right." Thalmas nodded. His eyes darted to the flower: The petals faded to white. "That's all I need to ask, Daric. I'll relay this to the Tromon primes. Consider the matter put to rest." He straightened, drank the rest of his cider, and set the cup down on the table, then took up the flower and slid it back into his coat pocket.

The next morning, after a late breakfast, Daric climbed the stairs to the fourth floor and walked down the hall to Merode's room. During the night he had decided on this, and now the walk had the aspect of a dream being lived out.

The door was halfway open, covered with pictures of flowers and ancient buildings—*postcards*, he would learn they were called.

Merode was sitting on the edge of a canopied bed. A bird stood on the side of her hand. A sparrow. She gently touched its head—the head flinching, so quickly that it had moved before it seemed to move. Daric watched, admiring her confidence with it.

Trying to affect a simple look of curiosity about the room, with its bright wallpaper and the creme carpet underfoot, its many bookcases and trinket shelves, Daric stepped inside.

Beside the window were two objects like giant gray eggs.

She looked up briefly, then back to the bird.

"There. Let the salve sink in. And try staying away from Big Crow." Cupping it, she stood and walked past Daric into the hall, to the aviary next door. Daric had followed, lingering while she tended to four other birds, finally joining her on the narrow patio to toss seed over the rail, down to the crows, a black rustle on the grass below. "They're called *raven avernus*," she told him plainly. "They exist in only three places in the Wilderness and this is the nicest they have it, by far."

The conversation had run out with the seed.

After dinner, he approached her in the study. She was sitting by the fireplace, a half-dozen books scattered on the carpet behind her. She looked up, then went back to reading.

He sat in the second-nearest chair, and moments later (spent watching the blue flames in the fireplace) asked her what she was reading.

"About old Triton." She turned the book toward him, pictures of long-limbed people wearing capes, riding crystal wheels. "The three families and seven hierarchies, the lords and ladies. Tromons, Kraters, and the Sfericambrii." She flipped ahead, too quickly, then set the book down, looking directly at Daric. She said simply, "Father says you're ancient, that you stepped right out of history."

Daric had been unable to reply.

"He likes talking like that. You'll get used to it."

A week later, sitting with Daric on the swings, she had told him, "We're prisoners. Both of us. I'm his daughter but I'm an ancient, too. The world makes no sense of us."

·   ·   ·

"Father!"

Merode walked into the second room of the Sanctuary; Daric followed. The ceiling was low, made of black rock marked with faint gray symbols. Helioglyphs. According to Thalmas the Sanctuary had once stood on Ganymede, an ancient temple. He'd dug it from the ground rock by rock, and reassembled it here.

"There he is. There you are!"

A table to their right was covered with pictures, rocky landscapes—what looked like asteroids.

One picture was a stone hand grasping at the stars. The transmission cusp on Ixion.

Daric's heart stuttered.

"Now you're the late one, Father!"

Ahead, with a clapping of dusty palms, Thalmas appeared, ducking under the lintel. "Record time, Merode. Daric." He wore a dusty long blue jacket. Approaching the table, he pulled a bundled cloth from his side pocket. He set it down, then dragged over a stool, though a stool was already there.

"I can make this a short meet, Father. We didn't waste the afternoon. Daric worked on his reading, and I finished my text assignment."

Daric could hear her smile, though he did not turn to see it.

"Excellent." Thalmas eased himself on the stool. "And, Daric, how are you coming along with reading?"

Daric nodded, then, "I finished the first book today."

"Very good." Thalmas reached into his side pocket, withdrawing a sonic brush, square and black, white on one side. He set it gently on the table, beside the bundled cloth, then glanced up, over his shoulder—seemingly at a crystal box on the opposite table. "Merode, the light, please." He pulled back the corners of the cloth, uncovering a flat white rock.

"Where's that from?" Merode tapped the globe beside her. As it floated across the room to Thalmas's upheld hand, everything on the table seemed to tilt, leading Daric's eye to the picture of the cusp.

"Beta Nine-nine-three." Thalmas drew the globe closer with his fingertips, then flicked it free.

"How old?"

"From 100 A.E." Thalmas turned the piece in the light.

"Could I look at it later?"

He nodded. "If you treat it with care. You left the Acteon fragments out."

"Because I'll be working on them tomorrow," she replied. "Bright and early."

Thalmas scratched the rock with his thumbnail; a bit fell away, to dim orange. "Leaving them out risks contamination, Merode. Even a minuscule amount of dust . . ."

"But dust won't harm them. They're crystal."

Thalmas turned to her, looking at her throat. "Merode, using the artifacts is a privilege. You simply must follow my rules." He patted the stool beside him. "Up here, Daric, please."

"I follow most of them."

Intent on ignoring the cusp, Daric climbed up and folded his hands on his lap. Thalmas was whisking the brush lightly along the rock. Daric could smell dust; he nearly sneezed.

"You've been with us almost a month, Daric."

"Twenty-nine days," Merode clarified, somewhere behind.

"It's December, in the ancient calendar. What was called *Christmastide.* We've healed you well, haven't we? How did you do today? Any headaches? Any troubling dreams?"

"No," Daric said, a lie.

Thalmas scratched the rock with his thumbnail, orange flakes raining on the tabletop, the piece becoming silvery and flat, the size of his thumbnail. "Merode, if you have a moment, would you see to the Acteon pieces?"

She exhaled through her teeth.

Daric resisted the urge to turn and look at her, looking down at his lap instead.

"It won't take but two minutes, dear."

"You want to talk to Daric alone."

"Merode, there's no need for dramatics. Please, if you could turn on the dust fields, too."

She mumbled and walked off into the Sanctuary, scuffing her shoes.

Thalmas seemed about to speak, then switched on the brush, gently whisking it across the rock.

"This was very ordinary once. A coin of the realm. Now quite rare." He held it up to the light.

Daric resisted the urge to glance at the pictures, the cusp.

"*Platinum*—very common on Earth in those days." Thalmas tapped it on the edge of the table; another bit fell away from a curved edge. "All the refined metals were eaten by the storm, of course. This was found on Callisto, in the ruins of a Doge temple. Do you know about the World Prime, Daric?"

"It's the capital . . . of the Heliocracy."

Thalmas nodded, placing the coin flat on the table, leaning close to pick at it with his thumbnail. "Nearly the size of our Jupiter, and sentient, alive. Their technologies have eaten away the planetary mantle. I made the journey almost ten years ago. It shines, like a jewel. Terrifying, really." With his thumb, Thalmas rubbed the face of the coin. "Every particle alive at every moment, listening to the suns, the *wisdom of the singing suns*, they say. And the citizens are its partners. Plexus Foley is the template for their empire, a hundred planets along this edge of the galaxy."

He turned the piece over beneath his eyes: It was small, flat, dim silver. "Holding on to what remains of this system is a constant struggle for us. The Krater-Tromon took it gladly, as caretakers. Our duty. We promised to watch the storm on Earth and maintain the few cities for their amusement. The Heliocratic minds could visit Mars and the Scythe, safe within the fundamentals. Inhabit the locals, experience the thrill, the terror, of the ancient life."

The air crackled: the dust field being turned on.

"And all the while we could do what was most important—preserve the history." Thalmas tapped the piece, brushed it with his thumb. "There's a group of us, Daric, within the Krater-Tromon. We call ourselves the *Sifters*. Have you heard that name before?" Thalmas glanced over.

"No," Daric said (both remembering and trying to forget Sofie trotting alongside him on Ixion—*Are you with the Sifters?*).

"We're unknown to the worldglass. Peer Tromon is our benefactor. A good benefactor to have. He joined many hundreds of years back. He once told me he'd nearly left with the Sferi-cambrii. Instead, he joined the Sifters." Thalmas laid the piece on the table. "Without our actions, artifacts like this one would be lost, remade by the storms. And in a larger sense, the home system would be lost. In step with the Helio worlds. At best, like Triton throughout, changed at the very core, the past erased, re-worked on a molecular level." Thalmas drew the light globe closer, throwing the piece into relief: a coin, stamped with a pro-file. "As it stands, we care for it, on behalf of the Heliocracy. We tell them the system is a ruin, unsafe. The Wilderness of Ruin, we call it. Keep away, let us watch the storm, and all the while"—a chime sounded; a small light winked on beside the table; Thal-mas took brief notice of it—"we rescue. Without us, Daric, all of the *ancient ancient*, all traces, would be lost. And the gens would be everywhere. Not just on Earth's moon and the port cities. Our system would be *raised*, in step with the core worlds."

Merode appeared, tugging on Thalmas's jacket. She was ar-ranging a sprig of small flowers in his lapel.

"What's this, dear?"

"Trying to brighten you," she said. "But it's not working."

"I appreciate the effort." With the heel of his hand, Thalmas swept the dust and fragments into a pile.

Merode lifted the coin. "A dime?"

"Yes."

She regarded the face stamped on one side, scraped it with her thumbnail. "I made up some of that solvent, Father. You should use it."

He barely looked up. "I will."

Merode set it down with exaggerated care.

Thalmas looked over at the blinking light, as though for the first time. He gestured to it. "We've received a telltale in the house, dear."

She said nothing.

Thalmas turned to her. "Could you . . ."

Her eyes dimmed, and she seemed about to say something, then turned and stalked out, stomping up the Sanctuary stairs.

Thalmas shook his head, moved the light globe farther back, flicked it free, then moved the brush farther back. Daric looked down at his own hands, then, quickly, at the pictures, the cusp.

"Were you going to use it, Daric? The cusp?"

His stomach became ice.

Thalmas looked over: calm blue eyes.

Daric shook his head. Then, "No."

"But you knew what it was?"

He nodded.

Thalmas turned back to the piece. "They're all over the Wilderness. Darius liked to say he could stride from planet to planet, across his empire." He began making adjustments to the brush, though Daric knew his attention was still on the cusp, and on Daric.

Daric moved as if to rise from the stool.

"While you're here, Daric, I have a small favor from you. Something for my studies." Thalmas climbed off the stool and walked to the opposite table, to the crystal box. "Simply an impression of your hand."

The cusp.

"A quick procedure, absolutely painless. I promise."

Daric swallowed, tasting acid.

"This contains fluid that solidifies when given a current, and retains an impression. Here . . ." Thalmas set the box on the table in front of Daric, and fumbled off the lid. The fluid was gray. Thalmas took Daric's hand and unbuttoned the shirtsleeve, rolling it back. "I promise, Daric. It's rather cool right now, but there's no discomfort. If you would, please."

Daric crooked his arm and allowed his hand to be put into the chill fluid, which seeped between his fingers and held him firm, as if in a clasp. "Now, just this . . ." Thalmas touched the other side, and the box hummed, the fluid warming around Daric's hand, under his nails.

He fought the urge to pull free, while Thalmas stared down at the fluid changing from gray to white.

"Good." The hum stopped. Thalmas helped him pull his hand out.

It felt bare, cool in the air.

He flexed his fingers.

"That will be all for now, Daric. Why don't you go find Merode. Tell her I'll take the dinner chores."

The mansion, a five-storied crescent in opposition to the grounds, looked strangest at dusk, the inward curve of dim white stone looming up, with one hundred forty-three windows reflecting the fiery shell.

He found Merode just inside the hall. Her hair was tied back with a white ribbon. She stood looking up at a burnt-out light, a vacuum bulb, tapping it gently with her finger.

She didn't acknowledge his approach.

"Merode?"

She continued on, past pools of light, her shoes whisking over the carpet's red and gold crescent pattern, a design echoed in the wallpaper—called *wainscoting*—that covered the upper portions of the walls.

Catching up, he said to the back of her head, "I'm not doing anything for Thalmas anymore." His voice was harsher than he'd intended, but still she didn't look.

At the main hall she turned right.

"Merode?"

She stopped at a door, pulled it open, and stepped through. A globe illuminated a stairwell leading down to a storage hall. "Close it if you're coming," she said over her shoulder, with one hand drawing the globe down the stairs.

Daric complied, hurrying into cooler air and shadows, down the stairs after her, to a narrow, crowded hall. Straight-backed chairs were stacked one on the other, beside dusty oil paintings in decorous golden frames, trays of silverware, rugs rolled up and tipped against the wall—things that would be brought upstairs when they had guests over, Merode had once told him; and boxes of supplies, in which she was now rummaging.

A faint chime: She had retrieved a lightbulb, and now held it up to Daric.

He said, "I'm not doing anything for Thalmas anymore."

She looked at him directly, then set the bulb down on a box and brushed past Daric, drawing the globe with her, its light pooling against the tall door at the end of the hall, shining on the high and low locks.

"Merode?"

In her hand was a long metal key. Ignoring Daric, she slipped it into the high lock, then the low lock. Bolts clicked. He stood back as she pulled open the door.

The lamp didn't penetrate far: furniture, a stack of chairs, long tables like those in the dining room laid one on the other, the end of a bed tilted against a dresser.

Daric followed her in. He nearly tripped against boxes stacked beside the door, and became aware of a high ceiling, an echo.

Dust tickled his nose, like particles against his sheen. His heart began to pound.

"Merode?"

Daric tried to fathom her eyes, but she was gazing into the room. She was breathing hard.

There were portraits on the wall, or perhaps stacked near the wall, dim faces looking down, like the ghosts aboard the *Pyre*, watching as he and Merode walked around rolls of what might have been wainscoting, between tables and more chairs, then stacks of boxes, across the room to a table where rested five shapes, side by side, covered with brown sheets.

She flicked the globe free, then pulled off the first sheet—dust swirling against the lamp, an acrid, sour scent—revealing a rounded glass container, a dim shape becoming clear. Matted fur against the glass—an animal, afloat in cloudy liquid, its arms half-raised, yellowed fingernails against the glass, and between them a face, pale and shrunken, with wrinkled skin and wide, startled eyes.

He whispered, "What is it?"

She wiped the glass. Goose bumps on her skin and the dust breaking free. Beyond her fingers the face becoming clear, an angry brow, small eyes edged with white mucus.

"Merode . . ."

"One of his dendrii."

She wiped more of the glass, making clearer the stiff dark fur at the throat.

Daric glanced up at the other four containers.

Quietly, Merode said, "They're him."

The shadow of her hand made the eyes blink.

Pale blue eyes, staring straight up. Thalmas's eyes.

Daric stepped back. Merode was silent, still touching the glass, and the dust still falling. He looked away, into the shadows of the room.

A moment later: "Merode, could there be century roses here?"

She might not have heard.

To her back, he said, "I'm looking for two of them. One red, one blue. Thalmas might have gotten them on Ixion, when he got me."

Merode took her hand away. "Daric, what did he want? What was so important?"

Daric thought for a moment. "He wanted . . . to take a cast. Of my hand." As he raised it she looked over, briefly. He added, "To study the cusps."

He lowered it, flexing the fingers, which barely tingled now.

Merode retrieved the sheet, flung it back on the container. "This was the best he could ever do, no matter what he says."

"Merode . . ."

Avoiding his eyes, she drew close the lamp and walked past him.

"Merode?"

But she was quiet, quick, the light stuttering near and far on tables, chairs. As they reached the door he said, "Merode . . . could we leave here? Could we leave the Estate? By ourselves?"

She turned, walking backward, her face lit upward smiling, and bright green eyes. "We'll talk at midnight."

During dinner, she ignored his significant glances.

Thalmas had made vegetable stew, which was delicious, as well as fresh-baked bread, and chocolate cake for dessert. He acted cheerful to Merode, thanking her for cleaning up the Acteon pieces, asking about her current studies. Merode acted equally cheerful to him.

Afterward, she refused to talk to Daric about anything beyond the routine.

When the clock struck twelve Daric climbed out of bed in pajamas and socks, ventured out into the dim hall, down one flight of stairs to her room. She opened at his second knock, ushered him inside. She wore a yellow T-shirt and shorts. Across the room, a lamp shone over the two eggs. "I thought you'd fallen asleep, Daric."

Her room seemed unnaturally still at this hour, dark beyond the window. Her desk lamp lit a coin on the blotter: the silver dime.

Daric approached the eggs. They were taller than he, with a dull shine. "Eighty thousand Citizens. Some five hundred blocks, three districts. Five parks." At some gesture of Merode's, a seam appeared in the left-hand egg, the upper portion sliding back, revealing tousled sheets.

"Go ahead, Daric."

He climbed in with a little difficulty, onto warm sheets. Then she was beside him, both braced by the curving shell as the top folded back over, and Merode's hair tensed, rising up to tangle overhead. He was vaguely frightened, his heart pounding, but calmed with Merode so close, her voice, a whisper: "My name is Thetis."

Daric blinked, gazing up and around.

To all sides were lofty buildings of pale glass and stone. People were everywhere—crowds like those in Oppidum, crossing the high bridges between buildings, milling beneath grand edifices of wrought iron, through this plaza where Daric now stood—unraised, ancient people in colorful clothes moving past Merode in a yellow dress, different from the girl who had lain down beside him, somehow older, taller, and more serene, her hands folded in front of her as she smiled and nodded to the passersby, to her Citizens.

She turned to Daric, the light catching in her green and gold eyes, as a railcar flashed beyond her shoulder. "Dizzy?"

He shook his head, studying the folds of his white cravat, his dark suit and shoes. His hands seemed larger, as though he were holding them close to his face. He was older, too.

"Pleasures of the season, Lady Thetis." A gray-haired man in a black suit bowed to Merode, then moved off.

"We'll have to take the trolley, Daric. We're on the Pacific Walk." Beneath the dress, she was much like the floating woman on the *Pyre*, with a rounded chest. "I put the broochek beyond those buildings in the distance, see the azure one—the blue one? That's the Civic Auditorium, then there's the bowery park."

They walked through the crowd. Silvery orbs floated here and there, and as they collided or touched the ground, they chimed in bright, conflicting tones.

And the crowd, passing: ". . . said to her, we'll take the liner to Ulna, spend the holiday there . . ." ". . . disappointing, the acting was dreadful, really dreadful . . ." "Seventeen, without doubt, if not twenty . . ."

Dazed, he slowed, finding it hard to walk for a moment.

An orb floated past and Merode reached for it, scooping out the silver liquid, which rang and chimed as she held it: a flurry of tones as she tossed it toward the crowd. Daric thought he heard the KayTee tones inside it, all mixed up.

He felt a sharp pain behind his eyes, and remembered the egg and Merode asleep beside him.

"It gets easier," she said, over her shoulder. "There's the trolley!"

The car was perched on a track that climbed in a broad arch, above the streets and smaller buildings. Inside, a crowd of ten or fifteen milled, chatting; when Merode stepped aboard they bowed. They made room.

The floor was a filigree of crescent moons, the ground visible beyond it. As the car lurched into motion, Merode fell against him, her hair tickling his face in the sudden breeze. She straightened.

"Good afternoon, Lady Thetis," said a plump woman.

Merode nodded and said brightly, "Hello, madame."

"Lady, we're all looking forward to the seasonal performance."

"It'll be a grand shindig. *A Christmas Carol*, it's called."

"Ah. Wonderful."

How tall am I? Daric wondered, staring once more at his hands.

Everyone in the car was shorter than he was.

Daric looked past his shoes, at glittering lakes and parkland, square white houses, and tiny people milling about.

"Merode, what did you mean? What you said . . . in the basement. About the dendrii. How that was the best he could do?"

Squinting down at the city, she said, "Didn't they tell you?"

"Who?"

"The chids. On that asteroid."

"Tell me what?"

"He made them. All the chids."

Daric nodded, trying to read her older face, the eyes, which glanced quickly toward him, then away.

"To repopulate the system. Ancient humans. First he made the firsts, but they didn't work out. Then the seconds. He's up to sevenths, now. But he didn't make me."

The car began to curve and drop.

"Sometimes people think he did."

The car set down gently on the grass.

A Citizen said, "Out and about, Lady Thetis."

"Out and about, Chandler Beatrice," Merode said brightly, gesturing for the other passengers to disembark first. She smiled at Daric—suddenly so familiar about the eyes that Daric lingered, staring after her.

"C'mon, Daric."

"Oh," said another passenger. "Look at it!"

Overhead a dark shape blotted out the sky.

Daric squinted.

"Yes, that's your broochek."

He recognized the head and mandibles against the sky. In the distance to either side were the massive legs, lost behind buildings that spanned the park.

"It was hard placing it," Merode said. "Crowd control was difficult. I had to close off this entire district."

They walked across the grass, into shadow. Some citizens saw Merode and bowed, before resuming their watch. Daric likewise looked up. Blinking against the ache in his eyes, he asked, "Is it awake?"

She nodded. "It just doesn't want to talk. Broocheks are like that. Remember I had to freeze its legs. Not for long, though. Just until we escape." She looked over and smiled at his expression. "Yes, Daric. We can at least try. Father's leaving on an expedition. I'm sure of it. We'll have the Estate to ourselves in a few days. I can steal sheens from the Sanctuary, and time out the entrance fields." She searched the nearby park. "Right now, we need a phaeton. Driver!" She hailed a short wheeled cart clattering down a cobblestone path.

"Lady Thetis."

To the old man on the front seat she said, "We need a lift, Driver Lowell!"

"Of course, Lady Thetis."

When they climbed into the open compartment, onto plush velvet seats, the phaeton actually lifted, gliding over the parkland, rising past silver orbs—whose music was caught and torn by the wind—up to the black and purple mass of the great broochek, the mandibles yawning to either side of the pinched head, surrounding a colossal smile of pointed silver teeth.

"A little higher," Merode told the driver.

They passed from shadow, up level with one of the widely spaced eyes, compounded and brilliant, scattering flecks of light on Merode as she leaned forward and tapped the driver on the shoulder. "This'll do, driver." She stood. "Oracle! Are you awake?"

The broochek gave no response.

Daric called out, "Shade, it's me! Daric! Can you hear me?!"

Nothing.

"Shade! It's Daric!"

The eyes dimmed, then flashed tremendously; a voice roared: *"DAR-IC."* The sound of it carrying across the city, as thunder, with faint shouts and cries from below.

"It's me, Shade!"

"DAR-IC!"

Merode, with her hands over her ears, called out, "Oracle, you must quiet down! You're frightening my Citizens!"

The mandibles moved, creaking, raining flecks of black metal. "YOU ARE DARIC!" it said, more subdued, though Daric felt it through the phaeton's floor.

He yelled, "Shade! We're on Triton! Do you understand?"

"THE OPTICALS . . . IN THIS BODY. THEY'RE FALLIBLE . . . DARIC. NOT INTENDED FOR USE . . . AS A GIANT."

"But I'm here, Shade! We're going to get you out!"

The mandibles yawned wide, then came together with a *clang.*

"Shade, I've called out for Grandpapa, in the Myiepan forest! There was a burst of light."

The broochek groaned. "I CAN NO LONGER . . . MOVE MY LEGS . . . DARIC."

"Shade, I was on Myiepa. I saw a light, a burst of light, when I called out Grandpapa's name."

The giant mandibles opened; the eyes flashed. "GRAND-PAPA'S ... GOAL."

"What do you mean?"

"TO ... RID HIMSELF ... OF THE CENTURY SEAT. TO ... PROJECT HIS MIND ... ONTO THE MYIEPAN MATRIX."

"Shade, so he's there, now?"

The eyes flashed. "YES."

"Can I call him?"

"IF JONAS ... WAS SUCCESSFUL ... THEN GRAND-PAPA LIVES IN THE STARLINES. THAT WAS THE REASON ... FOR THE DRINK IN OPPIDUM. YOU WOULD BE GIVEN THE SPORE. BUT NOT THE PRIMER. GRANDPAPA WOULD BE ... YOUR PRIMER."

Daric grimaced at an ache behind his eyes.

"HOW LONG ..." the broochek groaned. "HOW MANY YEARS HAVE I BEEN HERE?"

"Not too long, Shade. About thirty days."

"MY EYES ARE ... BETTER. YOU LOOK ... MUCH OLDER."

"I'm not. We're on Triton. In her city."

"I am Thetis," she called out.

"YES," the broochek said, its eyes flashing. "YES. I AM AWARE OF THETIS. THIS IS HER CITY. SHE GREW ME."

"Shade, how do I contact Grandpapa?"

"CALL OUT ... HIS NAME. HE WILL ... FIND YOU."

"Could he help me find Jonas?"

The mandibles clanged shut. "IF THE MIND IS ... INTACT. AS ALWAYS A PROBLEM ... WITH GRAND-PAPA."

"Then he can get help for us?"

"IF THE MIND IS INTACT."

Daric's legs were weak; he leaned against Merode, who called up, "Oracle, we'll come back later."

"LADY THETIS . . ." the broochek called out, and the phaeton jerked to a stop. "LADY THETIS, I WISH TO ASK . . . FOR MOVEMENT."

She called up, "You'd trample my city, Oracle! You'll have to stay this way awhile longer. Just a bit, and then we'll bring you out. I promise. Driver, take us down." She leaned close to Daric, saying, "Hold on to the rail."

He clutched it. The phaeton slowly dropped, turning, clinking down on the cobblestone walk.

Citizens stood on the black-speckled grass, wielding umbrellas. She leaned close. "You should wait outside 'til I'm done. I won't be long. I want to see my librarian."

He nodded.

She stood up and helped Daric from the carriage. "We should only talk about this here. Even if we're sure he doesn't listen to us."

He nodded, rubbing his forehead, grimacing.

"Say aloud, that you want to leave the city."

"I want to leave the city."

Her face wavered, fading as the city drained from the air around him, sounds, sights, falling away to silence, to cotton sheets beneath him.

He stirred, touched his forehead, but the ache was gone. Merode lay beside him, strands of hair trailing up, trembling on the grill, her face peaceful, empty, the girl he knew lost inside the city. Daric shut his eyes and turned away, listening to the sluggish rise and fall of her breath.

Thalmas was late for breakfast. Unshaven, with tired eyes, he wore a rumpled white shirt and gray trousers, and carried a telltale's ivory wafer under his arm. "Good morning, Merode, Daric."

"Good morning."

"Busy night, Father?"

"Yes." He said no more, his back to them as he cooked some coffee. Daric and Merode exchanged glances. Thalmas poured a bowl of wheat cereal and asked them about their plans for the day, as he did every morning, though this morning he didn't seem interested.

"You're bringing a telltale with you?"

Thalmas nodded at the wafer. "I hate to. But I'm expecting an important query."

He hurriedly ate. Afterward, he told her, "I expect to be all day in my work, dear. Let's skip the three o'clock meet. But I'll want to hear all about your projects at dinner."

His shoulders sloping more than usual, Thalmas walked outside, down the patio stairs, crossing the lawn toward the pine.

"He only carries a telltale before something big—usually an expedition. If so, he'll be gone for maybe a few days, or a week."

Daric leaned closer to her. "Can we go to the city?"

"Tonight."

"There's a library there? You said it was connected to the Triton trove. Would it know about the starlines? About the shell?"

How far away were they? He had wondered last night in bed, unable to sleep. Maybe the worldglass didn't block them, maybe just the shell. So they were just beyond the shell.

"We can't talk now, Daric. But we'll see my librarian tonight."

He nodded.

After breakfast, walking the grounds, Daric realized that all of it—the mansion, the lawn, the fountain, the white stone path— was *temporary*.

If I could just get outside, I could catch the lines, go to Myiepa. Talk to Grandpapa in the starlines. Or Bele Gra'Vize.

Daric sat down by the maple tree, remembering the lines and numbers, the voices in the ivy.

Tonight, he thought. Not too long, and I'll get to see Shade again.

He pressed his palms in the grass, settled his shoulders against the trunk.

Merode's library. What would it know about the starlines? Whether the starlines went into Triton, or stayed outside the worldglass.

He drew a deep breath and opened his eyes.

Or about Darius? Starswarm? The Scales.

Penthesilia?

Daric tried to relax his shoulders. Now the day would be longer than ever.

"Pleasures of the season, Lady Thetis." A tall, gray-haired lady in a silver and yellow dress bowed, then rejoined the murmurous crowd walking the length of a promenade; the men in black-and-white suits, the women in glittering gowns. On all sides tall buildings were silhouetted against red and pink clouds.

"We're later tonight," Merode said.

He blinked, watching the crowd, who were smiling, in good cheer, most moving in a general direction along the promenade, some milling about the flower tenders.

To his left, through the towers, the broochek darkened the sky.

"Do you want to see your broochek?"

He shook his head. "Can we go to the library?"

"Of course."

He studied his own crisp black sleeves, white cuffs, the yellow flower stuck to his lapel. Her jeweled hand appeared, adjusting the flower as though it were one of Thalmas's, falling out.

Merode—the older Merode, with a diamond crown—smiled at him, her eyes flashing as a railcar rushed beyond her shoulder.

A plump man with curly brown hair approached and raised

his hat. "May I do the honor of accompanying you to the play, Lady Thetis?"

She smiled. "We're on other business. Urgent, I'm afraid. But it's my wish that you enjoy the performance, sir."

The man smiled, nodded, replacing his hat. He walked off.

To Daric she said, "The library's this way."

Ahead, people were stopping, then sliding away with sudden swiftness, sliding off in ranks, as if caught in a downstream current.

A moving walk.

Merode and Daric stepped on, gliding quickly beneath towers, beneath flashing railcars. Soon her eyes widened, and she said, "Now, Daric. Off the path! This way."

Across an empty plaza, around a fountain whose centerpiece was a statue of Thetis with upraised arms, to a flight of marble stairs leading to a tall white building, full of curves. A glass door in the center, twice as tall as Daric—and Daric was tall here.

He pulled it open for Merode, then followed her into a dim, circular chamber, onto a floor tiled with a portrait of Thetis, dusty hues of blue and white forming her profile, yellow the hair that snaked out beyond the farther side.

Along the curving wall were statues, the first of luminous orange, becoming darker along the line, to blue, then gray.

She walked to one of the many scattered small tables and pulled out a chair, gesturing. As Daric sat, a figure stepped from the shadows, a tall woman with long white hair, serene blue eyes. She bowed. "Lady Thetis."

Merode said, "Good evening, Miriam."

"Lady, we've made progress on your latest trove request. I've also prepared a schematic on your Estate's barrier."

"Good. Miriam, we have a new request—about the Myiepan spore. Does it reach Triton through the worldglass?"

"I will access the trove, lady."

"This gentleman is a guest. He has some research to do, while we attend our projects."

Again, the Librarian bowed. "What did you wish to research, guest?"

"Old history," he said.

"Very good. Which period?"

Daric looked to Merode. "Before the *ancient ancient*. Before the Storm."

"The oldest period, Miriam."

"Very good, lady."

The Librarian gestured at the line of statues; the gray one at the far left stirred, stepped down, the sound of it resounding above. The statue was tall and dressed in chiseled robes. Closer, Daric could see faint fissures of blue.

Stopping beside them, the statue bowed, then looked to Merode. "Might I be of service, Lady Thetis?" Its voice was like cold raindrops on metal.

The Librarian said, "Help our guest. He wishes to research your trove."

The statue nodded.

"We'll be back in a bit, Daric. Just ask for what you want. Any form. Images might be the place to start."

Merode walked off with the Librarian.

The statue stared down at him. "What did you wish, guest?"

"Images."

It raised its hands. "Very good, guest. Name the subject, please."

"Darius. The Leader."

The statue lifted a hand. The air shivered behind it, the ghost of a tall, wiry dark-haired man with large dark eyes. Unfamiliar.

"His real name was Artashata. He was said to have been *andron kallistos kai megtistos*, the most handsome and tallest man in Asia, known also as the Great king, and Les Six."

Daric was about to speak, but another image crowded the air, blocking off half the library. "Here is his procession. It was led by holy fire tended by Zoroastrian priests and three hundred sixty-five youths, as many as days of the year." A line of figures, slowly moving in place.

How old is this? Too old.

"The white horses are drawing the empty chariot of Ahura Mazda," the statue recited, its metallic voice thinly echoing, "followed by a great white horse sacred to the sun, then ten chariots embossed with gold and silver, preceded by elite regiments and the king himself, as you see there, his cloak ornamented with gold hawks—divine birds of primeval legends, the royal standard carried by the Great King and the symbol of the Tree of Life, *axis mundi*. He was defeated by Alexander in . . ."

"Wait," Daric said. The statue's head inclined.

"This isn't him. It's too early."

The image dissolved.

"I'm looking for Darius. The Leader, of the *ancient ancient*."

The statue's shoulders dropped; its head inclined. "Many apologies, guest. But I am the most ancient of days, and this is the Darius I have."

Behind it, a second statue stirred, stepped down. This one was entirely shorter, more rounded. As it walked toward them it nodded to the older statue returning to its perch.

"Guest?" This one was a woman with coils of stone hair, and a smooth, cold voice.

"I wish to know of Darius, the Leader."

"I have Darius, but no reference to Darius the Leader."

He was never called Leader, Yellow Daric had said.

"Show me Darius."

She nodded, her eyes widening slightly.

"I'd like images. The earliest one you have."

She gestured, and the air shivered, taking shape above the frieze of Thetis: a wooden house, a lawn, on which knelt the boy, dark-haired, with narrow shoulders, his back to Daric, his arm subtly moving, head slowly turning.

Daric recognized himself.

"Taken in Paris, guest, in the period known colloquially as the *ancient ancient*, though the actual date is lost." A moment later the statue added, "Shall I proceed in chronological fashion, with the first tier of images?"

"Yes."

Another moving image of the boy kneeling amid a garden and whirring bees, clearly with Daric's face, but the expression was somehow different, like Yellow Daric on Earth.

The boy clutched a magnifying glass, and smiled.

"How old was he then? Is there a date?"

"It is purported to be millennium two A.D., though there is doubt about this. Records that far back are often corrupt. Shall I continue?"

"Yes. Faster."

She gestured.

He shifted forward in his seat. In a succession of images the boy grew up, taller, a harder face seen from different angles, in different landscapes—rolling hills, a crystalline city, a mountainside—but always the face gazing out. Becoming Jonas's face, without his silver nose, without his smile, and occasionally—in flashes—didn't seem like Jonas at all.

Jonas wearing a winding black robe, standing before a yellow and black flag.

The man—sometimes Jonas, sometimes not—aging, his face growing more somber, while the vistas surrounding him became more fantastic—crystal structures stained with a red sky, ranks of soldiers.

Jonas seated on a tall white throne.

"Stop. What is this? When was it taken?"

"Year Zero, modern. The coronation. An image echoed famously on Neptune's moon Miranda. Would you like..."

"Keep going."

"Yes, guest."

Jonas, standing on a slope of red rock.

Mars.

Red rock gave way to forests, and the wild sprawl of the Chryse castle; the grounds marked with intersecting lines on the white rock, curves and dotted angles, with the tower shadows casting across. Then came tumult, disaster; bleak white winds, a storm, the ocean engulfing the land—Darius had sunk his Chryse castle under the waves.

An older Jonas, his face more gaunt, standing against a curved rock horizon: an asteroid. Even older—the Darius on Earth—surveying long lines of troops reduced in the distance to yellow and black bands.

Then, suddenly, young Jonas with short black hair, against a line of trees. Not earth, but ancient Mars: Phobos haunted the sky above, an oblong gray moon.

"Are these in order?"

"Chronological order. This was taken shortly after Darius's return from Delphi Prior, colloquially known as *Parson's Planet*."

"Keep going."

Darius standing beneath a transmission cusp. The broken hand grasping at the stars. Beneath a yellow sky, another cusp, with Darius stepping from the palm, his body surrounded in a white glow.

"We've reached the end of the first tier. Shall I proceed to the second?"

Daric nodded. More images came. These were of crowds. Of the tall white throne with Darius seated. Of his image cast huge upon walls of a huge city, glaring down at the crowd. Again, the throne room, with a crowd gathered before him, heads bowed, hands bound. Closer, the crowd in purple robes, with wounds in their foreheads, raw and bleeding, directly above their eyes.

"Wait. Who are these?"

"They are Mori, guest."

Mori. Thola Nee Montyorn.

Sitting forward, he said, "Show me more about them."

The statue raised its hand, as though gathering in the image; it disappeared. Another of an old woman, the third eye in her forehead.

"A cult contemporary with that era. They protested Darius's use of storms on Mercury Scythe and Deimos in 200 A.E. He allowed them to leave the settled system. They departed in ancient ramjet ships and were not heard from for five hundred years. Word came in 700 A.E. that they had settled the planet Edler-Haynes, in the Orion system."

The statue reached to the empty air and plucked the eye, a black oval, and held it out. "This is the *Spiri beetle*, native of the planet Edler-Haynes. It bonded with the Mori in the Ten-Year-Struggle."

Closer, Daric could see its glossy shell, and a wriggling underneath—filaments of some sort.

"The creature fixes itself to strong bone—usually the skull." The statue lifted it to its own forehead, and the black oval stayed there, fixed. "It threads its viral lines throughout the host system." The statue tipped its head demonstratively. "Certain properties of spatial and temporal folds are known to occur." The statue smiled, and its teeth began to glow. "The spiri uses the body as an antenna of sorts, bathed in the radiation of its home star."

"Show me more images."

He looked closely at the people in their purple robes, standing in a chamber of old, arching stone; another of rolling green and gold hills, the double suns; a group of Mori, each with the third eye, peering past him; then figures in black tending a pond filled with the Spiri.

Daric grimaced: His headache was worse.

"Can I see more of Darius?"

More images came. The younger Darius who was like Jonas, aging slowly from different angles. The tall man with the cruel smile.

Another cusp, on another planet, this time Darius stood nearby with Starswarm, and a woman, too. A tall woman turned toward Darius, her long black hair tied with silver wire.

Again, the woman, her arm now laced with his.

The floating woman. From the *Pyre*.

Daric swallowed.

"Stop," he said. "Who's that?"

"Alissia Gra'Hague," the Librarian replied. "Darius's companion from 275 to 321 A.E., She won fame for the discovery of the planet Myiepa in 265 A.E., on which her ship *Beneficent Argonaut* crashed, and which she later purchased, in 276 A.E., founding the void mariners."

His eyes ached; he shut them.

"Do you wish to access data on Alissia Gra'Hague?"

Daric shook his head. "No." He sat back and rubbed his eyes, pinched the bridge of his nose.

Daric walked outside, into an empty plaza under a dark, starry sky. Overhead a railcar flashed along, and the towers shuddered in its wake with pools of yellow light.

His eyes burned.

Alissia Gra'Hague.

What could I have asked her?

As he walked along the plaza he was joined by another figure in the mirrored wall, a tall man, familiar.

Darius.

Halting now to stare at Daric, as Daric stared at him.

Alissia Gra'Hague, the floating woman.

What had she called him on the *Pyre*?

Daric rode the swings. Overhead the strands were silver and dim blue, with a mix of yellow: early afternoon.

Thalmas had been in the Sanctuary since breakfast. He'd barely talked to them, enough to say he would be involved until dinner. Plenty of time for Merode to search the Estate for the sonic punch—*a high intensity beam*—recommended by her Librarian.

Daric tugged on the chains, going higher.

Dearest.

He returned to the *Pyre*, to the music room, where she floated, black hair pulled back and twined with silver wire, her sly eyes.

Dearest.

Blue was your favorite color, like the cooling suns.

(While he walked the halls of the *Pyre*, ghosts on either side bowing and nodding, to the gray disk that shuddered beneath his boots, carrying him up into the music dome.)

"You're remembering."

Alissia Gra'Hague, who bought the Myiepan planet. Who founded the void mariners and disappeared long ago.

The way her blue eyes came alive when she spoke, or smiled.

"You're the best of him, the best of Darius."

"Daric?"

He straightened, dragged the toes of his shoes in the dirt.

Merode stepped from the poplars. She squinted toward the Sanctuary. "He still in there?"

"Yes." Daric folded his arms around the chains.

She sat on the other swing, clutching a small silver globe with black dots along the side, a yellow cap on top.

"Is that the punch?"

She nodded. "He had one in a display case, in the second-floor study. Hasn't used it in years." Merode turned it upside-down; it was partially hollow, large enough for Merode to slip her hand inside. It began to whine. She glanced at the Sanctuary. "Miriam couldn't get all the information on the shell. It was in the Triton trove—classified. But she's pretty sure there's a field just inside that blocks the starlines. She thinks it can be disrupted, if we use this at the highest intensity."

"Will it leave a mark?"

Merode shook her head. "She doesn't think so. But we'll do it on the far side, near the maple tree. Watch. Here's the lowest setting." She pointed the cap at the swing's rusted chain; the chain trembled, leaving a link polished silver.

"Ready, Daric?"

He nodded.

They jumped off, climbed up the pine island and down the other side, past the fountain, following the curve of grass to the opposite corner of the Estate, and the maple tree.

Daric looked over his shoulder.

"He'll be in there for a while, Daric. Now . . . we're supposed to keep it absolutely steady." She knelt on the grass, elbows against her sides, aiming up. "Stand clear."

Daric stepped back, staring up at the shell, the silver strands beyond the branches.

The punch whined. A gray spot struck overhead, vibrating purple-white. "There!"

He held his breath, braced for the lines.

"Anything?"

A moment later, he shook his head. "No."

She switched it off. The spot faded back to silver. She moved closer to the edge, with the shell arcing down toward the brick wall, and tried again, for a longer time, but still nothing; then another spot, just above the wall. Nothing. No starlines.

"Miriam said to try as high up as I could. We could bring it up to the roof?"

Daric looked at the tree. "Let me try." He took the punch, barely fitting it into his side pocket.

She understood. "Be careful, Daric."

He grabbed a branch overhead with both hands and hauled himself up, finding the knot in the trunk with his shoe, climbing onto the lowest branch, first with his knee, then his other shoe, reaching higher, testing his weight, then standing up into a realm of branches, climbing higher, one branch, two, aware of the shell beyond the slender branches and shoots, the brilliant silver strands.

Carefully, he turned and leaned against the trunk, and looked up.

Bracing himself—squaring his shoulders, with the pick against his chest—he sighted and steadied, then squeezed the trigger. In the shell above the spot struck, and he held it, keeping it on the wavering yellow and purple strands, trying to stay balanced with Merode looking up from below as the strands flexed and darkened, exploding into numbers, into lines.

87437 29186104916 37528133271

Falling back—dropping the pick, which clattered down—he caught a branch, another, held by numbers but his shoe slipping, found a branch to stand on and crouched, letting himself down branch by branch, jumping down.

. . . *oh Myiepa oh Rhea oh Alendra Six oh Tarsus oh Cyprine Two . . .*

"Daric?"

With her help, he sat down.

. . . *oh Barnum Five oh Cybele oh Tethys . . .*

The air full of lines from all directions, fixing him beyond the confines of the Estate and Triton, to the nearby worlds and the solar system, and the arc of Heliocratic stars.

The ivy underfoot, high purple treetops and rows of trunks stretching into the distance.

Myiepa.

Breathing hard, Daric stared down at his suspenders, his

brown trousers, his shoes lost in the ivy, yellow-haired leaves. He knelt, swept his hands across the leaves, then plucked one off. Regarded the waxy green surface, the faint veins, the yellow hairs along the edge.

But no voices, no information leaping out of the shadows.

Daric looked up and around. This was the forest as he'd first seen it, before the drink on Ixion.

He stood, squinting in the distance, suddenly wanting to run. He cupped his hands around his mouth. "Grandpapa!"

He turned in place.

Louder: "Grandpapa!"

There! A flicker of light, fainter than it had been aboard the *Pyre*; an echo of that sphere that had rushed outward through the trees. Gone, now.

But he had the direction.

He began to run, his heart thudding and the blood tight in his ears, trees whipping past, rows marching on either side.

"Grandpapa!"

Ahead the light returned, more diffuse, a different kind of light, slanting through the canopy. Sunlight. Trunks at angles, trunks on their sides, tangled limbs. A low-lying haze over beards of purple foliage.

Fallen treetops.

And he was irresistibly rising, blinking at silvery blue light, and the branches of the maple tree.

"Daric? Did it work?" Merode was kneeling beside him.

He could barely nod. He was lying flat. He sat up against the trunk. The lines were all around him. He couldn't read the names, couldn't hear the voices, but the lines were there, the numbers all around.

"Daric?"

Didn't she feel them?

"You're smiling."

"I was there." He caught the lines, held them, familiar. "My Grandpapa . . . he's there, too. I know it." He tried to stand. She had to help him. The starlines vanished three paces from the tree.

"I'm all right."

She helped him to the kitchen door. "I'm going to my room, Daric, to check on the birds. Just like a normal day."

He nodded. "I'll try again later."

Merode left. Daric poured himself some orange juice and sat down at the kitchen table. His heart was beating fast.

I can go back. I can call out again, find the light. But what if the light's gone? Nearly gone? I can mark a tree. Scratch the bark. He looked down at his pants, his suspenders, took hold of the buckle.

Grandpapa, I'll find you.

Daric stood up, paced the kitchen seven times, then returned to the tree.

"Grandpapa!"

The light, nearly invisible but for the corner of his eye.

Daric approached the tree to the right of the proper row, and began scratching with the buckle, gouging out two lines, an arrow pointing at where the light had been.

He began to run. It seemed farther away than before, but eventually the fallen trees appeared.

Gasping, he reached sunlight—two suns, yellow and blue, overhead—hot against his face and hands. He clambered through the limbs, up and over, the humming in his ears like sunlight, as he stumbled down into a rectangular clearing.

"Grandpapa!"

He gained his breath, heart pounding, staring around him. A

glint to his left, at boot level. He brushed away leaves and branches, uncovering a bright, translucent cube.

Inside, a fish gazing blindly out.

One of *Daric's* fish from home, with blue scales and dull, protruding eyes—frozen with Grandpapa's finger by the lakeshore, months ago.

"Grandpapa?" He straightened, looking around desperately.

Stepping back, he nearly crushed another cube, another fish gazing out. "I'm on Triton, Grandpapa. I've been here for . . . for a month." Daric pulled back branches, reaching in. "You need to tell Jonas."

He turned, squinting down. "Grandpapa! Grandpapa . . . I was captured on Ixion! By the KayTee! I'm in the Estate and . . . Shade's here. He's a broochek . . .

"Grandpapa!"

I'm going to wake up.

He stumbled around the clearing, uncovering fish—three, four of them, and more in his periphery, but no gold or silver. I'm going to wake before I find him.

"Grandpapa!"

I'm too excited. I have to concentrate, or I'll . . .

He knelt and pulled aside the branches.

"Grandpapa!"

Until he arose, irresistibly.

Waking to the late afternoon shell.

Daric sat up against the tree. He breathed deeply. He watched the sparrows on the edge of the fountain.

I can go back now. Catch the lines, fall through them. Fall through them. He shut his eyes, tried to calm himself but his heart was beating too fast, thick in his ears.

I can go back. I can.

*9872349   82349878837987982   98729384792873987
9283798274982739*

The sound of a door sliding shut.

He opened his eyes.

Thalmas appeared beyond the edge of the mansion, walking across the grass toward the pine, dressed in his dark suitcoat, hands in his pockets. Something followed at his left shoulder, smaller than a bird, wings flashing.

Thalmas was talking.

Daric stood up. When Thalmas rounded the pine he began to run, quick across the grass, past the kitchen door, the long line of windows, the door to the main hall, up the slope into the trees. Damp twigs and branches underfoot. On the other side Thalmas walking with his head bowed, saying, "I understand . . . what it *could* be . . ."

The insect had long translucent wings. A dragonfly. A weeform.

Daric moved closer.

"Hiding out . . . scheming," Thalmas was saying, and a moment later, harshly: "*devastation . . .*" Passing the swingset. "Started ten days ago . . . By all indications the ancient *Pyre . . .*"

Starswarm!

Thalmas stomped down the Sanctuary stairs.

Starswarm, he thought, it was about Starswarm. Starswarm's looking for me. And Thalmas knows.

Heart pounding, Daric turned away, walked through the pine island, his thoughts turning and turning, down the other side, across the lawn.

I need to try again. I can do it.

When he reached the maple tree he sat down, drew a deep breath—intensifying the sourness of his stomach—and shut his eyes.

Remembering Thalmas's voice: "this *devastation . . .*"

He reached for Ixion's line among the others.

He dropped his shoulders, breathing deeply.

I will never give up the search for you, Starswarm had said.

Relax.

He shut his eyes, aware of the pounding of his heart.

I can do it.

Birds cried out.

Daric opened his eyes: sparrows darting up from the fountain; beside it, a small steady flicker, narrow wings. The dragonfly— the weeform—zipping back and forth, close to the ground, circling the fountain, then along the white stone path, in Daric's direction.

Daric stood up. He walked away from the maple tree, toward the kitchen door. Halfway there the dragonfly flew alongside, wings faintly humming, bulbous eyes fixed on Daric.

When Daric stepped through the kitchen door it zipped off.

He hurried down the hall to the stairs, up the four flights to Merode's room and the aviary. She was sitting at her table, working on a piece of crystal. "A key," she said, "for the main door. What's wrong?"

He told her about Thalmas and the dragonfly.

"It's a Citizen. Father had a butterfly over once, one of the Tromon elite. But I've never seen a dragonfly here before."

At the window he searched for it. "Thalmas was talking to it about Starswarm. My ship."

Merode pressed her forehead to the glass. "It's another sign. An expedition."

"My ship's trying to find me."

She stood up, tugged his sleeve. "Then you have to try again, Daric. I'll keep watch."

He reached the clearing out of breath, looking into the trees on all sides, past his fish, sure that somewhere here . . .

A gold glint, deep within the branches.

He stopped.

"Grandpapa?"

Slowly he knelt, reaching toward it, a gold glint, snapping off branches, brushing aside leaves to reveal the dented gold crown.

The top of a gold head.

Farther, a golden arm, and a hand grasping at leaves. A jade hand, one finger missing.

Grandpapa's torso, arms flung wide, head turned sideways, dim ruby eyes.

Daric touched the cold metal.

He sat down heavily, thinking, I can't call Jonas. Aloud: "We're prisoners."

A while later he stood, climbed back out of the clearing into the forest. He walked, waiting to wake up, his thoughts turning and turning. Then he noticed a sound. Like gears grinding. It had been there for some time, to his left, making music. Familiar.

From pole to pole and planets wide . . .

The Leader's anthem.

He ran. He called out, and halted, listening. Ran again. But it was always ahead.

I'll wake too soon, he thought. I won't find him.

"Grandpapa! Are you here?"

From directly ahead, trills and beeps.

"Grandpapa!"

A golden flash, deep within the forest.

A faint voice: "Jonas?" Grandpapa's voice.

"Grandpapa, it's Daric!"

"Jonas?"

"Grandpapa, listen! It's Daric! I'm on Triton! At Thalmas Green's estate!"

Behind him, another voice said calmly, "Daric?"

He turned to find a figure close by, tall and golden, with a featureless face. "Do you remember me, Daric?"

Sisteel Nee Portia.

The lower half of the face tugged at the corners, suggesting a smile, while the forest trembled with silver light, and Merode's voice, close and clear, said, "Wake up, Daric. Wake up. He has visitors!"

She jostled his shoulder.

Sisteel.

He stood, confused, on the edge of panic.

Sisteel—with Leften Tine?

"Daric? C'mon. He has visitors, in the study."

"Who are they?" He hurried along the path behind her.

"I didn't see them."

They reached the kitchen door and quietly slid it open, stepped inside. Voices vaguely echoed from the hall. Daric heard Thalmas, angry, then a second voice, bright and strange, then silence.

They snuck into the hall, then through the music room into the library, nearly opposite the study. On hands and knees under the long table, toward the door. Daric was first, leaning around the edge. From this angle he could see partway in: the study's lamps were casting shadows across the carpet.

"Utter annihilation! Throughout the entire system!" This second voice had a metallic undertone.

"If this *is* a storm entity," said Thalmas, farther in the room, "then I don't understand how it left Earth. Leften assured us the storm was successfully contained."

"It was, Thalmas Green." A third voice, calm and cold, and entirely familiar. Leften Tine. "Nonetheless the boy escaped. With the ancient ship, the *Pyre*."

Thalmas: "I questioned him under ash-light that first night.

The events on Earth were hazy to him, typical with the sort of strain he's been through."

"There's not been a proper sifting of the boy's mind."

A pause.

Thalmas: "Lord agrees with me, I think, that the risk of damage is too great. His neural lattice—which is ancient, Lord, surely the remnants of a shade—makes it difficult. I was only able to remove the recent information he'd acquired on Ixion. His row is catalyzed—replication didn't work. A sifting would be foolhardy, perhaps dangerous to him."

Leften: "We're speaking of catastrophe, Thalmas Green, unless the entity can be contained. The risk of damage is outweighed."

A pause again. Then Thalmas said, "Lord, I beg you. The boy is of *absolute* importance—absolute. We must demonstrate . . . respect, and gain his trust."

"I understand Thalmas more than you, Tine," said the second voice, a ringing tone, as the shadow swayed strangely up the wall. "He's read his Prazeel. He knows the ancient legends."

Merode whispered, "Peer Tromon."

The thing appeared, shot through with lamplight.

Seemingly spun from liquid glass, taller than Thalmas, it undulated across the carpet on hundreds of tendrils, translucent yellow, green, red, and blue, casting a mix of colors on the carpet. "You're careful, Thalmas," it said, a metal and glass voice. "Cautious. Marks of the Sifters, I know. In this instance, care and caution might lose us the Ambry. Before we can . . ."

Thalmas, angry: "Rush, and we could lose it anyway!"

The thing froze, brittling to silver.

"Forgive me, Lord," said Thalmas, with a quake in his voice. "I'm passionate about the ruins, as you know."

Leften said calmly, "Perhaps, Thalmas Green, you are too protective of the boy, your hero reborn?"

The thing swayed into motion and color.

Thalmas's shadow on the wall. "Lord—Peer—your aide speaks without proper respect."

As it raised a silvery tendril, the shadow withdrew. "I've long trusted her opinions. She speaks with our interests at heart."

Silence, then for an instant the thing went rigid, its tendrils becoming the symbol of a sun. The room falling quiet. Then it relaxed, flooding with colors, and walked spiderlike end-over-end along the wall, out of sight. Hoots and clucks followed, and heavy shuffles. Six short creatures, eyes averted, heads stooped, shambled into view. Small wrinkled faces in brown fur.

Dendrii. Monkeys.

"Nine of your sites have been lost," Leften Tine said. "You were once quite protective of them."

The dendrii wore bulky gray uniforms with black collars and a red cross at the chest, black boots.

Peer Tromon replied, "But Thalmas has the most precious of relics, now, remember, Tine."

"I agree. And he's aware of what remains, as yet. Soon it will come to Charon."

"Lord Tromon, do I have no say in this?"

One of the dendrii looked up, into the hall.

Merode whispered, "Daric!"

Something jabbed his back. Daric jumped, turned—a dendrii looming behind them, with a triangle of white fur on its forehead, and pale blue eyes under a thick brow. *"King boy."* A strangled voice, a growl. *"No listen."* It pushed past Daric into the hall, where Leften Tine now stood.

She was taller than he remembered, long-limbed, entirely smooth and aglow, the placid face gazing down, rippling. A doppel.

She smiled.

Behind her, Thalmas shoved his hands deep into his jacket pockets. "Merode, you and Daric go outside *now*."

• • •

But they snuck inside, running up the side stairs, to Merode's room.

"Daric?"

He hurried to the gold egg, found the seal.

He climbed inside; she was right behind him as the shell folded over. The city assumed the empty air; a different location, street level, in darkness, with white flakes falling through fog.

To the older Merode, Daric said, "Can I access the library directly?"

Citizens appeared bearing packages, stamping through the white foam. They smiled as they passed, tipped their hats, mumbled greetings.

She nodded. "We can access the trove. Like real Citizens in the worldglass."

"How?"

"Simple. Say aloud that you want to visit third."

He nodded. Before he could speak she added, "It'll be strange, we'll see everything. Then you only need ask for the Triton trove and *think* your question. When you're done, think clearly that you wish to leave. I'll go first." Speaking up into the snow, she said, "I want to visit third," and vanished.

Even her footprints were gone.

"I want to visit third."

The falling snow began to rise, the street receded, railcars flashing far below, then the city was beneath his eyes, beneath his hand. He became aware of the Triton trove, existing inside the green currents of the worldglass, in weblike patterns of thought which—

Daric?

—guarded from invasion—

Daric?

—against a resurgent Storm, or the gendarme.

Are you there?

Merode's voice, from all directions.

I'm here, Merode.

Ask your question.

I want the Triton trove, he thought.

History. Old history. Ambry. Tell me of Ambry. Darius's Ambry . . .

Something was given to him: Pluto and its moon Charon, swinging round each other through the void; the moon growing larger, dark rock silvered with the distant sun, soon a landscape, dim and barren.

Tell me of Darius's Ambry. The Leader's. What is it?

Tell me of Ambry.

Concentrate.

Daric? Someone's taking us out.

Too bright: burning behind his eyes.

Daric was suddenly himself, cowering behind his hands as the shell folded back, and a dark face with entirely dark eyes leaned close.

Merode stiffened beside him.

The dark face and sharp teeth, the writhing silver wires, wild gray hair.

Joom took hold of Daric, long arms lifting him up and out of the egg. The dendrii stumbled back, making room. The dragonfly circled above.

Thalmas was at the door with Leften Tine. "Merode, I'm taking Daric on a trip. We shouldn't be gone more than a day."

Merode was struggling out.

The white-furred dendrii shoved a suit toward Daric. *"Urs!"*

Daric struck it away. On all sides the other creatures hissed, showed their teeth.

"Back!" Thalmas said. "Tak! Down!" The dendrii ducked. "You *will* be careful with him!" Thalmas took the suit from the white-furred dendrii, then knelt beside Daric. "It's a sheen, a voidsuit. Like the one you wore before."

A black suit, a red cross on the breast.

"I'm going, too, Father!"

"No, Merode. You're staying here."

She took it in the eyes, like a sting.

Leften Tine said, "We can dress you ourselves, boy."

Daric unbuttoned his shirt with shaking hands, pulled off shirt, trousers, socks, and shoes. He stepped into the suit, struggling into the sleeves, sealing it, then found the tab and pulled the sheen up over his head—looking at the dendrii, not looking away.

Leften gestured. Joom stepped up behind Daric. The dendrii watched, looking from Joom to Thalmas, who nodded and left the room with Leften. The dendrii milled about then—goaded by the white dendrii Tak—followed, half behind Daric as he walked along the hall, down the stairs and the main hall, approaching the black doors.

The procession halted. There was a commotion as the dendrii gathered up equipment, Thalmas conferring with Leften Tine. Then Thalmas spoke quietly and the doors hummed open on a pale chamber; he and Leften stepped inside.

Following, Daric looked back to see Merode at the end of the corridor. The door shut; the walls brightened.

As doors opened ahead, the party continued on, each chamber brighter, until the final doors opened on a rush of brilliant green light, a chiming breeze.

Daric hesitated. Joom was suddenly at his side, smiling down, holding something out to Daric.

A small hand.

The fingers torn at the tip, blackened below, the back raked, as if by claws.

My hand, he thought.

"As you can see, My Glory, we need the actual."

Smiling his terrible smile, Joom gestured Daric through the door.

5

EXODY

The city was farther away than before, a distant surge of color, with upward bright curls under the arching world-glass and the sound of it in the air, a shimmering, inconstant chime.

...oh Myiepa oh Rhea oh Alendra Six oh Tethys oh...

Following Leften Tine and Thalmas across a field of blue brick, Daric caught the starlines, the numbers and voices—

...oh Barnum Five oh Cybele oh Pluto...

873487 29387293487298374 9287349827439287340129743098

—and held the local system, thinking *Charon*, then *Ambry*.

...oh New Io oh Isidis oh Coeus Alpha oh...

Thalmas, in his lumbering gait, was gazing up at the world-glass, as Jonas had often searched the clouds for rain.

Charon, Daric thought.

Ambry.

...oh Parisbeta oh Regio oh Onomule oh Paul IV...

When I get outside, past the worldglass, maybe I'll get the information . . .

Suns and planets beneath my feet.

At the far end of the field was a square of glimmering silver; no—a silver cube floating over the brick, hugely.

He sensed a red line.

It was the *Talus*.

As he tried to read it dozens of crystal spheres darted in from both sides, halting in the air above. Vague long figures in colorful clothes leaning forward, perhaps bowing, though Thalmas took no notice, trudging now along the brick. Leften Tine's only response was to glance smoothly back at Daric, then look up behind him, smiling.

Daric turned—the dendrii ducked. The front of the Compound was broad dark stone, eerily solid against the city. A crystal sphere floated there. Inside, a figure raised a long silver arm and seemed to drop a bit of greenish gold that turned end over end; a dragonfly, coming to life, flitting toward him.

The sphere darted away.

Thalmas looked back. "Daric?"

Was it the same dragonfly?

"Remember what I told you about the Sifters, Daric?"

The chiming had become louder. Daric looked up at the nearest spheres, the long faces, wondering if the chiming was their voices.

"These are students of history, of the *ancient ancient*."

Some were obscured by clouds of weeforms inside their spheres, moving in strange patterns.

He looked down at the brick. Shapes darted below the surface, some small and bright, close by, others larger, darker, flowing underneath the field. He focused on his boots, trying to ignore the commotion all around. He began counting his steps, at one hundred looking up to find the *Talus*, a silver wall stretching wide, rippling like water, taller than the compound, the upper edge sharp against the green tides.

"The ship catches us," said Leften Tine, a moment before she was drawn into the air. Thalmas nearly stumbled, looking back as the force seized him. Then Daric floated up, much as Sisteel and Joom had long ago floated down to the Tharsis plain.

"Welcome home, 'fink," murmured Joom beside him.

The silver cube churned with blue flecks: it gave no reflection and radiated a coldness. As Daric was drawn through, the chiming air became a roar, tickling his ears.

Then silence.

0938 02384 0238402 092834 0298340928340 209384 02983409

A square room, dim blue.

"Daric?" Thalmas motioned him out of the way as the dendrii stumbled in, then the hounds, low and black, claws clicking on the floor, sharp snouts seeming to smile.

"Tak!"

The white-haired dendrii bowed to Thalmas.

"Go to quarters."

... oh Mercury Scythe oh Mars oh ...

Daric caught the lines. *Charon*, he thought. *Ambry*.

"Look at his eyes, Thalmas Green. He is with the spore."

... oh Sisteel Nee Portia 928 928739487293874 ...

Six hounds had gathered before Daric, standing exactly side by side, their ears sharp and tall.

"You promised us a cabin."

She nodded. "Of course, Thalmas Green. My engineer will help you. Down the corridor appearing ... there."

"You're tracking the *Pyre*?"

"It waits near the remains of Ix, as before."

The dragonfly circled the room, then flew up, into the ceiling.

Thalmas patted the pockets of his long coat. "When we land, I'll want the Sifters kept back, and away from Daric."

In response, she put her arms at her side and floated up into the ceiling.

Joom gave something between a grunt and a laugh, tendrils flicking.

Thalmas gestured. "This way, Daric."

Not far down the corridor—as Daric expected—they came upon Sisteel Nee Portia. She straightened, and gave a slight bow.

"Engineer, show us to our cabin."

Blank face nodding, her familiar, somehow kind voice said, "This way, sieurs."

Following Thalmas, Daric caught her line, brighter now, name and numbers. Looking back he found the white walls closing in behind them.

"I want Joom kept away," Thalmas told Sisteel. "Do you understand?"

"Of course." At a gesture from Sisteel, a portion to their left faded on a small, low-ceilinged room of solid white walls, a tiled floor. Two couches stood side by side.

Sisteel was silent as they stepped inside. When Daric glanced back, the opening was gone.

"I apologize, for the suddenness of this trip." Thalmas ponderously sat down, calm blue eyes appraising Daric.

Daric sat on the other couch. He caught the lines, Triton and distant Mars, Earth, Neptune, Mercury Scythe. Earth with spiders still scurrying: the warning.

Who was on board? Sisteel and Leften Tine. And the dragonfly—who was it? Peer Tromon? And Joom, and Thalmas. Six dendrii. Six hounds.

There came a rustle.

Looking over, he found Thalmas pulling a small case from inside his coat, prying off its lid. Nestled inside was an insect made of gold, tall, with a triangular head and long arms crooked near the end.

Like a cricket, Daric thought.

"I don't know how much you heard, Daric." Thalmas prodded the thing with blunt fingers. "Our destination is Charon, Pluto's moon." He touched his throat, staring down. "To a place called the *Ambry*."

Thalmas's voice was echoed by the cricket, which stirred, forelegs twitching, the tiny head turning on the green felt. Thalmas said quietly, "Yan tan tethera."

The thing froze.

"It lies far below the surface. Your forebear protected it well. We've been able to forge a path through the vestibule creatures, and maintain it with shields. We've excavated down to the drop but can't open the lock."

"You tried," Daric said.

After a pause, Thalmas nodded.

"You tried with the cast of my hand. But it was torn up."

"Who told you this?"

"Joom. He showed me."

Anger darkened Thalmas's eyes. He fumbled the case's lid back on. "The cast of your hand was damaged, yes. It didn't open the lock, and there's a price to be paid for trying. Over time— how long has it been, eight years?—we've lost many souls, Daric, not to mention the mechs, and my dendrii." He tucked the case into his pocket, and looked at Daric. "Whatever's inside the Ambry is the most important piece of your family's history. The *key* to understanding your great past, and your heritage. There have been stories, Daric . . . myths, come down to us in old books, in clouds of data. It may hold the crux of the *ancient ancient*, preserved." He paused, staring down. "I promise, Daric, no harm will come to you. I won't allow it. We'll be back on Triton tonight."

The floor shuddered; Thalmas jumped, grabbed the edge of the couch as the ship began to rise, a sudden acceleration.

. . . *1090328450982304985209345092384509826073025702398* . . .

Daric shut his eyes. Past the worldglass.

Ambry, he thought. *Charon*.

Nothing.

Gravity remained; they were not shunning the rock.

Thalmas tugged the sides of his coat then lay down, a dark hump, boots jutting to either side.

The starlines moving, vivid—

    ... 982734983 98237492874981 98273498274986734987 2 ...

    ... oh Neptune oh Mercury Scythe ...

—the *Talus* soaring away from Triton and the other lines becoming stronger, names and numbers, and something else ...

"The cast I made of your hand—it was damaged because it wasn't entirely *your* hand. Do you understand?"

Neptune, far behind. The system, turning.

"There's a series of corridors into the surface of Charon, with the Ambry at its end. A series of doors that will open to your hand, or your voice. Unlock them, let us see inside. Then we'll go home, I promise."

Daric grimaced: The starlines had begun to bend, change places—

5640686068737969873

       24878374987

23498779236   5   46540654066540654065

40654   0654548484

       6482736482736540654466504654654

68 1346   464   0866   8597268   4668468

4   7   4

—stitching, strangely, insisting they were many places at once, near Mars, near Callisto, at the edge of the asteroids near Mercury Scythe beyond Venus—impossible movement.

Impossible movement, to throw anybody off their trail.

"Do you believe me, Daric?"

To throw Starswarm off their trail.

Disoriented, Daric lay down, clutching the sides of the couch, overwhelmed by lines, a shifting tide of numbers.

And somehow, Grandpapa. Everywhere, Grandpapa.

Pluto nix bee-five-five.

The lines settled. A moment later Daric relaxed his shoulders and reached for the numbers, sensing the ship moving toward Pluto, slowing. Then came a sudden jolt. The ship stopped, on nothing, with no starline below: Charon had no shrine.

Thalmas stirred and, striving to sound calm, said, "Daric, are you all right?"

Daric sat up. Staring at the wall, he was really staring at the lines, at Pluto and the inner worlds, then out toward the Helio-cratic stars, looking for Grandpapa.

"You're a true mariner, I think. I can see why Jonas gave you the information at a young age."

He said, "It wasn't Jonas."

From his outer pocket Thalmas took an airlace, and fixed it around his own neck.

Did Thalmas wear a sheen? How *raised* was he?

The wall opened. "We have arrived, Thalmas Green." Leften Tine stepped in. The *real* Leften, Daric decided, studying her silver and blue suit, and the gold airlace at her neck.

Not doppeling from Triton.

"How did the boy handle modulation?"

Thalmas patted his coat pockets, and in the same tone he had often used to chide Merode, said, "Where is the *Pyre* presently?"

She smiled. Daric watched her face, remembering how it had once rippled with her smile, a mask floating on the surface of its lake. "Near the remnants of Ix, as before. Though I think Lord Tromon and the others hope for an appearance. They're eager to see the ancient bloodletting, from a safe distance."

"I'll want to personally check the fields."

"They're like your tourists, Thalmas Green."

"Leften," Thalmas said, looking at her directly. "Peer told you to follow my orders to the letter, nothing more."

"*To the letter*. From your trove of ancient languages. We will pretend it means little to me, Thalmas Green. Your dendrii seem shaken by the voyage. Perhaps you should tend to them." She stepped out.

For a long moment, Thalmas sat with his eyes steady on the floor. Then he stirred. "You'll stay here, Daric. Try to rest. I won't be long."

With no starline below, no view outside . . .

"Is there a window. Could I see out?"

Thamas fingered the ring at his throat, then stood up, and in a steady voice, said, "I'm not sure. But if it's possible, I'll arrange it. A moment, please." He stepped into the corridor, returning shortly after with Sisteel.

"Could you give him a window?"

She nodded. "Of course, sieur." As she glided past him, Daric looked for an expression to tug at the gold mask. She stepped to the opposite wall and traced a circle with her index finger. The wall darkened, fading onto stars and dim rock, low hills limned with silver; a curved horizon; the sun, nearly as remote as the stars.

"Try to rest, Daric." Thalmas shuffled off. Sisteel followed without looking back.

The door faded.

Daric approached the window. The longer he stared the more color emerged from the low hills—the silver becoming yellow, the brown becoming dark red with hints of blue. And the hilltops themselves were flat in places, too angular.

He caught Pluto, remembering how he had roamed here after leaving Earth. Sitting in the music dome on the *Pyre*'s back.

83767   2865051850958   28356   2349   6382154832756928
5283765982

Where's Starswarm? And Alissia Gra'Hague? Would she know about the Ambry, and think to warn Starswarm back here?

There was movement on the horizon. Faint, it had been there all along, like something stirring in a breeze, something darker than the sky. A sharpness, fluttering back and forth. He remembered the sandfink on its shell, the hundred legs pawing at the air.

Somehow he knew it was the Ambry. Its presence was the reason why there was no shrine here.

The Krater-Tromon wouldn't allow it.

There came motion below. Small figures venturing onto the rock—Thalmas, his coat shimmering at the edges. Leften Tine walking behind him in long, floating steps, easily overtaking him. Then four dendrii advancing fitfully, hunched, wearing bulky white suits with red triangles on the chest, their faces flashing as they looked here and there. They dragged long poles that flared at the top, though at an angry gesture from Tak they straightened up.

The poles flashed, stitching a net of light.

Nodding broadly, Thalmas gave a downward motion with his left arm. The light died. The dendrii lowered their poles and once more milled about on the rock.

Thalmas and Leften seemed to confer. Daric saw Thalmas gesture to the distant motion—the Ambry—then turn back to the ship, staring, as though waiting for something to appear.

A sphere popped into view, floating over the rock. Then another, and a third. Twelve in all. Not spheres as they'd been on Triton, Daric realized, but ghosts of spheres, with ghosts inside. Twelve figures who seemed to gaze at the silent scene around them.

Again Thalmas and Leften conferred, ignoring their audience. Leften looked over at the ship and raised her arm.

The stars vanished.

Gone, pure blackness above the curving horizon.

Daric fell against the window, groping inwardly for the lines that weren't there—utter silence. Then the stars reappeared. Slightly different. He had time to think, *Charon's moved, like Ix*, and they winked out again.

Lines gone, too, then back, slightly different with the different stars, with faint light flickering on the rocks below, gone then back, again and again, the faint sun beating back and forth across the sky.

Modulation.

—oh Jupiter Mars oh—

—11874 737278484 7383

280937 4932874 9—

—Pluto Mercury Scythe Neptune—

—89293847 298743923874—

—Neptune Cyrpisia oh—

Planets, numbers mixing up.

The spheres, too, were popping in and out of view.

Swallowing, blinking against the dizziness, Daric caught the sun, lost it, caught it again, and again, never too far away.

Below, in the flickering sunlight, Leften resumed walking, then Thalmas, lumbering after, then the dendrii, distracted by the changing sky, their poles dragging in the dust.

Daric pushed himself away from the wall, found the couch, sat heavily. He struggled to feel Grandpapa on the lines. *I have time*, he thought. *I can find him on the lines. I can try.* He lay down, struggling for calm. Eyes darting back and forth, with the lines. *I need relaxant. Like the stuff I had on Earth, in my suit.* Breathing deeply.

Just a little, and I can reach Myiepa.

A moment later he sat up, then stood and stepped toward the wall. It faded.

Sisteel stood on the other side. "Hello, Daric." The mask was gone. Her eyes were wide and dark, and she smiled.

He nodded.

"You're having difficulty, aren't you?"

"Thalmas told me to rest. But I can't."

"Do you understand what's happening—the modulation?"

"They're moving this planet. Like what Quint did on Ixion. Only back and forth."

"Yes."

"So Starswarm can't find you."

She smiled. "Can't find *you*, Daric. You'll get used to it, or more used to it. Even I find it difficult sometimes. Can you walk?"

"I think so. But I need to rest 'til Thalmas comes back. I need a relaxant, like the stuff on my old voidsuit." He pointed to his forearm, where the tabs had been before.

After a moment she gave a slight nod, following him inside. "You don't have long, Daric. Maybe a quarter."

"He told me to rest."

She studied him with wide brown eyes. "They don't know how busy you've been with the Heart."

Daric said nothing.

"I'll have to give you a stimulant if they come back early."

He nodded.

She knelt beside his couch, reached into her belt, and withdrew a crystal, looking at Daric, then touched it to the back of his hand.

"With the suns, Daric."

Familiar calm flowed through him, and he could only smile as the cabin faded, darkening to the purple canopy of the Myiepan forest.

To his eyes the nearby trunks were shifting, the ivy transposed with leaping shadows, barely noticeable in the distance.

"Grandpapa!"

The domical vaults were steady overhead.

He cupped his hands around his mouth. "Grandpapa!"

A yellow wink in the distance, brightening.

Arms out, Daric began to walk toward it, began to run, nearly snagging his boots in the shifting ivy but pushing on, the light of double suns streaming through a break in the canopy.

Only as he stumbled into the clearing did he realize the change.

The fallen trees had been removed, replaced by a lake— completely steady in the stuttering forest—within which swam Daric's fish. Stunned momentarily into silence, he stared down. Then roused himself, and called into the distance, "Grandpapa!"

Perhaps due to the relaxant, or the lack of a shell blocking the stars, his voice was unusually strong, echoing back to him from the aisles all around, along with a faint undertone, bright like the suns overhead.

"Grandpapa! I'm at the lake!"

And with the echo came a sound volleying in through the trees, like horns in his dream of ancient Mars, a single tone bending up, an echo bending, too, heralding the sudden movement in front of him.

A golden man stepping from the trees.

Darius, made of liquid gold, kicking through the last of the undergrowth, adjusting his gold cravat. He grasped the upper edges of his long coat and smiled broadly, beaming. "Ah, my boy, my boy, I've found you at last." His voice was no longer a grind of gears but unloosed, supple, with a faint metallic echo. "You are Daric, and I am I, your Grandpapa."

Unable to reply, Daric stared at the face, familiar from the old man on Earth, from Jonas; the piercing eyes and long nose, the smile that was pleasant now, yet in Merode's library could turn dreadful.

Hands on hips, Grandpapa looked up at the suns. He sang, " 'From pole to pole and planets wide . . .' " Shaking his head, with the sunlight glazing his chin.

"Grandpapa, I need your help."

He looked down at Daric. "It's good to finally see you, my boy." He offered his hand but could not grasp Daric's. "You're ... here and there, boy."

"Grandpapa, I've been kidnapped. I'm at the Ambry."

"How does it go? ' 'Cross warp and weft'?" he asked, noticing the trees. " 'From pole to pole and planets wide, 'cross warp and weft ...' " He turned away from Daric, gesturing. "An enchanting planet, this. And I've seen them all lately, seen them *entire*, as I flit along the lines."

"Because of Alissia," Daric said. "She found Myiepa. Alissia Gra'Hague, right, Grandpapa?"

Grandpapa shook his head. "No, thanks to Jonas. Dear Jonas who boosted me in his arms—and I his father—boosted me into the starlines, into this." He nodded appreciatively.

"Grandpapa, where is Jonas?"

Grandpapa began to speak, then pressed a finger to his lips. "You would want to go to him?"

"I need his help, Grandpapa. I'm on Charon, at the Ambry."

Grandpapa shook his head. "You would go to Jonas. And forget the *Plan*."

"Grandpapa ..."

"No, he spent too much time searching for you, my boy. But then I find you here, where you belong." Grandpapa gazed around, gesturing at the forest, the lake, and the fish.

"I need you to contact Jonas, or the void mariners. Can you talk to them, Grandpapa?"

The golden figure laughed, eyebrows jumping up. "Talk? To them? If only they would listen."

"There's only four people guarding me here, with a dendrii, and the hounds."

"Too many plans confuse us, Daric."

"If you want me to follow yours, you'll have to help me

escape! I'm on Charon. They're going to make me open the Ambry. Grandpapa, what is it?"

Grandpapa scowled. "Too many plans, young Daric. Ambry's are beside the point."

"But none of the plans can work until I'm free! Right, Grandpapa?"

Daric thought, I'll wake up.

"A forest! Trees all around, young Daric! Reminds us of the Plan, does it not? The Great Plan!"

"What is it, Grandpapa?"

"What? Why, nothing less than the finding of a single tree. The tree of us. The original tree that was once our original self."

Daric nodded, trying to remember Grandpapa's story. "They found it, didn't they? It was . . . the leaves were . . . weeping."

Grandpapa shook his head.

"It was planted somewhere, but nobody knew where, until the leaves began weeping."

"No, my boy. You heard that from Jonas—I remember! Yes, but he told it wrong. The other version is much sadder." The gold eyes widened. "They buried the Leader, bark and branch and brains, somewhere in the Limbus Realm, my boy!"

Daric shook his head. "But . . . nobody knows where that is!"

Still smiling, Grandpapa said, "Nobody has had *my* help before."

Daric looked away, exasperated, trying to think. "Jonas searched, and he didn't find it. And Alissia Gra'Hague, she was lost trying to find it, wasn't she?"

"Yes, yes. You're right. Alissia! My rose, lost so long ago. Good work, boy. That's the key! I'd nearly forgotten my love, Alissia."

"Grandpapa. I can help you with the Plan once I'm freed. But I'm on Charon. You'll have to contact Jonas, or a mariner. To help me get free."

Grandpapa was humming, then, under his breath, said, " ' 'Cross warp and weft of . . . stellar . . .' "

"Starswarm is looking for me. Do you remember Starswarm?"

"Starswarm? Of course!" Grandpapa jumped up. "Good! You can call her."

"How, Grandpapa?"

"Hmmm." Grandpapa stared down at his hands. "Activation! You must activate any device that belongs to us."

"I had the Defenses, but they were taken away—I think they used it as a lure. Starswarm destroyed Ixion. And other asteroids and moons . . ."

Grandpapa began walking toward the forest.

"Grandpapa . . ."

"You must call Starswarm. Simple as that. With her help you must free yourself from Charon." Grandpapa stopped, then turned and knelt down, so his face was level with Daric's. The eyes, suddenly lucid, the irises so bright a gold they were nearly white. "You must trust me, Daric."

"Grandpapa . . . I can't."

But Grandpapa straightened again and continued on, into the forest, dismissing Daric's calls with a wave of his hand. Soon he was a gold glint among the trees, gone.

Daric stood for a time watching.

"Daric?"

He jumped, turned.

Sisteel stood beside him. "It's time."

Thalmas was crouching beside him. "Daric?"

Daric sat up on the couch. Thalmas had not yet turned off his airlace: His features were vague behind its flow, a forehead without wrinkles, eyes flat and pale blue. "We're ready for you."

Daric stood up, among the bewildering lines.

"Here..." Thalmas held the cricket, its tiny head turning back and forth. He brought it close to Daric's collar, and the cricket grabbed hold. "This will help me talk to you, Daric. Can you walk?"

Daric pulled away when Thalmas offered his hand. He followed Thalmas into the corridor, which opened up before them, delivering them to the square blue room, where Leften and Joom stood conferring, with Sisteel nearby.

For a moment, Sisteel's eyes met Daric's. She asked Thalmas, "Sieur, do you wish me to go? To help the boy?"

Leften said, smiling, "We risk no other personnel, Sisteel."

"Yes, Leften."

The dragonfly appeared, flitting down through the ceiling to the back of her outstretched hand.

"This is Thalmas Green's expedition. Give the boy his airlace."

Sisteel approached. Thalmas's attention was divided between Sisteel and the dragonfly on Leften's hand, as Sisteel slipped the ring around Daric's neck and activated it.

Daric blinked against the cool air.

She leaned close and touched his forehead with two fingers. "With the suns, Daric."

She stepped back. He barely nodded.

"This way, Daric."

Following Thalmas, he nearly stumbled.

"Your monsters could carry him," Leften offered.

"We'll keep a slow pace, Daric." Thalmas moved to the wall—ducking, as though to clear a lintel. Daric followed, finding himself a great height above the ground, slowly dropping.

As his boots touched down, dust rose around him.

Hills stretched out to the curving horizon, and overhead the stars flickered, madly.

"All right, Daric?"

Thalmas spoke through the cricket; Daric could feel it stirring against his neck.

The dendrii waited in a loose group, clutching their poles, with Tak in front—his white triangle of fur seeming to glow from the airlace.

Beside them the hounds stood side by side.

"Let's go."

At a gesture from Thalmas the hounds set off, in perfect step, darker than the faint, erratic shadows they cast, loping two abreast across the rock. Tak followed, then Thalmas and Daric, with the rest of the dendrii behind.

While the audience of ghosts watched from their crystal spheres, winking in and out of view with the stars. Soon they were left behind.

The hounds led the party, noses to the ground. Muttering, Daric presumed. On the scent.

He found the dark motion on the horizon, the spiky leaves swaying back and forth. As he followed Thalmas over a slight hill, he could see a constant sputter of light deep within the black; though perhaps it was a reflection of the stars.

The ground was rockier, portions almost entirely flat. Buckled lines and corners nearly overgrown with veils of rust—and as they climbed over another squat, angular hill, Daric recognized the ancient ships, all around. Wrecked long ago, the *bones* of ships like those on Ixion. Mounds that once were hulls, winking with windows now dim crystal under dust.

And ahead, a blackness that looked like a forest, swaying back and forth, full of dark motion, with the flicker of light brighter, sputtering yellow and orange.

Two fainter lights now became visible. The hounds loped in that direction.

The dendrii ahead of Daric stumbled. Tak pulled it up, then looked fearfully back, hurrying along.

Thalmas looked at Daric and touched his throat; through the cricket on Daric's shoulder he said, "Tired?"

Daric shook his head, noting the strain in Thalmas's voice. "We're almost there. They . . ."

Ahead of them, the hounds halted.

In unison lifting their heads, ears sharpening.

Thalmas stumbled. "Freeze!" He grabbed Daric's arm and gazed up at the stars. "Protection!"

Bolts of light jumped from pole to pole, forming a shield over the party. Thalmas pulled Daric close while the dendrii spread out on all sides—teeth clenching, eyes wide on the sky—and the hounds rose up to howl, soundlessly.

Thalmas clamped his arm painfully. "Steady." Gazing up through the flickering lattice.

Daric expected to see a shadow pouncing down.

"Tine!"

Her cold voice: "Thalmas Green, the *Pyre* is attempting an approach."

The moment stretched, with Thalmas gazing up, the dendrii shifting from foot to foot, gaping, and the hounds frozen on their hind legs, ears sharp, snouts pointing at a section of the sky. The snouts barely moving. Tracking.

"Is it gaining?" Thalmas was trying to sound calm. "Tine?"

Beyond the shield, the stars began flickering faster.

Leften appeared, a ghost beside Thalmas, slowly swaying. "Modulation has been increased, Thalmas Green."

"It won't stop looking."

She smiled, and looked up with them at the stars. "Nonetheless, the *Pyre* is now losing ground. Quintillux has deployed the child's cloak near Mercury Scythe. It calls to the *Pyre*."

A moment later the hounds dropped down, ears going flat.

Thalmas relaxed his grip on Daric's arm.

Leften smiled, and faded.

"Tak! Shield off!"

Tak jerkily bowed. The brilliant net vanished.

"Continue!" Looking down at Daric, his face vague behind the airlace, Thalmas said, "Almost there."

He took Daric's hand.

Walking, Daric had to look down to avoid the flickering stars and the starlines, staring at the dendrii's boots and the dust with starlines jumping, trying to trip him. He began to count but gave up. The forest was closer, black fronds swaying under the stars, with two lights directly ahead, glowglobes floating on either side of a path.

As they reached it—the forest now towering above them, more active—the dendrii stopped, some peering ahead down the bone-white path, some looking back.

Through the cricket, Thalmas said, "The vestibule is made of creatures. Infernal machines, like the Grawls they say exist on Earth."

White poles were sunk every few paces along the bone-white path.

Thalmas gestured to Tak, who barked silently to the other dendrii. They regrouped, wide-eyed, some chewing absently, two in front of Daric and three behind.

The shield was activated.

The hounds started off, then the dendrii, ducking. Thalmas took Daric's hand and led him forward. As Daric's boots touched the path a great violent surge struck the field overhead. Sparks and brilliant blackness.

Tak pushed a dendrii forward.

To either side, in the tangle, the writhing black was nearly purple in places, with piles of what looked like gray bones. The path was not entirely flat, as though the machines had been cut or burned away; and it was not entirely straight, beginning to zigzag.

Surrounded entirely, Daric had lost sense of how far they had come, when the hounds froze and once more stood up on their hind legs, keening at the hidden sky.

"Report!"

Daric stared up through the branches.

"Keep going! Leften!"

The hounds dropped, and continued on, but with snouts aimed at the sky.

She appeared, walking beside them. "The *Pyre* was not fooled for long. Perhaps Prazeel's myths are correct. There really are thaumaturgists and seers aboard." She watched the sky with them. "It was closer, but our movements have become wider." A moment later she said, "We've lost it again."

The hounds dropped back down.

Leften vanished.

Ahead through the sparks and dark foliage, a steady light. Thalmas turned to Daric, offered a smile that quickly died with the sudden thrashing behind them. A spark, a rush, dendrii falling: one lying on the rock, cut entirely in half at the waist, gazing at the fan of blood spreading out; and a second dendrii crumpling, one leg shorn. Shield sparking.

A black limb flowing in, cutting, sparking.

"Forward!" Thalmas motioned to Tak, then began dragging Daric—nearly stumbling himself—along the trail. Daric wrenched around to see Tak hesitating, lifting the wounded dendrii, and behind them a rush of dark limbs flowing like liquid, writhing in snapping shoots and branches along the trail.

Daric was dragged from the forest, into a clearing.

Globes lit a ramp angling into the rock. Halfway down, a ripple of dust betrayed an atmosphere cap. Thalmas stumbled down after the hounds, with Daric nearly falling, gravity tugging, through a layer of dust climbing his boots, legs, waist, closing with a pop over his head.

"Quickly!" Thalmas's voice echoed wildly off the walls: "This ramp has its own field! Tak!"

Reaching the ramp Tak fell, rolling with the wounded dendrii down the ramp. Thalmas struck off a panel on the wall, pushed a switch. Darkness thrashed at the top, sparking, but advancing no farther.

The dendrii's agonized howl tore the air.

"Tak, bring down!" Thalmas said, struggling to keep his voice steady.

Lamps floated at the end, lighting a small room of black rock, a gray door, and a yellow and black panel beside it.

Tak half dragged the wounded dendrii, tracking blood down the ramp.

"Down," Thalmas said.

Red froth bubbled at its lips.

Tak laid the dendrii down. The thing looked pitifully up, yellow eyes narrowing in pain.

The others scattered back, grunting, smacking their lips; a pole clattered to the deck.

Thalmas knelt and made a gesture over the dendrii's eyes, and said softly, *"Yan tan tethera."*

The dendrii sank back onto the rock, gave a rattling groan.

With his thumb, Thalmas closed its eyelids. He stood up, blankly gazing at the room around them, then at the ramp, the rasping shield, against which a blackness swelled.

The dendrii grew more quiet.

Leften Tine appeared. She barely took notice of the creature. "There's no passage out, Thalmas Green."

He ignored her, looking at Daric, then the door.

Wiping sweat from his forehead he stood up, and tried to take Daric's arm. Daric pulled back.

"Daric, try the door, please. Put your hand on the square."

Daric approached it. It was similar to the door on Earth.

He raised his hand, and touched the yellow and black square beside it.

The door sighed open onto shadows. Thalmas shone a light on a dark, downward corridor.

"Very good," he said quietly, still catching his breath. He looked around to the hounds, then to Tak, and finally back to Daric. He touched the cricket at Daric's throat, which stirred. "Daric, I'll be with you at every step. The dendrii and a hound will go with you. As I said before . . . you only need follow these passages to the Ambry. Use your hand on the plate, and if that doesn't work, ask the door to open. Once you find the Ambry, simply set this cricket down and return here. By then, Leften will have us out of here. We'll be home before dinner." Thalmas added, "And you'll have company at the Compound. Two century roses I brought back from Ix. Your friends, Chev and Mila."

Daric said nothing, and ignored Thalmas's steady eyes.

Thalmas turned to the five dendrii, who were shifting from foot to foot. "Don't rush him."

Tak nodded.

"Ready, Daric?"

"As your Leader would say, *bonne chance.*" Leften Tine smiled, her face undulating. "And *bonne chance* to you, Thalmas Green."

"You will cut a path through the rock, Leften."

"Certainly."

As Daric stepped through the door, the walls brightened with yellow lightlines.

The dendrii hesitated, then one by one stepped inside, licking their teeth, blinking at Daric, followed by three hounds, and the dragonfly winging overhead.

Behind them the door closed; there came a subtle change in air pressure.

"Good, very good. Continue at your own pace, Daric."

Tak, watching steadily, gestured him on with yellow claws.

Daric began walking, feeling the gravity tug, walking more quickly now—the dendrii hurrying to keep up—counting his steps.

110 . . . 111 . . . 112.

He reached a new door, with another yellow and black square beside it.

The cricket said, "Daric? Simply open it like the last. You're doing well."

This door, too, opened at his touch. The hound slinked inside with Tak behind it, trudging into shadows. Tak turned, his eyes alight, gesturing. Daric followed, into a hallway that brightened suddenly.

Behind him, a shriek, cut off.

Daric turned. Only two dendrii were there, hooting, gaping at the closed door.

Thalmas asked, "Daric?"

The dragonfly darted close to his shoulder.

"The door shut," Daric said. "We lost two dendrii."

Faint, from Tak's collar, "Tak! Onward!" Cheeks puffing, blinking rapidly, Tak waved Daric on. When they reached the next door, Tak held Daric back while he stepped through.

The process continued for another ten doors, each corridor about a hundred steps long, angling down. Finally they reached a different door: more narrow and polished, reflecting their approach.

Like the door on Earth. The one leading to the Machineries.

"Ask it to open," Thalmas said.

The dendrii stood on either side.

He said, "I am Darius."

The door slid back on a small room.

An elevator.

I have to go alone.

Tak shifted nervously from boot to boot, the hound walking in circles, while the dragonfly suddenly flitted inside.

It turned, watched Daric with bulbous eyes.

A moment later Thalmas said, "Daric, step inside."

But it won't work, Daric thought.

Tak stepped in, the dragonfly settling on Daric's shoulder.

It won't work with anyone but me.

"Order the doors to close. Tell it you want to descend."

"I am Darius. I wish to descend."

The doors remained open.

"Ask it again."

"I want to descend. I am Darius . . ." To Thalmas: "I have to go alone."

A pause, then Tak's collar made a noise. Tak stepped out, squinting at Daric, gray tongue licking blunt teeth.

The dragonfly and the hound remained.

"Continue, Daric."

"But . . ."

"It should work, now, Daric. Try it."

Daric stared at the hound, which likewise stared up. "I am Darius."

The doors shut on the wide-eyed dendrii.

The walls brightened with yellow and black stripes. In the air came a strange, reedy sound, like a tree's voice. Then another, deeper, and a third, lower still. The fourth was Grandpapa's reverie. *String Quartet Primus.*

In a tiny, rasping voice, the dragonfly on Daric's shoulder said, "No tricks, child of Darius."

Peer Tromon.

Daric said, "I want to descend!"

The room plummeted.

·   ·   ·

"Daric?" said Thalmas, through the cricket. "Are you all right? You've stopped."

Daric leaned against the wall, still feeling the drop, dizzy.

"We have you near the core. Daric?"

He straightened. The door slid open on shadows.

"Don't do anything else, Daric. Just let me look."

But he stepped from the elevator, onto hard floor; the click of his boots kindling yellow lights nearby.

Immediately the hound was at his side, a pointed nose nudging his leg.

The air stale, and cold.

"Do nothing else. Daric, do you understand?"

The hound was trying to force him back into the elevator; the dragonfly buzzed his hair. He brushed it away, discerning blue lights below the yellow ones, hexagonal blue lights, all around.

He raised his boot and brought it down, the echo kindled more yellow lights.

He walked farther in.

"Daric!"

The hound followed, while the dragonfly winged up, out of sight.

At his shoulder, Thalmas said, more calmly: "This isn't safe, Daric. Leave the others and come back to the surface."

Daric peered at the blue lights. He walked toward the nearest. The blue lights were windows looking into—

"Come back to the surface, Daric."

—looking into a blue glow, which in turn held a faint shadow.

And within the shadow, a twinned gleam, of eyes.

He tried to focus on a single window but felt his attention scattered—to the shadows all around into the distance, as his heart began to pound.

Eyes, looking out.

He walked closer.

Thalmas said softly, "They're your brothers, Daric."

Blue shadows, curled up. And within the shadows, magnified by glass, were the eyes, wide and empty above slight noses and mouths, hands clutched below.

"Daric, we always hoped for this. Living history. Untainted, in cold sleep since the *ancient ancient*."

Daric sensed them, all the eyes surrounding this chamber.

"I'd always hoped. There was much in the legends, Daric. I'd collected data in the Sanctuary, and mapped, and planned for it."

Looking to the far end, the corner, and a stone hand—a cusp.

"Daric, you can go back to Merode now."

He plucked the cricket from his armor. The head turned back and forth, legs twitching. Daric grabbed a leg, bent, twisted, wrenched it off, then set the cricket on the ground, on its side. The cricket twitched. Faint: "Daric."

When he began walking toward the cusp the hound leapt in front of him, crouching, entirely dark but for its smile, its sharp teeth. Remote from fear, he pushed past it, and the hound growled low then leapt at his throat, was suddenly struck, lifted high in a cloud of white light—tossing its head from side to side—flung high, falling as fire, scorching, tumbling as a cube, a smoldering black cube.

"My Glory."

The tall figure stood before the racks, dressed in a familiar square hat and red robes.

The long face with white eyebrows.

"My Glory, you have returned." Smiling, the Curator bowed.

Daric studied the Machineries, finding row upon row of weapons, like those Mila and Chev had found on Ixion. Ancient-style projectile and beam rifles, black and gray and silver. Beside these were uniforms, dark suits and cloaks.

And in the far corner, the cusp.

"A stupendous renewal, My Glory?"

The Curator approached, growing smaller with each step.

"Don't . . . grow smaller," Daric said.

With a nod, the Curator stopped beside Daric, staring down. "You lack Defenses, My Glory. Allow me to outfit your current form."

"No, I . . ."

"There is much activity outside, My Glory. It would be advisable, if I may . . ."

The dragonfly was suddenly at Daric's eyes, buzzing as he turned, brushing at it, staggering back. "Curator!"

There came a whir, a pop, and the dragonfly with sizzling wings dropped to the floor.

The Curator stared down, then gestured to the racks. "If you will, My Glory."

"Curator . . ." He caught his breath.

"What is your desire, My Glory?"

He turned, looking at the blue windows.

"My Glory?"

Daric said, "Destroy them."

The Curator raised an eyebrow. "Them, My Glory?"

Daric gestured.

The Curator's face registered no surprise. "The zygotes?"

Daric nodded.

The Curator shook his head. Almost sadly, he said, "I am afraid I cannot, My Glory. I am prevented from harming the zygotes or their stasis containers, and directed, with all the energies at my disposal, to prevent others from harming them." The Curator smiled, adding, "The single exception being you, of course, My Glory." Bowing, his face lost beneath the square hat, the Curator floated backward.

Daric walked to the crystal racks. Weapons, ancient like those on Ixion, or older. He recognized some from his history lessons:

simple knives, swords, spears. Guns, like those he'd seen in Merode's library, though these were older, and entirely familiar. A black rifle tipped with a fan of black glass.

He lifted it down, located the trigger, then lugged it to the center of the chamber.

He turned, looking up and around at all the similar eyes, the similar curled forms, receding into the distance.

Faint: "Daric?" The cricket was struggling across the floor toward him.

"Curator, can you call Starswarm?"

"The *Starswarm Pyre*? Yes, My Glory. It has been making a rather haphazard approach for some time."

"Do it."

A whirling tone like the theremin, echoing back to him.

"The beacon is activated."

Daric bit his lower lip, then struggled the weapon up under his arm, holding it close to his body. He raised the fan. His eyes roaming the stasis chambers he pressed the trigger, and fierce light leapt, guided by his hands, sweeping back and forth, a sudden rain of sparks and blue mist.

He stopped, stepped back, choking, then began once more, sweeping the chamber, the floor sizzling and steaming into the distance, through smoke to the far side as he raked the floor, walking backward now to the Machineries, leaving blue steam and shadows.

He stopped, and was sick, on his knees.

The Curator appeared beside him.

"My Glory, the *Starswarm Pyre* has the signal, and is attempting an approach."

Daric nodded, thinking suddenly of Alissia Gra'Hague. He stood, trying to clear his head. Something moved near his boot—the cricket. He stepped on it, crushed it down.

"Curator?"

"Yes, My Glory."

He faltered, then said, "Can you turn on the transmission cusp?"

A hum.

"Activated."

"Can I choose a destination?"

The Curator shook his head. "This is the last link, My Glory, and can only return you to the previous."

Coughing, Daric said, "Don't communicate with Starswarm. Not at all. Understand?"

The Curator bowed. "There will be no communication, My Glory."

Dropping the rifle, he gathered his cloak about him with suddenly shaking hands, pressed the stud on his necklace, then staggered toward the cusp. Behind him the Curator said, "My Glory, it has been an honor to serve you."

Daric stopped before the portal in the palm. He remembered the gendarme in Oppidum, the void through which he would fall forever. But everywhere else was death, so he stepped forward—

—onto a field of ice-bound craters, beneath the vast face of Saturn.

23498 4 0938 40598345097180 73209579 218640 98160591874 Tethys, the starlines confirmed.

Lines, numbers, and voices, and all of them fixed in the sky.

He turned, expecting destruction at his heels. The palm was dark. Overhead, icy stone fingers clutched at the stars.

Daric looked around at glinting blue craters and the curved horizon.

He stood up, still dizzy though the lines were back, were stable; dizzy like those moments after turning in place on the shore at home, dropping to the grass with the ground pitching and yawing.

At first, the bodies seemed like two rumpled white crosses a short distance to his left. In black suits decorated with the KayTee cross, faces down, one with a leg twisted unnaturally, the ice around both full of blue footprints and scuffle marks.

Daric searched the starlines, found no warnings, no indications of settlements, no mariners. Nothing.

Turning to the cusp—whose palm was icebound blue except for a damp square where the portal had been—Daric looked for a way to change its settings, call up another destination.

They can't come through, he told himself. The guards are dead.

Around the cusp, in the distance, a strange ship floated over the ice. It was hard to make sense of with his eyes, perhaps made of bright wood carved into ripples and hollows, gilded with gold lines.

Not a KayTee ship, he was sure.

He shut his eyes briefly and found only the empty line of Tethys. No mariners.

His heart began pounding.

But it isn't their ship. Isn't.

Walking around the cusp, he found her standing just ahead, watching him with three oblong eyes, long black braids twining on the ice around her.

Thola Nee Montyorn, outlined in white fire.

She reached into her dark cloak—the hem scattering ice crystals at her feet—and pulled out a century rose, offering it to Daric, showing no surprise as he stepped forward and took it.

She turned to her ship.

After a pause, Daric followed her across the ice, to the ship, through a portal in the rippling hull into a low, quiet chamber. It seemed made of smooth wood, with rounded archways leading farther in, and all of it intricately carved and patterned.

The door shut behind him.

The glow faded from her cloak as she turned. "Welcome."

Daric could not reply. He stood holding the rose, staring at the strange chamber, feeling the cool rush of the airlace across his face. He turned it off.

"Do you know where you are?" she asked.

"Tethys."

At a gesture from Thola, a planet materialized in the air between them. White and blue, heavily cratered. A flashing point of light marked their position.

"We make do without the shrines," she said. Her cloak rippled on her shoulders, and tensed.

With her hand she drew the planet toward her, then cast it aside; it darted into the distance; gone. Golden lines pierced the chamber, and on the lines were tiny planets growing larger as she reached for them—Neptune, reached for and discarded; the black mass of Pluto, and then Charon.

She regarded it, turning it in long fingers, until a spark of light was revealed.

"Do you know what will happen?" she asked calmly, then let go of the globe. It remained in the air between them.

"You should sit down, child. There." She pointed to a hollow in the wall behind him, a chair of sorts. As he backed toward it a sudden astonishment seized him: in the starlines, numbers quickening, the line of Charon winking out.

While in the air, the planet crackled, and faded.

Thola Nee Montyorn watched without surprise. "Others will be here soon, child. I must work the ship."

Starswarm destroyed it. Thalmas and Leften, Sisteel . . .

Numb, with a weight stealing over his body, Daric sank into the chair, staring at the rose in his hand, some time later realizing that the starlines were moving. Tethys and Saturn soaring off.

Thola returned. Vaguely staring at her cloak, the dark material patterned with purple flowers, he caught the warnings from home like spiders, trailing numbers, Charon destroyed.

She reached for the rose. "Allow me."

But he held on, glancing up. Her eyes widened. "We have to take her to Parson's Planet."

Thola nodded. As he let go, she took the rose. "It lies along our path. You can feel that, can't you?"

He nodded, catching its line, even as she summoned a great gray world in the center of the chamber. It was accompanied by four smaller worlds stacked one by one beneath, as the lines verified; blue and white, green and white, yellow, and fiery red.

"The tier of worlds," she said. "The winding river." Drawing the planets close to show Daric the structures between. "We will take those steps together, Daric."

He looked past them, to the starlines. They were leaving the system behind.

"Would you like to see out?"

He nodded.

The display vanished. She led him to a larger room, with a round portal set deep in the wood wall. He walked to it. The lines told him this direction was home. He found the sun with his eyes, just another star. Mars, Earth, Mercury Scythe, invisible.

Remembering the key Darius had placed inside him, he tried to find it.

A voice behind him said, "Where am I?"

Penthesilia stood transparent in the middle of the room, in a purple dress as before, long red hair, widening eyes. "Daric? What's happened?" She slowly blinked. "Where are we?" And blinked again. "I can't find my trove."

Thola Nee Montyorn reclined in the curving wall. "You have a new trove, child."

"Daric?"

Quietly, "Hello, Pen."

She approached him, her pale red eyes searching his face. "Where are we?"

"On the ecliptic," he told her. "One-five-five-seven-one." He caught the Earth and spiders scurrying. Warnings about Earth, warnings about Charon. "We'll reach the Onomule colonies soon, I think, and Vectra. Three-nine-two." Mars and Triton were no more important than the others now. Oppidum and the Tharsis plain, the Compound, somewhere in the stronger lines of the Heliocratic worlds, the lines of mariners. He wanted to show them to Penthesilia. Instead he let them go, *looked away*, looked at her. She seemed worried, glancing around at the ship, at Thola, moving up beside him by the window.

He said, "We're taking you to Parson's Planet."

Her profile, as she blinked, and beyond her the sun was just another star. Home was lost, reduced to lines and numbers.

"Thank you, Daric."

Merode and Shade, in lines and numbers. Jonas and Grandpapa, and home. Gone but still there, with the web of shrines, and the numbers.